Hawker's lenses picked
shape that flapped to
drawing circles over th
the lagoon. The bino
something more drama... ...came into view. It was a
human hand, a pale, wasted, forlorn thing, reaching
up in despair out of the thick brown sludge. Hawker
adjusted the glasses to give himself maximum close-up
and saw that the hand was inches away from a tiny
round object.

It was a golf ball.

Also by the same author:

TOUCH PLAY

MARTiN INiGO

STONE DEAD

SPHERE BOOKS LIMITED

A SPHERE Book

First published in Great Britain by Sphere Books Ltd, 1991

Photoset in North Wales by
Derek Doyle & Associates, Mold, Clwyd
Printed and bound in Great Britain by
BPCC Hazell Books
Aylesbury, Bucks, England
Member of BPCC Ltd.

ISBN 0 7474 0204 3

Sphere Books Ltd
A Division of
Macdonald & Co (Publishers) Ltd
Orbit House
1 New Fetter Lane
London EC4A 1AR

A member of Maxwell Macmillan Pergamon Publishing Corporation

Too long a sacrifice
Can make a stone of the heart.

W.B. Yeats

To the memory of Sam Ryder

Chapter One

Don Hawker often wondered why he drove such appalling cars. There was always something drastically wrong with them. It wasn't only a question of money. Even if he could afford to buy a new car, it would arrive with some basic and irremediable faults. Hawker did something to motor vehicles. He imparted his sense of personal chaos to them. They shook, rattled and rolled. Bits fell off. Dents and scratches appeared for no apparent reason. Windows stuck and doors refused to open without grievous bodily harm. A Hawker car was by definition a travelling mud pack. Dirt and filth were months deep. The concept of the car wash was quite unknown to him and he had never raised a soapy sponge in anger. Maintenance was something that happened at the garage during one of the irregular services. It was an article of faith with Hawker that you did not lift a bonnet unless it was a dire emergency. As a driver, he was a disgrace on four wheels, a one-man act of defiance against the invention of the internal combustion engine.

The traffic jam on the M1 gave him ample time to reflect on his unhappy relationship with his Vauxhall Cavalier. The radio did not work, the clutch squeaked every time he depressed his foot and one of the windscreen wipers left a dark rainbow whenever it swished to the right. He surveyed the sleek limousines all round him and heaved a sigh of regret that soon

1

gave way to a grunt of acceptance. Hawker could never be comfortable in any of this gleaming modernity. A clapped-out car was his natural milieu. He relied on its very unreliability. He was the motoring equivalent of an arthritic who has come to love the aches and pains of simple locomotion. It is cruel to deprive such a martyr of his suffering.

Drizzle intensified to heavy rain as he turned on to the M6 and headed north. He soon picked up a sign for his first port of call. Fifteen minutes later he left the hissing racetrack and swung into Corley Services, one of those mirages of false hope and high prices that greet the weary traveller on the motorways of Britain. Ignoring the car park, Hawker followed the road as it curved around towards the petrol station, then he braked, changed gear, flicked on a weak-willed indicator, veered to the left and went out, illegally, through the service exit.

A narrow road ran for a hundred yards or so, flanked by fields of tufted grass. The Dog Training Centre on the corner had noisy inhabitants. Hawker let the indicator pulse feebly again as he went left, then immediately right into Rock Lane. He rumbled on past the farm buildings until he saw the house he was seeking.

Corley Hall was a large but rather nondescript building that stood at the rear of an acre of walled garden. It had begun life as a Tudor farmhouse, been extended by successive owners, then had lost its distinctive character in the last century when its front and sides were rendered. Half-timbering was buried for ever beneath aggressive pebbledashing. History had been painted out in a blaze of white.

Hawker went up the drive with the garden wall on his left and the farmyard on his right. It was afternoon. The cows were just paying their second visit of the day to the milking parlour. Two dogs scampered around

2

uselessly. A bellow of rage suggested that the farmer was not a happy man. The Cavalier came to a halt beside a Renault and its engine died with a groan of despair. Hawker took his bags from the boot and hurried across to ring the doorbell, glancing over his shoulder as fresh howls of fury came from the milking parlour where the farmer was evidently having an uneasy time with his beasts.

The door opened and Hawker met his host.

'Mr Starrett?'

'Call me Norman.'

'How do you do? I'm Don Hawker.'

'You don't need to tell me that.'

'Oh?'

'Recognised you immediately. Even after all these years. I used to enjoy watching the athletics on the telly. I can still see you going past the lot of them on that last lap in the Commonwealth Games. Great race!'

'Er, Mr Starrett . . .'

'Norman, please.'

'Could I possibly step in out of the rain?'

'Of course, of course. How stupid of me! Come in.'

'Thanks.'

Norman Starrett stood back to admit his new guest to the passageway, then showered him with apologies. The owner of Corley Hall was a tall thin angular man in his sixties, a retired accountant with a manner that was at once pompous and ingratiating. Hawker felt that he was being simultaneously patronised and flattered and decided that, on balance, he preferred the condescension. It was the obsequious Norman Starrett who watched television.

'Good journey?' asked the older man.

'Miserable.'

'Know what you mean. I hate motorways.'

'Then why do you live so close to one?'

'It has its advantages.'

'How far away is The Belfry?'

'Twenty minutes if you put your foot down.'

'Never dare to do that in my car.'

'Allow half an hour then.' He put his head to one side to appraise Hawker more carefully. 'Well! I never thought I'd be welcoming the great Don Hawker into my house. You look much bigger in real life.'

'I eat a lot.'

'But you're still obsessively fit. I read that in an article about you. Don't you train every day?'

'I like running, that's all.'

Starrett launched into a monologue about another televised race in which he had seen his guest run. Hawker sighed inwardly and regretted his decision to book in at Corley Hall. The place had been recommended to him as quiet, inexpensive and convenient. There had been no mention of a garrulous host whose mind was an action replay tape of Hawker's athletic triumphs. Help was at hand. The loudest expletives yet roared out of the milking parlour. Starrett's face darkened.

'Leech!' he grunted.

'Who?'

'My neighbour. Brian Leech.'

'Good lungs.'

'Noisy devil!'

'Doesn't sound like the friendliest of men.'

'He's not.'

Starrett shot a rueful glance in the direction of the farmyard, then he conducted Hawker along the passage and into the well of the house. Corley Hall was far more interesting on the inside, oozing character and showing all the signs of sympathetic renovation by somebody who cared for their property. Hawker followed his host up a wide flight of stairs that were surmounted by a carved oak balustrade, then they went along a low corridor that obliged both of them to duck. A small door at the far end was opened to reveal a rickety staircase that spiralled up into the attic.

Hawker's room was the biggest and most comfortable of the six on the upper storey. It contained a double bed, a wardrobe, a chest of drawers, a mahogany desk with an upright chair beside it, and an old leather armchair. A colour television stood on a coffee table in the corner. The washbasin looked brand new. Hawker was reassured. The place was impeccably clean. White towels lay across the foot of the bed and a vase of flowers brightened up the whole room. The double-glazing reduced the surging motorway traffic to a distant buzz.

Starrett switched back to his lordly mode.

'You're staying in a listed building, you know.'

'Am I?'

'Yes. We're in all the architectural histories.'

'I see.'

'Then there's the literary association.'

'Literary?'

'George Eliot.'

'Ah.'

'Hall Farm in *Adam Bede*. It's based on Corley Hall.'

'Indeed.'

'George Eliot knew the house well.'

'Did he?'

Starrett was on to the mistake with relish.

'George Eliot was a woman,' he said with a smile of rebuke. 'Her real name was Mary Ann Evans. One of our finest novelists. She was born not far away.' He lapsed back into hand-washing servility. 'So you're not the only celebrity we've had here. George Eliot beat you to it.'

'What was her time for the five thousand metres?'

Starrett gave a hollow laugh before backing out so that his guest could settle in. Hawker made a mental note to give the other a wide berth during his stay. It would not be difficult. The assignment which had brought the journalist to the Midlands promised to be an engrossing one. The Ryder Cup would keep him well clear of the attentions of Norman Starrett.

Hawker glanced around the room and noticed the Gideon Bible for the first time. He also saw the binoculars that were standing on the window sill and he moved to pick them up. His room afforded him a panoramic view of rolling fields that swept up to Corley Rocks, a jagged outcrop of sandstone that was topped by more agricultural land. Down to the left was a strip of housing that curled off towards Keresley Pit in the middle distance. The incongruous juxtaposition of farm and coalmine made him blink in astonishment.

A much bigger surprise awaited him. Lifting the binoculars to his eyes, he focused them on the M6 which was snaking its way southwards in a blanket of rain, then he panned slowly to the right. As his gaze moved across the seven-acre field immediately opposite the house, he noted the slurry lagoon that disfigured the pasture, a deep pit some forty metres square, surrounded by banks of earth into which a barbed wire fence had been set. All the effluent from the farm gathered in the lagoon and slowly evaporated in the keen air.

Hawker's lenses picked up a distinctive black and white shape that flapped to and fro. It was a lone magpie, drawing circles over the field before swooping across the lagoon. The binoculars traced its flight until something more dramatic came into view. It was a human hand, a pale, wasted, forlorn thing, reaching up in despair out of the thick brown sludge. Hawker adjusted the glasses to give himself maximum close-up and saw that the hand was inches away from a tiny round object.

It was a golf ball.

*

Norman Starrett was lurking in the kitchen when he heard his guest hurtling down the stairs. He rushed out in time to see the hefty figure descending at speed towards him.

'What's the problem?' he said.

'Call the police!'

'Why?'

'There's a dead body in the field opposite.'

'Are you sure?'

'Call them!'

Hawker went out through the door and sprinted down the drive as if he were just coming round the final bend in a race. He went across the lane and in through the five-barred gate that had been left open when the herd was brought out of the field for milking. Charging across the muddy surface, he went up the bank of the lagoon and looked for a break in the barbed wire. He found it at once. After squeezing through the gap, he went down the slippery incline with the utmost care, then worked his way along the edge of the slurry until he came to the hand that had attracted his attention. Close up, it looked more pathetic and lifeless than ever, a five-fingered symbol of a grotesque death. It was a man's right hand. The golf ball was now out of his reach for ever.

Starrett, meanwhile, had been galvanised into action. He rang the police, gabbled his message, snatched up an old umbrella from the cloakroom, then put it up as he scurried out of the house. Familiar yells from the milking parlour made him stop and consider. The farmer would have to be told. Much against his will, Starrett mounted the struts of the steel fence and cocked a leg over. When a dog came yelping across at him, he kicked out viciously.

The body was a shapeless lump below the surface of the sludge. Hawker crouched down to scrutinise it but he made no attempt to touch it. That was the job of the police. The magpie landed on one of the fence posts behind him and watched the proceedings with offhand interest. It took to the air again as an angry voice approached the lagoon. Brian Leech did not take kindly to being interrupted. With Starrett at his heels he squelched across the field in his gumboots, venting his spleen at full volume.

'What the hell's going on!'

'He saw a dead body in your field.'

'There'll be another if he doesn't get off my land. He's trespassing. Bloody nerve!'

'This is serious, man.'

'There's a hole in the barbed wire,' said Leech with a fresh burst of outrage. 'Look! Up there. One of my cows might have fallen into the lagoon!'

He clambered up the bank and glowered at Hawker, who stood up and turned around. The farmer was a short stout man of middle years with broad shoulders that had been rounded by a lifetime of toil, and Popeye forearms that were exposed beneath the rolled-up sleeves of his greasy dungarees. A flat cap hid a few remaining wisps of grey hair. The face was a dark red beetroot of hostility.

'Who are you!' he demanded.

'I saw him from the house,' said Hawker.

'That gives you no right to come barging in here.'

'There's a corpse down there.'

'I own this bloody land.'

'Fine. You get him out.'

Leech started to rant wildly and Starrett did his best to calm his neighbour down. Hawker ignored them both and studied the dead body once more, trying to work out exactly where and how it had been thrown into the lagoon. The row was still going on behind him when the sound of a police siren was heard. Even Brian Leech was nudged into silence for a few moments.

8

The white Range Rover turned into the field and bounced its way towards them. As it skidded to a halt, two uniformed policemen leapt out and ran towards the lagoon. A second siren could be heard in the distance. The magpie had flown off to the safety of the huge monkey-puzzle tree in the front garden of Corley Hall. Don Hawker was left alone to answer awkward questions, but he had his story all worked out. There was only one thing that he would not mention.

The golf ball was now in his pocket.

Police vehicles arrived from all directions, one of them with an ambulance on its tail. The field became an impromptu car park for the Warwickshire Constabulary. There was a great deal of animated discussion, but very little was actually done until a senior CID officer reached the scene. Summing up the situation, he took charge with an alacrity which suggested that he had spent the whole of his career just waiting for a case of this nature to fall into his lap. There was an air of well-rehearsed decision about him and his orders were obeyed instantly. Two policemen pulled on waders and went down into the slurry to extricate the corpse as best they could, finding it extremely reluctant to leave its fetid resting place. The explanation brought an involuntary groan from some of the onlookers. Trussed up with ropes, the body was weighted down by a large boulder that had to be cut free with a knife.

When the dead man finally emerged into the light of day, the stink was quite noisome. His head had been smashed to a pulp and one of the arms was twisted up at an unnatural angle. Caked blood mingled with the sludge. The driving rain revealed additional damage as it slowly cleaned the cadaver for inspection. Norman Starrett retched violently.

Murder drew its usual audience. Attracted by the commotion, dozens of people came out of the houses along Bennetts Road North and stared over the hedge. Others watched from their bedrooms. Corley Hall itself was turned into a grandstand as guests and staff pressed their noses to the upstairs windows. The farmer's wife came waddling anxiously over. Two cars, a lorry and a curious motorcyclist stopped in the lane. The police tried to limit the intrusion and waved some of the spectators away. After erecting a ridge tent, they placed the body on a sheet of heavy-duty polythene and pulled it under cover. Forensic experts moved in to search the lagoon. The corpse had its first faltering conversation with a pathologist. A photographer flashed away.

Don Hawker gave a brief statement to a Detective Sergeant. Then, incredibly, as if they were at some social gathering, one of the uniformed policemen sidled over to the former athlete and started to chat about the Olympic gold medals that Hawker had won in Montreal. The horrid proximity of death did not deter him from asking for his hero's autograph. Hawker refused in disgust.

As thick yellow tape was tied across the gateway to the field, Brian Leech protested vehemently. The dairy herd was due to come back into the field after milking and the farmer would not accept that his own land was now out of bounds to him. He could not have been more irate if his cows had been slaughtered on the spot, and the police had to threaten him with arrest in order to quieten him down. Leech's venom found another target and he confronted Hawker with blazing eyes.

'This is all your fault!'

'Hardly.'

'Who asked you to come here?'

'Free country.'

'I'll bloody remember this!'

Hawker squared up to him and believed for a second

that he would have to parry a blow but the farmer thought better of it and stalked off to share his wrath with his wife and his animals. Starrett treated his guest to another flurry of apologies but the latter waved him away and became aware that he was now soaked to the skin. He was excused by the police and went back to Corley Hall at a steady jog, ignoring the waved fist of Brian Leech and going straight into the house and up to the privacy of his attic room.

After locking the door behind him, he took out the golf ball, washed it under the cold water tap, then dried it carefully in a towel. He was quite untroubled by the fact that he was withholding evidence from the police. They had plenty to keep them occupied. He held the gleaming white sphere up to the light. It was a Wilson Ultra 432 and it was personalised with its owner's initials: G.L.

Don Hawker had no idea to whom it belonged or why he had obeyed the impulse to slip it into his pocket, but he felt a surge of excitement that made him tingle with a kind of macabre pleasure. The golf ball set up all sorts of intriguing questions.

He knew where he might find the answers.

Chapter Two

The Belfry lay at the very heart of England and, for three fateful days in late September, it was due to pump the lifeblood of world golf as the finest players from Europe and from the United States of America fought a pitched battle to win the Ryder Cup. It was not the most popular venue. Used for the same event in 1985, the Brabazon course attracted a lot of criticism from both teams, and wails of protest from disappointed spectators who felt that the viewing facilities were miserably inadequate. Now that the Ryder Cup had returned to The Belfry after four years, no expense was spared to bring the place up to scratch in every way. Over £8,000,000 was spent on the course, the park and the hotel complex, with nature itself being reshaped by the power of the cheque-book. When it opened its doors to the general public, it was going to be an infinitely better stage for the prestigious event.

Yet there were still dissentient voices.

'Shit!'

'Clip a mid-iron off the tee.'

'You kidding?'

'Safety first.'

'Nix to that!'

'How many more balls you gonna lose in the water?'

'As many as it takes.'

Tony Bianco had been cursing the Brabazon course ever since they started their practice round, moving on to each new hole with gathering frenzy and wondering what on earth he was doing with a golf club in his hands so early in the morning. Breakfast was still at least an hour away and he never played well on an empty stomach. It was chilly and rain was threatening. He longed to be back home in the Californian sunshine. Bianco took out yet another ball and placed it on the tee peg before stepping back to assess his shot.

His companion advised caution.

'Put that driver away.'

'No chance.'

'Go easy on yourself. Take a six-iron.'

'I like to attack a hole.'

'Show this one more respect.'

'Like hell I will!'

'Drop short of those bunkers then pitch in.'

'Who's playing this shot?'

'You are, Tony.'

'Then leave me be. I drove the green last time.'

'That was four years ago.'

Tony Bianco winced slightly, then gritted his teeth and addressed the ball. He was a chunky dark-haired man of thirty with a healthy tan. The pleasantly ugly face was usually redeemed by a confident grin, but he now wore an expression of morose concentration. During the last Ryder Cup match at The Belfry he had been the undisputed star of the American team, a supreme golfer at the very top of his game. His reputation had been tarnished since then and many people were starting to write him off altogether as a major force in the sport, but he retained Bob Jaglom's faith. As captain of the visiting team, it was his job to get the very best out of his twelve players. An early morning session with Tony Bianco gave him the chance to work on the man who was easily his most controversial selection.

'This is a par four, Tony.'

'Back off.'

'Don't even try for a birdie.'

'You giving me orders, Bob?'

'I'd never do that.'

'Then lemme have some room here.'

'Sure thing.'

Bob Jaglom smiled quietly to himself as he watched the other. They were on the tee at the tenth hole, the most treacherous on the entire course. It was 275 yards downhill, with a dog-leg right, to a narrow green that was set in a spinney and bunkered at the rear. What made it so intimidating was the long stretch of water that guarded it. Here was a gambler's hole which posed an irresistible challenge to a big hitter with strong nerves. There was no margin for error. The ball had to be hit straight and true along a thin corridor of space. Mistakes were cruelly punished.

Having found water three times in a row, Bianco tried to modify his swing so that he got a little less power but a lot more accuracy. His driver swished through the air in a graceful arc and the clubhead made a perfect contact with the ball to send it screaming down the fairway. It lost height and velocity and began the long descent to the water, but Bianco did not lose heart. He knew the true worth of the shot and he waited patiently as the ball flirted with disaster before hitting terra firma and rolling on purposefully to within three feet of the flag. Bob Jaglom let out a rich chuckle.

'I told you not to try for a birdie,' he said. 'So you go for an eagle instead.'

'Every time.'

'A shot like that would put terrific pressure on the opposition. If you can pull it out in each round.'

'Leave it to me, Bob.'

'Won't be a picnic out there. The Europeans have had two wins in a row now. They even beat us on our own patch at Muirfield Village. That means they'll be coming at us with their tails in the air.'

'They'll get my driver right up their ass!'

Jaglom ran a hand through the greying beard that complimented his long crinkly hair. The non-playing captain of the American team was a big shambling man with a soft and almost apologetic voice, but he was pure steel under the surface. He patted Bianco on the back as they marched down the fairway.

'I'm counting on you, Tony.'

'Stay cool. I won't let you down.'

'That cup has got to go back home with us,' said Jaglom. 'Only way to make up for what happened in Ohio last time around is to beat the pants off these guys. They can be arrogant bastards when they win.'

'We'll be the top dogs this year.'

'Wipe the floor with them.'

'It'll be a fucking massacre!'

Tony Bianco gave a harsh laugh. His blood-lust was aroused and he played much better golf on the remaining holes. Bob Jaglom was happy.

They were rolling.

Don Hawker ran along the country lane and tried to avoid the potholes and the puddles of water. He was wearing a tracksuit top, shorts and running shoes. His white socks were already liberally spattered with mud. Despite his great success on the track, he did not look or move like a natural athlete. His action was low, steady and frugal. Leaning forward from the waist, he pumped his arms across his chest so that his elbows jutted out ridiculously. His build suggested a boxer or a weight-lifter rather than a distance runner, yet his record belied his appearance. He might have lacked style but few competitors had his iron will and stamina. His craggy face was a mask of anguish, yet he had covered five miles at an unvarying pace without the slightest sense of effort. Burrow Hill Lane was to be his last lap.

He went past Keresley Rugby Club, up the incline and zigzagged his way around the bends. The hill steepened and he had to work hard to maintain his speed, shortening his stride and putting more thrust into his legs. When he reached the peak and the lane levelled out again, he was able to resume his normal rhythm and run along in the shadow of Corley Rocks. To his right were the fields that stretched down to Bennetts Road North and to the motorway beyond. He was given a bird's-eye view of the slurry lagoon, now festooned with police tapes to keep away any ghoulish visitors. A chain and padlock secured the gate. The field was empty. Not even a magpie.

Hawker reflected on the events of the previous day. Corley Hall had been presented to him as an ideal place to book into, yet within half an hour of being there he had found a dead body, given the police a false statement and incurred the undying hatred of a farmer. It was not the most auspicious start to an enjoyable stay. He was surprised when a large car loomed up unexpectedly on his left, tucked away among the bushes at the foot of the embankment. The sun was hitting the windscreen so that he could not see into the vehicle but Hawker had the feeling that it was occupied. He ran on at his chosen pace.

A long low, modern building popped up on his right to obscure the view. Muted cries told him that it was a cattery. He swung into Rock Lane itself and began the descent to his hotel, accelerating over the final hundred yards and turning into the drive as if he were breasting the tape at the end of a race. Running was more than a form of exercise for Hawker. It was a compulsion.

As he slowed to a walk, he caught sight of his Cavalier at the top of the drive. Not even heavy rain in

16

the night had been able to wash the thick mud from its bodywork. Across the boot, an illiterate hand had left him a crude message: PLOW THIS FEELD TODAY. Hawker looked around for the author and found that he was being watched from the farmyard. A tall gangly youth with straw-coloured hair and a half-witted grin of amusement was leaning on the fence. It was Malcolm, the resident farm labourer. He spat happily in the air then ambled off towards the pens to feed the young stock.

Hawker let himself into the house and went straight up to his room in the attic. He pulled off his tracksuit top, then grabbed his bath towel so that he could take a shower. Then he paused as he became uncomfortably aware of the fact that someone had been into the room and moved a few of his things around. There was also a significant change. The binoculars had vanished from the window sill and the Gideon Bible had gone from the bedside table. In their place, on the mahogany desk, was a well-thumbed paperback with curling edges. It was a copy of *Adam Bede* by George Eliot.

Someone was trying to educate him.

Sheila Dowling was an eternal optimist. Anybody else with her record of personal disasters would not have dared to tempt Providence so rashly, but she did so on a regular basis. Three marriages had ended in three divorces and left behind a confusing litter of children who competed madly for her attention with their respective problems. Other men waltzed in and out of her life all the time, but she still remained steadfastly on the dance floor in her best dress to beam at each prospective new partner with the innocent willingness of a teenager on her first date. Sheila was now fifty-five, a stout, striking, bosomy woman of middle height whose gushing maternalism did not completely blot out her girlishness. Having taken all the blows that life could direct at her, she was ready for more and she almost flaunted her defencelessness. She was one who had loved not wisely but too often.

Few people of her age would even have thought of opening a small hotel, and superstition would have warned them to avoid an establishment that had thirteen guest rooms. Sheila Dowling was not dismayed by the bad omen. She made light of her lack of experience, aptitude and finance, pitching herself wholeheartedly into the enterprise and dragging along whichever of her children she could persuade to work for her.

The Whitehall Hotel had many shortcomings but it also had its virtues. It was cheap, cheerful and run by a vivacious lady who was determined to be a friend to the whole world. Almost alone of the hotels within easy striking distance of The Belfry, it did not raise its prices for the Ryder Cup. Situated on the edge of Sutton Coldfield, it offered clean, if rather basic accommodation, and the kind of breakfast that set you up for the rest of the day.

'How many have you got here, Mrs Dowling?'

'Twenty.'

'I thought I saw a Chink on the stairs.'

'Korean. Four of them are booked in for the week.'

'North or South Korea?'

'Is there a difference?'

'They think so.'

Eric Fretton was up early for his first breakfast at the hotel. He was a small, rumpled, rotund man with echoes of the Sixties about him. The jeans, check shirt and denim waistcoat looked absurd on him and his weakness for badges only added to the general incongruity. Thirty years of unremitting work as a journalist had left him editing a monthly sports magazine, and one of the perks he relished most was a visit to the major golf events. By staying at the Whitehall Hotel he was able to defray expenses and have someone to watch over him.

'Are you sure you're warm enough, Mr Fretton?'

'Yes. Fine.'

'If you want an electric blanket, let me know.'

'In September?'

'Some guests feel the cold.'

'The Koreans?'

'I give them a hot water bottle each.'

'Do you tuck them up in bed as well?'

'Opportunity would be a fine thing!' said Sheila with a chortle that made her whole body shake. 'Now, sit yourself down, Mr Fretton, and I'll get you something nice and filling. None of this Continental stuff here. You can't beat a good old-fashioned English breakfast with all the trimmings.'

'I put myself in your hands, Mrs Dowling.'

'Promises, promises!'

Another chortle took her into the kitchen where the youngest of her daughters was in charge of the cooking. Eric Fretton nodded a greeting to the other guests in the dining room, then found himself a table in the corner. He settled down, opened his newspaper and lost himself in his contemplation of the sports pages. Other people drifted in and got a warm welcome from Sheila who was now serving the breakfasts on a large oval tray. The place was now buzzing with noise.

Eric was impervious to it all. As he flicked through the rest of his paper, his eye was arrested by a familiar photograph and it made him sit back in alarm. Don Hawker looked balefully up at him from beneath the headline of MURDER AT FARM. Since Eric employed the ex-athlete on his magazine, he read the report with a mixture of interest and foreboding. Hawker had an uncanny knack of finding trouble and he would not be

19

able to concentrate on his assignment at the Ryder Cup if he was involved in a murder inquiry. Dark shadows suddenly began to loom over the week ahead and Eric heaved a sigh.

Hawker had done it again.

'Mind if I join you?'

'Eh?'

'Name's Hubert Stone. Phoenix, Arizona.'

'Oh, hello.'

'I guess you must be Eric Fretton.'

'That's right.'

'Hi, there.'

Eric shook the sinewy hand that was thrust at him and made no objection as the tall spare figure lowered himself into the seat opposite. Hubert Stone was a grizzled character in his sixties with shrewd eyes set in a face that had spent most of its life outdoors. Dressed in golf wear, he looked far too flamboyant for the quiet ambience of the hotel. The voice was deep and rich.

'So you're here for the Ryder Cup.'

'Yes,' said Eric.

'Sheila told me you were.'

'Sheila? Oh, Mrs Dowling . . .'

'Great lady!' said the American with a lecherous grin. 'She sure knows how to give a man a tickertape reception. I aim to get properly acquainted with her.' He became serious. 'You run a sports magazine, I hear.'

'That's right.'

'Doing a big feature on the golf?'

'Eight pages. Full colour.'

'Pity they'll have to be edged in black.'

'Why?'

'Because we're gonna roast you alive out there on that course, mister. We're gonna teach your boys a lesson that they'll never forget.'

'Don't bank on it.'

'Feel it in my old bones.'

'Rheumatism, probably.'

'We'll whip you to Kingdom Come.'

'I'll believe it when I see it,' said Eric levelly.

'Take my word,' insisted the other. 'That cup has got the U.S. of A. written all over it.' His chest swelled with self-esteem. 'I have the inside track on account of my niece. Glenn tells me everything.'

'She can't be playing in the Ryder Cup, surely?'

'As good as.'

'What do you mean?'

'Her husband is our secret weapon.'

'Indeed?'

'Tony Bianco.'

'But he's been struggling all season.'

'That doesn't count,' said the other dismissively. 'Tony always comes good when the chips are down. Prefers matchplay. Brings out the killer instinct in him. With Glenn in his corner, that man will be unbeatable.'

'We'll see about that.'

'Put your last cent on the result,' said Hubert Stone with fierce pride. 'America will regain the Ryder Cup and Tony Bianco will lead the way.'

'Are you that certain?'

'Bet my life on it!'

Glenn Bianco sat propped up in bed with the remains of her breakfast on a tray beside her. She was a long leggy blonde in her twenties with a cheerleader glossiness to her that made her look very American and very wholesome. The clinging silk robe displayed the shapely body at its most alluring. Even the pouting lips and furrowed brow could not detract from the regulation beauty. As she glanced idly through a fashion magazine, she was only half-listening to the monologue from the bathroom.

Her husband was in high spirits. Having ended his

practice round on a high note, he had come back to their room at The Belfry Hotel to have a shower and boast about some of the shots he had played. Tony Bianco could feel the adrenalin still pumping. He knew how lucky he was to be selected for the Ryder Cup team and he was determined to use the occasion to vindicate his reputation in the most signal way. A few hours out on the Brabazon course with Bob Jaglom had restored his belief in himself. He would find that elusive winning streak once again.

Stepping out of the shower, he grabbed a towel and went into the bedroom with his monologue unchecked. He was talking about his eagle on the tenth hole when he looked across at his wife and saw her lying there in the glistening silk. Golf fled from his mind. The towel was dropped casually to the floor.

Glenn Bianco kept her eyes on her magazine.

'Don't even think about it, honey,' she warned.

He bit back a rejoinder, glared at her for a moment, then stalked off into the bathroom and slammed the door behind him. It was becoming something of a ritual.

His wife allowed herself a smile of victory.

'Show me exactly where you were standing, Mr Hawker.'

'Right here.'

'And what did you do?'

'I looked through the binoculars and panned across the field. Then I spotted the hand in all that sludge.'

'Very observant of you, sir.'

'Any idea who he is?'

'We'll come to that, Mr Hawker.'

Detective Superintendent Frank Rayment was the CID officer who had taken charge at the scene of the crime on the previous day. He was a stocky man of medium height with a Hitler moustache in the middle of a pale unforgiving face and well-groomed brown hair. He was smartly dressed in a charcoal grey suit and shoes which had been covered in mud during the trek through the field, but were now gleaming once more. There was a professional air about him that was not dispelled by the Birmingham accent. He glanced across at his colleague and they had a silent conference for a full minute. Detective Sergeant Mike Impey was a baby-faced man with the physique of a nightclub bouncer. He had picked up no dress sense at all from his superior and opted for a crumpled brown suit that was much too small for him. Four ballpoint pens sprouted from his top pocket. A fifth was being used to take down the statement.

Don Hawker was less than pleased to be interrogated so closely. His room was just big enough for one guest. When it had to accommodate two detectives and a string of searching questions it became very cramped indeed, and Hawker was increasingly uneasy. Rayment tried to probe that uneasiness.

'You're not keeping anything back from us, are you?'

'Why should I?'

'You tell me.'

'I've given you a full statement, Superintendent.'

'Something is missing.'

'What?'

'I don't know. I just have this gut feeling.'

'All I did was to notice the dead body.'

'And get to it first.'

'Is that a crime?'

'Depends what you did when you got there.'

'I explained that.'

'Not satisfactorily.'

'Stop treating me like a suspect,' said Hawker.

'Stop behaving like one.'

Rayment's peremptory manner was backed up by a laser stare that was very discomfiting. Hawker shrugged his impatience and turned away to look out through the window while the policemen had another wordless conversation. Impey left the room but Rayment stayed for a last attack.

'We'll have to come back to you on this.'

'Why?' said Hawker in exasperation, turning to face him. 'I've been through it time and time again.'

'Something might have slipped your mind, sir.'

'Such as?'

'Who knows? Not every day you stumble upon a murder victim. I've seen dozens and it still makes me want to puke. Bound to leave you in a state of shock, Mr Hawker. When you come out of that shock, you might remember.'

'Remember what?'

'The bit you missed out.'

'There was nothing.'

'It'll come to you, sir.'

'Nothing, Superintendent.'

Frank Rayment picked up the copy of *Adam Bede* and turned it over to study the back cover. His face was expressionless. A slightly mocking note intruded.

'Didn't take you for a reading man, sir.'

'I'm not.'

'Ignorant lot, as a rule, journalists.'

'What's the IQ of the average policeman?'

'Coppers don't need an IQ. Just a good nose.' He handed the book the Hawker. 'Great story. Stay with it.'

'No thanks, Superintendent.'

'It's about a murder – and about the stupid lies told by the killer.'

'I can see why you enjoyed it.'

Rayment gave a mirthless laugh then swung around to go. Hawker's question stopped him at the door.

'Have you found out who he is?'

'Not yet, sir.'

'No clues at all?'

'We're pursuing various avenues of enquiry.'

'That usually means the police are baffled.'

'Don't underestimate us, Mr Hawker.'

'Have you established the cause of death?'

'Severe cranial damage.'

'The famous blunt instrument?'

'We'll let you know when we find it,' said Rayment with an edge. 'In the mean time, don't leave the area without our permission. We may need to put you through your paces again.'

'It would be a total waste of time.'

'Most police work is, sir. Boring repetition.'

'Then why bother?'

'Because you trouble me.'

'But I had nothing to do with the murder.'

'Possibly not.'

'I'm a complete stranger to the area.'

'So was the victim, sir.'

'What?'

'His teeth,' said Rayment briskly. 'He was still able to talk through them even though he was dead. There was some specialist dental work that is just not done in this country. So we have at least been able to confirm his nationality.'

'And where is he from?'

'America, sir. He's probably here for the Ryder Cup. Just like you. Now isn't that a coincidence?'

Don Hawker felt a thrill of real excitement.

He was on the right track.

Chapter Three

Intense media hype of the event led to an outbreak of
Ryder Cup fever, and The Belfry became the focus of
intense national and global interest. The world's
golfing press arrived like the Mongol hordes, with an
army of photographers at their heels. BBC Television
cameras took the best part of a fortnight to get set up
on their hoists at strategic holes, while the commentary
team had a choice of four positions on the actual
course. Police and security men were there in
abundance, as were referees, officials and marshals,
not to mention the scores of people employed in the
tented village to handle the merchandise sales points
or the public catering. The exhibition marquee
brought in even more staff; then there was the corps of
volunteers recruited to pick up any litter on the course.
Since the hotel itself was packed to capacity, hosting,
among others, both teams and their respective sets of
wives or girlfriends, The Belfry was throbbing with
life long before the spectators arrived on the first day
of play.

It all helped to build up the excitement, but it did
impose extra demands on certain key individuals. One
of them was the press officer.

'How's it going, Karen?'

'The jury's not in yet.'

'That bad?'

'My feet haven't touched the ground.'

'Who'd work with journalists!' sighed Eric Fretton.

'Only a masochist.'

Karen Maxwell was a slim lithe woman of thirty who looked as if she had stepped off the cover of a health magazine. Dark silky hair framed a face that positively glowed. Brown eyes had a mischievous sparkle, and the gleaming white teeth were usually on show in a friendly smile. Her duties as press officer at such a huge event were onerous to the point of being punitive but she carried them lightly and was quite imperturbable. Eric Fretton had always liked her and did not mind the fact that she was a good six inches taller than he.

They met outside the press tent to exchange news.

'What gives?' he said.

'Problems.'

'Angus?'

'A hole in one.'

'Is he playing silly buggers again?'

'I'm afraid so,' she said. 'He's decided that journalists are a bad influence, and forbidden his team to give any interviews.'

'That's madness!'

'No – that's Angus Cameron.'

'They should never have made him captain.'

'It worked on the last two occasions.'

'God knows how!'

'Oh, now come on, Eric. Give credit where it's due. Angus Cameron put an end to all those years of American domination of the Ryder Cup. We went almost a quarter of a century without a win. That's a whole career for most golfers. What more do you want?'

'A little humility.'

'From Angus? You've got to be joking!'

'Okay, okay,' he conceded. 'I know it'd be a tall order. I just wish he'd drop all that Field-Marshal

Montgomery stuff of his. We're up against the Yanks, not Rommel. Golfers are human beings. You can't treat them like enlisted men in a combat situation. They need freedom of movement.'

'They also need discipline.'

'Not that kind.'

'Why not just admit it, Eric?'

'Admit what?'

'You don't like Angus Cameron.'

'I don't like his style,' he said. 'He was a great player in his day and one of the most consistent golfers I've ever seen, but that doesn't make him a leader.'

'Most people would disagree.'

'So what? I'm used to being in a minority of one.'

'Angus is the right man for a very difficult job.'

'Then why do something stupid like gagging his team? What's he afraid of, Karen? That one of the lads will let slip some juicy scandal for the tabloids or give away his master plan for beating the Yanks?' Eric extended his arms in a gesture of despair. 'We have our job to do as well. How can we give the European team our full support if we're not allowed to *talk* to them?'

'I put that same question to Angus.'

'What was his answer?'

'You'll have supervised access.'

'What the hell does that mean?'

'No private interviews.'

'And?'

'Press conferences controlled by him.'

'Christ!' wailed Eric. 'We're talking about twelve of the best players in the world. Surely they can be trusted to speak for themselves? Angus Cameron is a non-playing captain, not a bloody ventriloquist!'

'Stop exaggerating.'

'It's an occupational hazard.'

'What?'

'I'm a journo, remember?'

They shared a laugh, then surveyed the busy scene around them. With a couple of days still to go, the atmosphere was building steadily. Tension and excitement were in the air. The Ryder Cup had a magic all its own and the prospect of a hat trick of wins for the European team gave the event a special significance. Even the light drizzle could not dampen the spirit that hovered over the course. They spent a few minutes savouring it all before Karen Maxwell picked up the conversation.

'Anyway, your mag will be all right.'

'What do you mean?'

'Don Hawker. He'll get you an exclusive somehow.'

'That's what I'm afraid of, Karen!'

'He always lands a good story.'

'When he stays on the sports pages,' said Eric with a shiver. 'You read about this latest business?'

'The dead body in the slurry lagoon?'

'It could only happen to him.'

'Pure coincidence.'

'There's nothing coincidental about him, believe me. Why does he have to pick the one hotel in Warwickshire with a corpse on the doorstep? Because he's Don Bloody Hawker – that's why!'

Karen smiled and did her best to sound casual.

'I'm looking forward to seeing him again.'

'So am I. He should be here. Earning his salary.'

'And where is he?'

'Your guess is as good as mine.'

'If he needs any help, tell him to contact me.'

'Don't invite trouble.'

'That's what I'm here for, Eric.'

'You may regret ever saying that.'

'Mm?'

'Don Hawker will give you the kind of trouble that

you can do without. And lots of it.'

Her smile did not lose its tinge of affection.

Norman Starrett stood on his dignity and lost his footing slightly. He was not used to blunt questions from guests.

'I popped in for a few moments, that's all.'

'Do you change the beds around here?' asked Hawker.

'Of course not.'

'Then you had no reason to go into my room.'

'Look, I'm sorry.'

'And you had no right to move things around.'

'I didn't think you'd mind.'

'Well, I do.'

'I can see that now.'

'And why leave that copy of *Adam Bede*?'

'I thought you'd be interested.'

'Listen, Mr Starrett . . .'

'Norman, please.' A note of appeasement.

'Listen, Mr Starrett,' repeated Hawker. 'When I stay at a hotel – even if it's a listed building – I expect to come and go as I please, and to leave stuff in my room in the knowledge that nobody will touch it. As for bedside reading, I've been choosing my own books since I was about ten years old and I'd like to keep it that way. Okay?'

'It was only meant as a sort of joke.'

'It backfired.'

'I really do apologise.'

Thrown on to the defensive, Norman Starrett went through an elaborate hand-washing routine as he tried to mollify his guest. They were standing in the dining room at Corley Hall and the hotel owner was terrified that someone might overhear the complaints. Hawker's threat to walk out altogether had hurt the older man deeply. He fell back on an ingratiating smirk.

'Don't leave. Please.'

'Don't *make* me leave, Mr Starrett.'

'There's been an unfortunate misunderstanding.'

'On your part.'

'I accept that.'

'Good.'

'Is there anything else we can do for you?'

'Respect my privacy.'

'Nobody will go into your room again.'

'Is that a promise?'

'You have my word of honour.'

'One last thing,' said Hawker. 'Why did you leave those binoculars up there in the first place?'

Starrett was in even greater disarray now and he began to splutter as he rehearsed various answers in his mind. Control eventually asserted itself.

'It was a mistake.'

'A big one.'

Hawker nodded a farewell, then went out. His initial impulse had been to check out of Corley Hall and find somewhere else to stay, but two factors had weighed against that. Accommodation in the area was at a premium during Ryder Cup week and he knew how difficult it would be to locate another place at such short notice. More to the point, he wanted to stay close to the action. The key to the murder might lie at The Belfry but there were clues that would only emerge at the scene of the crime. It was vital to retain the base in Rock Lane.

Meanwhile he had an irate editor waiting for him on the golf course and he had to get across to him as soon as possible. Hawker came out of Corley Hall and walked towards his car, noting the graffiti on its boot once more. Something else then claimed his attention. It was a magpie, perched arrogantly on the wall immediately behind his vehicle and quite unworried by his approach. Hawker got within a yard of it, but the bird still did not move. Its bravery was its undoing.

There was a loud report and the creature exploded in a mass of black and white feathers, causing Hawker to step back smartly as the bonnet of the Vauxhall Cavalier was speckled with blood.

Smouldering quietly, Brian Leech tucked his shotgun under his arm and sauntered off towards the farmhouse.

He had made his point.

Hubert Stone was the only person left in the lounge at the Whitehall Hotel. With a half empty cup of coffee beside him on a low table, he sat on the edge of his chair as he searched through the last of the morning papers. They had not made pleasant reading for him. His eyes glinted with anger as he found yet another version of the news item that claimed his attention. He studied it very carefully then his jaw tightened. Cheap perfume wafted into the room with Sheila Dowling. She clicked her tongue and shook her head in mock disapproval.

'Are you still here, Mr Stone? I can see that we're not going to get rid of you easily, are we?'

The American regained his composure at once.

'Hi, Sheila,' he said, putting the paper aside and taking off his glasses. 'You look terrific!'

'In this apron?'

'You'd look terrific in anything.'

The famous giggle. 'Go on with you!'

'How come there's no special man in your life?'

'I'm between offers.'

'Maybe we can change that situation.'

'Now, you behave yourself!' she clucked.

'What happened to *Mr* Dowling?'

'That's a long story.'

'Tell me some time.'

'Oh, it would take hours.'

'I got all night,' he said with a frank grin.

Sheila laughed aloud and gave him a playful push.

'Stop it, Mr Stone.'

'The name is Hubert.'

'Learn to control yourself.'

'With a gorgeous gal like you around?' He stood up beside her. 'What say I buy you dinner this evening?'

'I'll be too busy cooking for twenty guests.'

'Tomorrow, then.'

'The same story, I'm afraid.'

'Don't you ever have any free time?'

'Not when we're fully booked, I'm afraid. It's a case of all hands to the pumps.'

'Where's the fun in your life?'

'I get by.'

'That settles it,' he said, slipping an arm familiarly around her waist. 'We'll just have to meet up after hours. A midnight feast in my room.'

'Mr Stone!' she protested.

'Hubert.'

'I don't fraternise with my guests.'

'But I'm not a guest, honey. I'm a suitor.'

She giggled again and detached herself from him to bend over the table and gather up the crumpled mass of newspapers from the table. Hubert Stone admired her body with a lustful gaze and stroked each generous curve in his mind. Then he remembered why he had been so interested in the papers that morning.

'Will you do me a big favour, Sheil?'

'Depends what it is.'

'I need to use a telephone.'

'There's one out in the hall.'

'Too public for my taste,' he said. 'I wondered if I could have the use of your office for a few minutes? I'm quite happy to pay for any calls I make. It's just that I need a little privacy.'

'It's very irregular.'

'Remember the Special Relationship.'

'Between Britain and America?'

'No, between me and you.' His face creased into a persuasive grin. 'How about it, Sheila? It would mean a lot to me. You won't lose by it, I promise.'

'Well . . .'

'The calls are both local. Name your price.'

'I wouldn't do this for anyone,' she said as she thought it over. 'But since you've been so warm and friendly, I suppose it'll be okay.'

'Thanks a million.'

'I'll show you the way.'

'I'm right on your heels.'

He followed her into the hall and along to the little office which was the administrative centre of the hotel. An old oak roll-top desk stood against a wall, with sheaves of paper all over it. Somewhere beneath the litter was an Amstrad word processor. The telephone was on a shelf right next to the desk. Sheila indicated it, then stood aside. As he flopped into the chair beside the desk, Stone noted the heavy iron safe in the far corner.

'Still got that little parcel I gave you?'

'It's locked securely away.'

'What if I need it in a hurry?'

'There's always someone on the premises.'

'Good.' He winked. 'Be seeing you around, Sheila.'

'Righto, Mr Stone.'

'Hubert, for God's sake.'

'I like to keep things on a professional basis.'

'You mean you *charge* for it?'

She let out a cackle and gave him a gentle smack of reproach before flitting out of the room. Stone's grin froze. He got up to close the door, resumed his seat and produced a card from his inside pocket. Reaching for the phone, he dialled the first number and was put through immediately. The girl on the switchboard at The Belfry Hotel connected him with the voice he had been waiting to hear for some days now.

'Hello?'

'Glenn? It's Uncle Huby.'

'Oh, hi!' Token enthusiasm.

'Everything okay?'

'Fine, fine.'

'How soon can we get together, baby?'

'Well, today, I guess.'

'I'm on my way.'

'Hold on there, Uncle Huby.'

'You want to play some golf, don't you?'

'Oh, sure I do.'

'Then what's the problem?'

'There isn't one.'

'See you in half an hour, then. Take care.'

Hubert Stone rang off before his niece could question the arrangement. He was peeved by her momentary reluctance but he could also draw comfort from the brief conversation. That comfort disappeared as he dialled another number. As it rang out, his eyes did not shift from the safe. Another switchboard girl in another hotel came on the line. He was put through to a gruff voice that was edged with hostility.

'Yeah.'

'It's me,' said Stone. 'I read the papers.'

'So what?'

'You goofed, mister.'

'Who says so?'

'I do. You blew it.'

This time he slammed the receiver down and sat brooding over it for a long time. He then crossed to the safe and drummed his fingers hard on the metal. Only one thing could rescue him from his simmering fury.

He needed to play some golf.

When he finally arrived at his destination, Don

Hawker made up for lost time. He checked out the press tent, he took and survived all the flak that his dyspeptic editor could throw at him, he contrived an interview on the hoof with Bob Jaglom, he walked the course, he assessed the form of the players out on their practice rounds, he befriended some of the watching wives and girlfriends, he noted the bird life and he even got a few words alone with Angus Cameron, the peppery little Scot who was at the helm of the European challenge. It was a useful morning. Karen Maxwell put the finishing touches to it for him.

'Don!'

'Hello, there!'

'Long time no see.'

'My fault.'

He gave her a hug and kissed her on the cheek. It was a few years since they had last met, though that had not been her doing. She had tried to contact him more than once but he had been evasive. Hawker had always been something of a loner. Events of the past few years had made him much worse.

'How are you?' she asked.

'Jogging along.'

'I was delighted when I knew you were coming.'

'Thanks. And congratulations.'

'On what?'

'Getting the job as press officer.'

'Fluke.'

'Rubbish! You're the ideal person.'

'Flattery goes a long way with me.'

He grinned but did not pick up the cue. Karen could see that the wound still smarted and she hoped that she was not opening it up again by her very presence. The thing which had kept him away served to draw her closer to him, and she took him by the arm to lead him in the direction of the driving range. They strolled along in silence, then paused to watch two of the

Americans, Gary Lapidus and Hal Mayo, hitting balls into the middle distance. The men were effortlessly professional, making tiny adjustments to their swing each time and working patiently at refining their technique.

Hawker was duly impressed by their commitment.

'How on earth do they do it?'

'The will to win.'

'There's more to it than that, Karen,' he said. 'If I go out on a golf course I always have the will to win, but that doesn't stop me making a fool of myself. My timing is hopeless.'

'What's your handicap?'

'A complete inability to master the game.'

'You can't be that bad.'

'Wait till you see me. When I go into a bunker, I'm trapped in the sand for ages. Hacking madly away as if I'm trying to dig another Channel Tunnel.' He indicated the two Americans. 'Yet look at these two. Wonderful swings. Perfect timing. Gary Lapidus is short, fat and older than me but he hits that ball straight and true without fail. Why is that?'

Karen shrugged. 'He's a golfer; you're an athlete.'

'Even Eric Fretton can beat me!'

'Always let your boss think he can win.'

'But he can. I'm a real duffer.'

'You'll crack it one day,' she reassured. 'It's only a question of sticking at it, and Elaine once told me that you had amazing stickability.'

The mere mention of the name made him wince visibly. Karen blamed herself and mumbled an apology but he shook his head. Gary Lapidus and Hal Mayo completed their stint on the driving range and went off together towards the putting green at the rear of the hotel. Hawker and Karen drifted after them, her arm now hooked affectionately in his.

'Sorry,' he said.

'It was stupid of me. I'd never make it in the Diplomatic Service.'

'Forget it.'

'Would you rather I kept out of the way?'

'No!'

'I'd hate to be a painful reminder, Don.'

'You're quite the opposite.'

'Am I?'

'Yes. In fact, I was hoping that we might be able to get together some time.'

'That would suit me down to the ground.'

Karen smiled and a friendship that went back many years was repaired in an instant. They made a tentative arrangement to meet that evening, then she glided off to the press tent. He watched her go and felt a stab of pain as he remembered how close she had once been to Elaine. At the same time he knew that Karen Maxwell might be the one person who could help him, who could take him back through some disturbing memories to confront the cold truths that lay behind them. While Europe and America waged war over the Ryder Cup, he might be able to fight a personal battle and achieve at least a degree of victory.

Laughter jerked him out of his reverie and turned his gaze to the putting green where an impromptu photo call was taking place. Hal Mayo and Gary Lapidus were posing in front of the cameras and keeping everyone amused with their badinage. Mayo was a tall rangy young Texan with a handsome profile and a film-star grin. As the reigning U.S. Open Champion, he was one of the undoubted strengths of the visiting team and a sure-fire hit with female fans of the game wherever he played. Lapidus was very different, a short stubby man of forty with a bald head and a rubber face. He was the self-appointed clown among the Americans, a witty wisecracking extrovert who could set the galleries alight with his antics and conjure a smile out of the most humourless situation.

Hugely popular with spectators, Gary Lapidus was less of a success with his playing partners who knew that his untiring jokiness was a means of unsettling them so that he could seize the advantage. In front of an audience or a camera, nobody was more comical than Lapidus, but his effervescence concealed a quiet ruthlessness that had kept him at the top for some fifteen years. He was the oldest, toughest and most experienced of the Americans with a putter of almost legendary reliability. Once he got on the green, he was lethal.

'Sink one for us, Gary!'

'Yeah. Hit a fifteen-footer.'

'Straight into the cup.'

'Show us the Lapidus touch.'

'You'll have to ask my wife about that,' he said.

The photographers laughed and crouched down near the hole so that they could get a good shot of the ball as it rolled inexorably towards its target. Lapidus twirled his putter between his fingers, pulled a face and shot out a stream of wisecracks that had them shaking with mirth. Pretending to accede to their request, he took up his stance and went through his celebrated ritual, sizing up the shot then taking two practice swings before tensing himself for the one that counted. As the cameras waited for him to sink the putt, he hit the ball absurdly hard and wide so that they all had to dive out of the way to avoid being struck. Two of them rolled on the ground and a third lost his hat in the confusion.

Don Hawker was the only person who did not join in the general hilarity. As the ball streaked towards him, he trapped it under his foot and picked it up. Something made it burn like molten metal in the palm of his hand. He saw that it was a Wilson Ultra 432 that had been personalised by its owner's initials.

The field opposite Corley Hall looked as if it had been planted with police officers and yielded a bumper crop. Uniforms were everywhere as the thorough search of the murder scene continued. Dogs were also being used in the hope that they might sniff out vital clues, though the prevailing odour was that of the effluent which was being slowly drained into sewage lorries so that the lagoon itself could be examined more closely. It was dull and repetitive work, yet it drew a small audience.

Malcolm was part of that audience. As he drove the tractor along Bennetts Road North, he had an excellent view of all the police activity. The field was to his left and he watched with a contemptuous sneer. Malcolm was returning to the farm with an empty trailer rattling along behind him, its noise – like that of the tractor's roar – suffocated beneath the massive blanket of sound that came from the earphones of his personal stereo. With his favourite Heavy Metal band pounding remorselessly away, he did not hear the vehicle that sped up behind him. It was a police car with its blue light flashing madly. Overtaking him with ease, it then swung in to the left and mounted the grass verge before coming to a halt.

Malcolm reduced speed so that he could have a more leisurely look at what was happening. Police interest was concentrated around a section of the verge that was directly opposite the lagoon. The field at this point was bounded by a thick hedge which was topped with a double strand of barbed wire. It seemed fairly obvious that this had been the probable place of entry for the murderer and his victim. The wire had been cut, leaving a two-foot holly hedge as the only obstacle. Once into the field, the dead body would only have had to be carried ten yards or so. Tyre tracks had been left on the grass verge and these were being photographed and discussed in great detail by the detectives. Every inch of the surrounding area was being sifted for evidence. Wearing thick gardening gloves, some of the men were even pulling up the nettles that fringed the holly hedge. They were determined to miss nothing.

The farm labourer smirked down at them. He hated the police and all that they represented. He despised them even more because they were crawling about the farm. Coppers always meant trouble. Malcolm had been waging a private war against them for most of his life. It was inevitable that they usually held the whiphand over him but this time it was different. He knew something that they did not and it gave him an odd sense of power.

When he reached the farmyard he alighted from the vehicle to open the gate, then mounted it again to drive tractor and trailer in. The dogs came bounding out to greet him, and one of them was allowed to leap up on to his lap. He fondled the animal and giggled.

'Look at 'em!' he said. 'They'll never find it.'

The dog barked an excited reply.

'I put one across the bleeders at last!'

The tractor was stationary but he jabbed his foot down hard on the accelerator and beeped the horn at the same time. Above the noise of engine, horn, dog and Heavy Metal rose a sound that had an almost eerie quality. He was laughing. Here was no simple expression of amusement but a wild and uncontrollable cachinnation that carried the timbre of madness.

Malcolm was triumphant.

Chapter Four

Angus Cameron was a man with a mission. Having led the European team to two consecutive victories in the Ryder Cup, he had set his heart on a third. Since he had already let it be known that he would stand down as captain after the current match, he was determined to end on a high note and carve his name deep into the record books. As a golfer in his own right he had had an illustrious career that included four major titles, but nothing gave him so much pride and pleasure as vanquishing an American Ryder Cup team. Cameron had played in the event himself on five occasions but he had been on the losing side each time. Defeat had been particularly bitter at Muirfield in 1973 in front of his own home crowd of fanatical Scots, and the enormity of that trauma had never quite left him. Only a third successive triumph could wipe away for ever the lingering phantoms of his earlier failure.

Angus Cameron was nothing if not peremptory.

'Six. Ten. Eighteen.'

'What about the other holes?' said Tom Pickard.

'They're all important,' said Cameron, 'but, in my view, the Ryder Cup will be decided on the sixth, the tenth and the eighteenth.'

'Water hazards each time.'

'Our hopes could drown at any one of them.'

'So could theirs.'

'If we put them under enough pressure.'

Pressure was a word that figured a great deal in the Cameron vocabulary and it was reflected in his hectoring manner. Even in the most casual conversation, he exerted intense pressure, and a full-blown argument with him was like trying to get the better of a tempest. Angus Cameron was a small, nervy, red-headed Scot with all the swirling aggression of a man who had had to fight against his many deficiencies all his life. Overcoming his diminutive size, he had learned to generate enormous power off the tee and to hit the ball as far as anyone in the game. When he was having a chat he still sounded as if he was swinging a golf club in anger.

'You and Rolf will lead off in the foursomes.'

'Suits me,' said Tom easily.

'They'll want to get off to a strong start as well, so you'll probably be up against Lapidus and Dressler. Or maybe Lapidus and Bianco. I think Bob Jaglom is still experimenting with the pairings.'

'He's got plenty of firepower to choose from.'

'So have we.'

'What's the word on Tony Bianco?'

'He's always dangerous in matchplay.'

'Lousy season so far.'

'Bob Jaglom knows what he's doing.'

'Still rather have you in my corner, Angus.'

Tom Pickard winked at his captain and sipped from his glass of orange juice. He was the tallest man in the whole contest, with rounded shoulders and a slight stoop, but he made every inch of his height count when he struck a golf ball. Now in his early thirties, Tom was a Ryder Cup veteran whose relaxed charm was always a morale-booster for the rest of the team. His big happy face was surmounted by a mop of tousled black hair. The Yorkshire accent had a soothing solidity to it.

They were having a drink together in the restaurant before being joined by the others. Angus Cameron was

43

his usual obsessive self and Tom Pickard was a patient but not uncritical listener. When he saw his chance, the Yorkshireman slipped in his request.

'D'you think you might reconsider this ban?'

'Eh?'

'Talking to the press.'

'They're a damn nuisance.'

'I know that, Angus,' said the other, 'but it does seem sort of . . . well, unrealistic. I mean, most of them are friends of ours. We mix with them socially and speak to them freely at every other tournament.'

'This one is different.'

'In what way?'

'I call the shots.'

'We don't want to antagonise the scribblers.'

'They'll get their stories. Through me.'

'That's what they're complaining about.'

'I know what I'm doing, Tom,' said Cameron testily. 'It isn't the golfing press that worries me so much. They know the score and get on with their job. No, it's the feature writers who cause the headaches. They're not here to report on the finer points of the game.'

'They want spice.'

'Exactly! And that's when the distraction starts. If I didn't clamp down, some of my team would spend more time giving interviews than working on their game. So I'll handle the press conferences my way and leave you lot free to get on with the real business.'

'And what about off-the-record chats?'

'Avoid them.'

'Even with Don Hawker?'

Cameron bristled. 'Especially with him. That man is a disaster on wheels. Keep well clear.'

'He goes in where it hurts, that's all.'

'Aye, he's a nosey bugger right enough.'

'Don also happens to be an old mate of mine.'

'Avoid him like the plague.'

44

'But he's collaborating on a book with me. I can't just cut him dead. We need to talk to each other.'

'Not for the next five days, you don't.'

'Angus, this is plain stupid!'

'No, it's the Ryder Cup.'

'Does that mean we have to take a vow of silence?'

'Frankly, yes,' said the other seriously. 'Nothing must be allowed to get in the way of victory. Complete concentration on the task in hand is our only hope. This is no ordinary match, Tom. It's a spiritual crusade. A vow of silence is only one part of the sacrifice you must make. I'd also suggest a vow of chastity.'

Tom Pickard smiled wickedly and rolled his eyes.

'Try telling that to my wife!'

After another testing practice round, they adjourned to the locker room to get changed. Bob Jaglom had the quiet assurance of a man who could see things developing in exactly the way he had planned. Tony Bianco was at his most ebullient and Gary Lapidus was firing off quips at his usual rate. The three men epitomised the mood of confidence in the American camp. Jaglom was encouraged to start making final decisions.

'I want you to lead off in the foursomes, Tony.'

'Fine.'

'Team up with Hal Mayo.'

'Any idea who we're up against?'

'Tom Pickard and Rolf Kohlmar.'

'No problem,' said Bianco with a grin.

'What about me?' asked Lapidus.

'I'm saving you as the sting in the tail.'

'Who's my playing partner?'

'Vance Dressler.'

'But the guy's got no sense of humour!'

'That's why I put him in with you, Gary.'

'He never laughs at my jokes.'

'You and Old Poker-Face will make a great combo. The court jester and the basilisk. My guess is you'll have to take on the Irish pair, Fitzgerald and Riley. You can put 'em off their stroke with your clowning and Vance can spook them with that Dracula stare of his.'

'Trouble is, he spooks me as well!' said Lapidus. 'Playing with him is worse than *Nightmare on Elm Street*.'

'You'll get used to it,' said Jaglom.

He gave them a few words of advice, then left them to mull over the implications of it all. Tony Bianco was bubbling with enthusiasm and delighted to be chosen for the opening duel in the contest. While appreciating the psychology behind his captain's decision, Gary Lapidus nevertheless enjoyed complaining about it and he made his colleague roar with laughter at his gibes. For the rest of the year they were sworn enemies on the golf course but the Ryder Cup turned them into the best of friends. They were representing their country and were intent on subduing the upstart Europeans by showing them what real golf was all about.

Gary Lapidus scratched his bald head and grimaced.

'Alma's not gonna like this one bit.'

'Why?'

'She was hoping I'd draw Hal Mayo so that she could follow us around and watch him flex his muscles. Alma's got the hots for that guy. It's those long legs and that Texas drawl.' He shrugged hopelessly. 'I told her not to marry a midget like me but there was no holding her.'

'Dressler's a good golfer.'

'But what woman could fall for that mug of his?'

'Only a blind one, I guess.'

'Hal Mayo is another story. Women go crazy over him. When he's around, the pussy doesn't just grow on trees. It drops off and bites him on the ankle.'

'That's his problem.'

'And yours, Tony.'

'How come?'

'Well, how do you feel about that gorgeous wife of yours trailing around after Glamour Boy? His chemistry never fails. She'll be turned on with the rest of 'em.'

'Glenn isn't like that,' said Bianco quickly.

'They're *all* like that, buddy.'

'Not my wife.'

'Wait till she gets a load of Hal Mayo.'

'Glenn has seen him before.'

'*This* close up? I tell you, he's deadly.'

'Knock it off, will you?' snapped Bianco.

'Hey, go easy,' soothed the other.

'Then cool it. Okay?'

'Sure, sure.'

Tony Bianco had been caught on a raw spot and he retreated into sullen silence. Lapidus waited until they were ready to leave the locker room together before he tossed a question over his shoulder.

'By the way, how *is* Glenn?'

'She's in great shape.'

'Haven't seen her around today.'

'Gone off with her own golf clubs.'

'On the other course?'

'No,' said Bianco irritably. 'The Derby course was booked up so they had to look further afield than The Belfry. Some club not too far away.'

'Who's she playing?'

'Her uncle.'

'Brave man. Glenn is some golfer.'

'It was Uncle Hubert who taught her.'

'Oh, I get it. He's her Svengali.'

'No,' said Bianco coldly. 'He's just a creep.'

Hubert Stone took out a five-iron and sized up his tee shot. He and his niece had driven the few miles to Maxstoke Park Golf Club in Coleshill where they found a pleasant if undemanding parkland course that was splashed with mature trees and lightly bunkered, with a lake that affected play on two holes. Stone was in his element. It was the ideal place for him to discuss the Ryder Cup.

'What's the feeling among the players?'

'They're sky high,' said Glenn Bianco.

'So they should be. We'll crucify the Europeans. Just look at our team, will you? Hal Mayo is US Open Champion. Vance Dressler won the Masters. And Gary Lapidus picked up the USPGA title for the second year in a row. Those guys are out on their own.' He gave a ripe chuckle. 'Then there's our secret weapon.'

'Who's that?'

'Tony, of course. Your husband.'

'Oh, yes,' she murmured.

'You don't sound very convinced.'

'Tony will do well.'

'I'm expecting big things from him,' said Stone with sudden urgency. 'He's the ace in the pack. I know that things haven't panned out for him recently but that crap is all behind him, isn't it?'

She shrugged. 'Yeah.'

'*Isn't* it, Glenn?' he pressed.

'Sure.'

'That damn nonsense is all sorted out.'

'Why don't we just play, Uncle Huby?'

'This is important to me.'

'Do you think that *I* don't care about it?' she said with a flash of spirit. 'Hell, it's my life.'

'So tell your old uncle the truth.'

'You know it already.'

'Reassure me, honey.'

'Back off, will you? Please.'

'I need to hear you say it, Glenn.'

'Look,' she said vehemently, 'it's *my* marriage. Why not let me get on with it my way?'

'Because we tried that, didn't we?' His manner

hardened. 'And we both know the result. I'm in on this in every sense so don't try to freeze me out. Don't forget who introduced you to Tony Bianco in the first place. *I* pulled all the strings. You were grateful enough to me then.' He softened. 'Now, don't let's fall out, sweetie-pie. I'm not asking too much, am I?'

Another shrug. 'I guess not.'

'So how does it stand between the two of you?'

'Everything is fine and dandy.'

'Convince me.'

'I can't, Uncle Huby. You'll just have to take my word for it. I made a big effort – we both did – and it's starting to pay off.'

'Do we get to see the real Tony Bianco again?'

'No reason why not.'

'Thanks, Glenn!' he said with feeling. 'I knew I could count on you. It means a great deal to me. I gotta lot invested in this Ryder Cup.'

'Too much.'

'Impossible.'

'Don't pin everything on Tony. He's only one player out of a team of twelve. Be fair to him.'

'Oh, I will. I'll be extremely fair.'

'Then stop going on about him.'

'But he's the key to the whole thing. If he inspires the team to win the Ryder Cup, then we all stand to make a killing. You, me and that golfing genius you married.'

'With your help,' she reminded.

'Very unselfish of me, really,' he said. 'Had half a mind to wed you myself but I decided to make the supreme sacrifice and put the game first. That's just the way it was. Business before pleasure. Tony Bianco was a much better bet as a husband but that doesn't mean I didn't have ideas about you.'

She shuddered inwardly. 'I noticed.'

'Don't let these wrinkles of mine deceive you, honey.

49

I still got plenty of red blood in my veins. Your Uncle Huby is still very much alive and kicking.'

'Let's get on with the game.'

'Then pay heed to all I said. Okay?'

'Okay.'

He showed his dentures in a grim smile that managed to combine avuncular affection with a seedy carnality, then he turned back to address his ball. Hubert Stone was an accomplished amateur golfer, and age had not robbed him of his technique and judgement. They were on the tee at the second hole, a 165-yard par three that presented him with the target of a two-tier green which invited a perfectly straight shot. Stone mustered his concentration before drawing back his club and injecting power into his downswing. The ball went high but directly on line. Comfortably missing the two bunkers on the right, it hit the turf and scudded to a halt some ten feet from the flag.

Glenn Bianco nodded her congratulations, then stepped up to place her own ball on the tee peg. Even in a plastic hat and light rainwear, she looked poised and elegant as she studied the shot carefully and worked out all its elements. When she was ready, she took up her stance, had one practice swing, then hit the ball hard and true. Its trajectory was much flatter than her uncle's shot but it was far more effective. Pitching on the soft grass, it bounced forward then slowed to a trickle before stopping only a foot away from the cup.

Hubert Stone slapped his thigh and whooped.

'Wowee! That was a Tony Bianco shot.'

He did not see the look of disgust on her face. Wrapped up in their personal battle, there was something else that he did not observe. They were being watched. A tall figure in an anorak was standing at a discreet distance from them and keeping check of their every move. He scratched his beard as the two of them headed towards the green. Something in his manner suggested that he was not interested in the golf.

A darker purpose had brought him there.

Don Hawker carried on as he had started. Spurning the idea of lunch, he went quietly about his job, collecting facts, garnering predictions and absorbing gossip. He was everywhere. He watched, waited, listened, probed, walked the entire course at least twice and followed his instinct. Hawker did all his best work when he was out and about. He was not an habitué of the press tent because he was not really accepted there. Most of the journalists were specialist golf writers, men who dedicated their lives to penning lyrical essays about a game they loved and which, in almost every case, they could play very well. It was a freemasonry that Hawker could never hope to penetrate. He was a rank outsider with nothing but contempt for the multiple snobberies and etiquette and élitism that lay at the heart of golf. It was too undemocratic for his liking and he was never at ease with its privileged class of scribes. They resented him as an intruder on private property and were not slow to prosecute him with their scorn and malice. Hawker ignored it all. He had a roving commission to work at any major sporting event and the Ryder Cup was as likely to throw up a dramatic story as any. Indeed, it had already turned up trumps.

He was on the verge of a scoop.

Eric Fretton caught up with him in the car park and looked at the Vauxhall Cavalier with distaste.

'When are you going to get rid of that heap?'

'When you pay me enough to buy a new car.'

'You'd only drag it down to your own level.'

'It goes. What more do you want?'

'It would be nice to know what colour it is under all that mud. Look at the filth on your headlights, man! That's a positive safety hazard.'

'I'll bear it in mind.'

Hawker slipped off his anorak and stowed it away in the boot of his car. Now that the drizzle had stopped, he put on a bomber jacket of pitted brown leather that would make him almost as incongruous a figure in the press tent as his editor. Hawker wore black trousers and a dark blue shirt with no tie. His stout walking shoes were scuffed from his perambulations.

'So what have you got so far?' said Eric.

'Not much.'

'Tell me the good news.'

'There isn't any.'

'Who's going to win?'

'Europe or America.'

'Big deal!'

'It's that close, Eric,' said the other. 'From what I can see, there's very little to choose between them. The Yanks may have the edge on paper but we have the home advantage and the certainty of a large patriotic crowd cheering us to the echo. I wouldn't risk my money on either team. It'll be neck and neck all the way.'

'That's my feeling. A real nail-biter.'

'What might tip the scales is the captaincy.'

'Angus Cameron versus Bob Jaglom.'

'They must pick the right men at the right time.'

'Angus is too much of a martinet,' said Eric. 'I rate Jaglom higher. He's the deep thinker. Angus is a master of attack but Jaglom is as cunning as a fox.'

Hawker nodded agreement. 'What will decide it is the singles on the last day. There'll be no place to hide any weaknesses then. Both teams will have to field everyone and that's when it will get really interesting.'

'And worrying.'

'Why?'

'They've got more strength in depth than us.'

'Don't write the Europeans off too soon, Eric.'

'I'm not. I still think we can pinch it. If our golfers

52

can play above themselves and get that vital bit of luck. Tom Pickard is on a streak at the moment, and Rolf Kohlmar won the British Open by four strokes. Denzil Evans, Colin Aitken and Ian Roslin won't let us down and we can always expect fireworks from Claudio Mundi. The two Irish lads are pretty solid, and Stefan Carlsson can be inspirational when he keeps his eyes off the ladies. Then we get into the danger zone.'

'Graham Lowe and Manuel Ingaramo.'

'Both new to Ryder Cup golf.'

'But both experienced professionals.'

'They could crack. So, alas, could Richie Llewellyn. He'll be struggling at this level. I know he's got plenty of Welsh passion but it takes more than *hwyl* to compete against the Yanks in a contest like this.'

'Angus Cameron forecasts a victory.'

'He would,' said Eric cynically. 'Don't forget that the wee man from Fife also forecast a victory before the five Ryder Cup matches in which he himself took part.'

'I've still got faith in him.'

Hawker locked his car and they made their way back towards the press tent. It was now early evening but people were still milling around everywhere. The sense of anticipatory delight was almost tangible. Hawker alone remained untouched by it.

Eric Fretton issued a forlorn warning.

'And try to keep your nose clean from now on.'

'Eh?'

'My old heart can't take it any more.'

'I didn't *intend* to get drawn into a murder case.'

'You never do.'

'It came with the accommodation.'

'Bullshit!'

'Cowshit, actually. Fathoms of it.'

'Stay somewhere else.'

'Everyone's booked solid, Eric. I have to stay put.' He grinned. 'Unless I share with you, that is.'

'Not on your life!'

'You can trust me after all these years.'

'I can trust you to put the mockers on everything, I know that! One thing I do insist on with you is separate accommodation. The Whitehall Hotel is a nice civilised place with comfortable rooms and a sexy landlady who stuffs us to the gills with monster breakfasts. If I let you in there, I'll be stepping over dead bodies.'

'Thanks for having such faith in me.'

'I pay you, don't I? What more do you want?'

Hawker laughed and they stopped near the hotel. He decided to test his editor's knowledge of literature.

'Ever heard of *Adam Bede*?'

'Is he a golfer?'

'No, he's a book by George Eliot.'

'Ah, now I've come across him before.'

'It's not a *him* – it's a *her*.'

'A transvestite novelist?'

'You're worse than me, Eric. Someone ought to improve your reading habits. Maybe you should swap rooms with me and learn about Warwickshire's finest writer.'

'I'm happy in my ignorance,' said Eric. 'Besides, I have a special reason for staying at the Whitehall.'

'That sexy landlady?'

'No, a man called Hubert Stone from Phoenix, Arizona. One of those crazy Yanks who piss down your back and tell you it's raining. He claims to have a direct line through to the American team via his niece.'

'And who is she?'

'Glenn Bianco.'

'Tony's wife?'

'Your deductive powers are amazing, Hawker.'

'I'd like to meet this Mr Stone.'

'Save yourself the trouble. He's a nutter.'

'All the more reason.'

'Look, *I've* got him covered,' said the editor. 'You

start sniffing around elsewhere. We're committing a lot of space and money to our feature on the Ryder Cup. I want you to unearth something that nobody else can.'

Hawker smiled. 'I guarantee it.'

Eric Fretton was less than reassured as he went off into the hotel. His leading writer consistently brought in good stories for the magazine but they were always riddled with danger and shot through with controversy. The portents were even more alarming this time around.

Don Hawker turned on his heel. Instead of going on to the press tent, he went quickly back to the car park and got into the Vauxhall Cavalier. Five minutes later he was crossing a hump-back bridge and swinging right before pulling up outside The Dog and Doublet. It was a small pub on the edge of the canal and it offered a degree of privacy that was quite vital. When Hawker went into the lounge bar, his drink was waiting for him on a table. A face looked up with a Yorkshire welcome.

'What kept you, mate?'

It was Tom Pickard.

Murder squad detectives had flooded Corley and set up an incident room in the village hall. Regulars at the old-time dancing on a Wednesday night were horrified that such a violent crime had taken place on their doorstep, but they were even more outraged that their ballroom had been hijacked by the police. Systematic house-to-house questioning got the whole village involved. There was a sense of deep resentment against what was seen as a kind of armed occupation. The unhurried pace of Corley life had given way to the urgent stride of a major criminal investigation. It was a communal burden.

Brian Leech and his family bore the brunt of the

police presence and it irked them. After yet another lengthy session with Superintendent Frank Rayment and Sergeant Mike Impey – 'When we can have our bloody field back, that's what we want to know!' – they were more hostile than ever. Their antagonism was directed towards their immediate neighbour and one of his guests. As they sat around the table in the kitchen, Brian Leech, his wife and his son brooded on the misery of their lot. Malcolm lounged in the doorway with a mug of coffee in his hand. Conspiracy stirred.

'Starrett is behind all this,' said the farmer.

'Yes,' agreed Roy Leech, who looked like a younger version of his father. 'We never had no trouble like this till he bought that house.'

'He's no countryman,' said Leech with rancour. 'He doesn't belong here with his high-faluting ideas and his fancy hotel. He should bugger off out of it and take his city ways with him!'

'Mr Starrett didn't do the murder,' said Olive Leech reasonably. 'He wouldn't stoop to anything like that. I think you're too hard on him sometimes, Brian.'

She was a short, anxious, bustling woman whose face and body bore testimony to a lifetime of unthinking drudgery in the service of her menfolk. Olive Leech was the one member of the household who was prepared to see other people's point of view and who understood the value of friendship.

'We should try to get on with them,' she continued weakly. 'Mr and Mrs Starrett may not be like us but that doesn't mean we can't be good neighbours.'

As usual, her comments were completely disregarded by the men. Their conversation rolled on without check.

'Corley Hall was a farmhouse,' said Leech. 'It's tied to the land. They should never have let him turn it into a flaming hotel.' Anguish changed his face into a beetroot again. '*We* should have had that place.'

'Yes,' said Roy. 'It's ours by right.'

'But that Starrett took it from us.'

'Bought it right under our sodding noses.'

'Who asked that bastard to come here?'

'We'll get him one day, Dad.'

'Someone ought to.'

'Don't talk like that,' bleated Olive. 'The reason we never bought the house was because we had no money. Mr Starrett did, so there's no arguing. Fair's fair, Brian.'

It was years since the farmer had stopped listening to his wife and he was not going to start doing so now. Besides, he was caught up in his dreams of revenge.

'Then there's that Hawker bloke.'

'Who?' grunted Roy.

'The one who found the body in the lagoon.'

'Oh, *that* clever sod!' He sniggered. 'Pity it wasn't old Starrett's body he found.' Malevolence took over. 'It says in the paper that Hawker was a famous runner. Well, he can bleeding well run away from Corley, I know that much! We don't need him here.'

'He's a guest at the hotel,' said Olive, swimming vainly against the tide. 'He's entitled to be here.'

'Hawker ought to be taken down a peg,' decreed Brian Leech. 'Serves him right for trespassing on our land.'

'Yes, Dad. And for staying next door.'

'He needs a good thumping.'

'At least.'

'Now don't get us into *more* trouble,' pleaded Olive. 'Why not just forget the whole thing?'

'He started all this,' said Leech ruminatively.

Roy nodded. 'We got his name. Don Hawker.'

'We got his name and number.'

'Let's just bide our time.'

'Brian!' said his wife ineffectually. 'Don't!'

'What are we gonna do to him, Dad?'

'I need time to think.' He glanced across at the farmhand. 'Malc is good at this kind of thing.'

'Any ideas, Malc?'

'You're in this with us.'

Malcolm rolled his coffee mug between the palms of his hands and let out a long low cackle. He emptied the mug with a gurgling sound before putting it in the sink and going back to the door.

'Let you know,' he said.

Malcolm was still laughing to himself as he left the house and went out to his own quarters in one of the outbuildings. The room was large but fairly primitive, with only a few sticks of furniture and a single bed. Three carpets failed to cover the uneven floor. Malcolm did not mind. Notwithstanding its gloom and its pervading smell of cattle feed, it was his own private lair and he loved it. One of its chief attractions was an unlimited expanse of whitewashed wall that lent itself to Malcolm's hobby. As he flopped down now on the bed, he surveyed that hobby with keen pleasure.

The walls were adorned with bits and pieces of motor cars. A number-plate hung next to a steering-wheel that was surrounded by a circle of stars which had been sawn from the bonnets of Mercedes. Engine parts of every kind dangled beside CB aerials, a rear windscreen, even a roof rack. One owner would still be wondering what had happened to the spare wheel from his Land Rover. Dozens of bemused drivers would still be puzzling over other thefts from their vehicles. Pride of place on the largest wall went to Malcolm's latest acquisition. On behalf of the Leech family, he had felt it important to strike back at the police in some way. One of their patrol cars now lacked the revolving blue light from its roof. In the cause of justice it had been extinguished forever.

Malcolm now turned his weird intelligence to the problem of Don Hawker. Hands behind his head and

58

ankles crossed like the effigy of a crusader, he let his mind play with various possibilities. Then he spotted a small area of empty wall directly opposite him and he started to snigger. He was thinking about a Vauxhall Cavalier.

An hour with Tom Pickard produced more hard fact and valuable comment than a whole day at The Belfry. Don Hawker plied his friend with questions and always got straight answers. The only thing that the golfer would not discuss was Angus Cameron's strategy for retaining the Ryder Cup, but that was not the journalist's main field of interest. Hawker was more concerned wth the personal stories behind the public event, with the way that each of the players was coping with the intense pressures being put upon him and with the roles of the respective wives and girlfriends. Tom Pickard was a mine of information that was delivered in a wry down-to-earth manner.

The two men talked the same language. Hawker had never been a professional golfer, nor even a useful amateur, but he had gone to the very top of his own sport and he understood the peculiar problems that afflict someone in that position. Pickard had become rich from golf, while Hawker had gained only minimal financial rewards from athletics, but they still had a bond which united them in a relaxed but caring friendship. Each of them had become – the golfer still remained – the elder statesman in his particular sphere. They exuded the wisdom that can only come from long experience. It was not perversity on the Yorkshireman's part that he had chosen Hawker as his co-author in preference to dozens of apparently more qualified observers of the game. Pickard knew that he could trust his colleague to be as honest and trenchant as himself. What Don Hawker lacked in style, he more than made up for in integrity.

Other customers were starting to drift in for an evening's solid drinking. Tom Pickard had chosen a quiet corner but he was already being pointed out by a few of the regulars. He emptied his pint glass and stood up.

'That's it for now, mate. Back to Angus.'

'What time is lights out?'

Pickard laughed. 'It's no joke, Don. If the Sage of Fife had his way, it wouldn't only be lights out. He wants us to become monks for the next four days.'

'What would your wife think of that?'

'I daresay she'd be tickled by the idea.'

'Why?'

'Sylvia's always wanted to seduce a monk.'

Hawker grinned, then finished his own drink before getting up and going out to the car park with his friend. The golfer climbed into his gleaming Rover and lowered the window for a last word.

'Why didn't you say that you knew Karen Maxwell?'

'Eh?'

'She tells me that you two go back a long way.'

'Yes, that's right. Karen was very close to . . . at one time. I haven't seen her for ages. I hadn't realised she'd got on so well.'

'Bright girl. She's a promising future ahead.'

'This job is a real feather in her cap. Karen must be pretty special to become press officer at an event like this. I bet the competition was terrific.'

'Karen had the best smile,' said Pickard flippantly. 'But you're right. It is an achievement for someone as young as Karen. Shows what tremendous potential she has. Someone must have put in a good word for her.'

'Friends in high places? That how she did it?'

'Why not ask her, Don?' He started the engine. 'I'll be too busy playing golf and trying to keep Angus at bay. See you around, mate. Take care.'

'I will – and thanks again, Tom!'

'Cheers!'

The Rover scrunched its way over the gravel and went off towards the little hump-back bridge over the canal. Hawker got into his own car, checked the notes he had made in his pad, then added some more. After consulting a map of the area, he then drove away himself, skirting The Belfry and following a tortuous route through country lanes until he came to The Cock at Wishaw. It was a much larger and more characterful pub than The Dog and Doublet, with a clientele that seemed to be evenly divided between courting couples and middle-aged regulars. One or two people half-recognised him, so he tucked himself away in an oak settle whose high side ensured his privacy. It was well over an hour before she came in.

'I thought I'd never get away,' said Karen Maxwell.

'Busy?'

'It's a madhouse over there.'

'You look sane enough to me.'

'An optical illusion,' she said, sitting down.

'What will you have?'

'Oh, anything. White wine, if they have it.'

'Coming up.'

While he bought a bottle of Australian Chardonnay at the bar, Hawker had the chance to appraise her properly. She was taller than he remembered and slightly darker, but the old attractions were still there. Becoming aware of his gaze, she met it with a twinkle of affection. Hawker had always liked Karen Maxwell. There was a time when she had been his wife's best friend. He still wondered why he had missed her so much at Elaine's funeral. A bottle of white wine might help to solve that mystery.

The first sip brought a smile of gratitude from her.

'Nectar!'

'Journalism drives you to drink.'

'I'm not surprised.' She savoured the wine again.

'One of the few compensations of this job. Talking of which, where were you last night?'

'Last night?'

'The Ryder Cup Ball was held at the NEC.'

'Not my kind of thing, Karen.'

'It was great,' she said. 'Angus Cameron and Bob Jaglom introduced their teams one by one, then we got on with the festivities. Gorgeous food, dancing and a super cabaret. You missed all the fun.'

'I was having my own share of fun in Corley.'

'Yes, I read about that. Any developments?'

'None that I know of.'

'What a shock it must have been for you!'

'I've had happier stays in hotels.'

They prodded the subject of the murder around, then turned back to golf. Karen provided some fascinating insights into the behaviour of the players in both teams as well as some searing criticism of their entourages. She was also an expert on the denizens of the press tent and was able to confirm that Hawker's name was being taken in vain with increasing monotony.

'That's why Eric brought me here,' he said. 'Because he knew that it would get their goat.'

'It's naked jealousy, Don. They can't get over the fact that you out-gunned the whole lot of them by getting the commission to work on Tom Pickard's auto-biography.'

'He asked me. It was as simple as that.'

'Not to them. You have quite a reputation, believe me. They talk about you as if you're a rogue elephant in a bird sanctuary.'

He was amused. 'Nice to know my presence is felt.'

'How is the book going, anyway?'

'It's still early days.'

'You'll enjoy working with Tom. He's a lovely man.'

Hawker agreed, then dived in with a blunt question.

'What do you know about Gary Lapidus?'

'Only the obvious things.'

'Such as.'

'He's one hell of a comedian.'

'There must be more to him than that, Karen.'

'Oh, there is. He's a driven man.'

'In what way?'

'That wife of his, for a start,' she said, warming to her theme. 'Alma. She's a real Jewish princess. Ten years younger than him and she loves to be pampered. Gary is desperate to succeed in order to please her and to satisfy his own high standards. Behind that rubber face and that jovial manner, there's a lot going on.'

'Is he neurotic?'

'Completely.'

'Popular with the other Americans?'

'Very.'

'Yet as black-hearted as any of them on the course.'

'Gary Lapidus can be a real killer.'

'We'll see,' he said reflectively. 'Do you happen to know when he arrived in England?'

'It was well over a week ago.'

'Staying at The Belfry?'

'Yes,' she said. 'He's put in more practice than the whole lot of them. That's what I mean about his being driven. Gary Lapidus has been out there every day, come rain or come shine. The public only gets to hear the jokes, but I've seen the hard slog that goes on behind them.'

'Is he a nice man?'

Karen Maxwell considered the question for some time.

'I'm not sure. I used to think so.'

'Did you see anything of him in the States?'

'Quite a bit. I worked on a lot of tournaments when I was over there. Gary is much better on his own turf. On the surface he seems like a really nice guy.'

63

'And deep down?'

A ruminative pause. 'I'd have my doubts.'

'Can you be more specific?'

'Not if I want to keep my job,' she said with a rueful smile. 'Golfers are my bread and butter. I just can't afford to bad-mouth them. Anyway, who expects any professional sportsman to be a saint? The pressures are far too intense. Something's bound to crack.'

'You say Lapidus has been here for some time?'

'Playing golf and placating Alma.'

'Anything else?'

'Sightseeing.'

Hawker wondered if the American had visited Corley Hall at any stage and studied it from the vantage point of the slurry lagoon. The golf ball in his pocket began to weigh like lead. He had nothing to go on but a hunch, yet his mind was now whirring busily. Alma Lapidus would be high on his list of interviewees the next day.

He topped up their glasses with more Chardonnay.

'So tell me about yourself, Karen,' he invited.

'What is there to say?'

'Start with your marriage.'

'I'd rather not,' she sighed. 'I've tried to blank out those two years completely. It was a dreadful mistake and that was that.'

'There must have been some happy times.'

'The day I met him and the day I left him.'

'Was it that awful?'

'No, it just seems so in retrospect.'

'You lived in Kansas, didn't you?'

'Nowheresville, USA.'

'Depressing.'

'In limbo for two years.'

'Is that why my letter took so long to get through?'

'Yes,' she said softly. 'I would have come, if only I'd known. Elaine was very dear to me. I felt rotten at

64

having to miss the funeral. Stuck in the middle of Kansas while a very special friend was being . . .' She touched his hand. 'I'm sorry, Don. I know you find it hard to forgive me. I should have been there. I might have helped.'

'It was a difficult time, Karen.'

'You ignored my letters.'

'I had to.'

'Why?'

Their eyes met across the table and he felt the pull of unacknowledged desires. Karen Maxwell was not just a link with the past, an emotional bridge to a beloved wife who had left him too soon and too violently. She was a beautiful woman who had been through her own kind of marital bereavement to find a zest and fortitude that had so far eluded him. Karen was an example and perhaps even a hope.

'It's ironic, isn't it?' she said.

'What is?'

'I hated America because it wasn't Britain. And where do I end up? Working at the Ryder Cup.'

'Them versus Us.'

'Torn between two worlds once again.'

'And paid to be impartial.'

'That's the worst part of it!'

He searched her eyes again and found a hint of welcome, but he was too uncertain to pursue it and so he guided the conversation back to more neutral topics. He needed time to get to know her again, to reconcile the person she once was with the one she had become. Elaine was still between them as a barrier as much as a bond. When they left Wishaw, they drove off in different directions.

Hawker had much to occupy his mind on the journey back to the hotel. The murder still bulked large. He felt that he had made progress but had no real evidence to prove it, and he was relying on intuition. Karen Maxwell was the crucial factor in the equation. Her vivacity might lift the weight of two dead bodies from his back. Through her position at The Belfry she might lead him to the man who dumped a naked body in the slurry lagoon, and through her role as a friend she might help him to understand why his wife had committed suicide.

He was so absorbed in it all that he did not observe the headlights which stayed in his rear-view mirror all the way from Coleshill. It never even crossed his mind that he was being followed by another vehicle. The M6 was fairly busy and other cars shot past him every few seconds, but there was one that had no urge to overtake. It was towed along by the Vauxhall Cavalier on an invisible rope some fifty yards long. Even when he left the motorway at Corley Services, he did not become aware of his shadow.

By the time he turned into Rock Lane, he had more or less persuaded himself that his problems were at an end. Fate had at last appointed a guardian angel for him. She liked Australian Chardonnay and loathed Kansas. She was keen to heal old wounds. Hawker realised with a shock just how fond he had been of her all these years. Even when Elaine had been alive. It was at once unnerving and oddly comforting.

Corley Hall stood silhouetted against the sky like a haunted house in a low-budget film, its grim outline offset by squares of light in some of the windows. There were five other cars in the drive and he had to park some way down it, tucking in close to the high wall. Instead of going straight into the house, he went across to the field opposite, stepping over the yellow police tape before clambering over the five-barred gate. For a reason that he could only dimly comprehend, he was being drawn back to the scene of the crime. As he made his way across the soggy grass, he tried to decide if the victim had taken that last walk

66

to the lagoon himself before being killed and stripped. Or had the body been dead on arrival?

He went on to the grassy bank and climbed up it to stare down into the dark noisome sludge. Most of the slurry had been drained away but the lagoon was slowly beginning to fill up again as the farm effluent oozed in. It was a particularly gruesome venue in which to die, and the symbolic implications were not lost on him. What was an unknown American doing in that part of the county?

Hawker was still grappling with possible answers when he heard the stealthy tread behind him, but his reactions were far too slow. Before he could even begin to turn, something hard, cold and vicious struck him across the back of the head and sent him plunging forwards. He felt a sharp pain in his chest then lapsed gratefully into an unconsciousness that was darker and deeper than anything he had ever known before.

Chapter Five

Sheila Dowling liked him. Despite overwhelming evidence to the contrary, she clung to the belief that she was an astute judge of character. If people let her down – and they did so time and again – she always explained it away as a momentary aberration on their part which did not detract from their essential goodness. Not even marital disasters and recurring romantic disappointments could dent her tolerance of human frailty. Her buoyant optimism carried all before it. When hotel guests misbehaved badly, or walked off with a suitcase full of her property, or did a moonlight flit without paying, she would never admit that her instinct was unsound. She was there with a warm and uncritical welcome for the next person over the threshold, convinced that he or she would be an excellent guest in every way.

Hubert Stone was a case in point. She liked him. He was what she called 'a character' and that enabled her to forgive a multitude of sins. In her eyes, the American had a gnarled charm which blotted out the fact that he was also brash, noisy, lustful and completely selfish. He could clear the bar in five minutes with his loud bragging, and only the polite Koreans remained on nodding terms with him during meals. Stone was an old tyrant, the sort of man who expected his personal needs to be given priority over everything else, and who achieved this end with a jocular bullying that stopped just short of intimidation.

'Can't a guy get a drink in this place?'

'Be with you in a minute, Mr Stone.'

'But I'm thirsty *now*.'

'I'll just serve this customer.'

'What about me?'

'Half a mo.'

'Don't I count for anything around here?' said the American with a self-pitying whine. 'Hell, I been out all day. Played two rounds of golf and walked my legs off. I need a stiff whisky, Sheila. Is that too much to ask?'

The Korean who was waiting patiently at the bar signalled his agreement that Stone should take precedence. Sheila Dowling gave the little man a shrug that combined thanks with apology, then she poured the drink and took it across to the table where Stone was sitting. The latter winked at her and grinned knowingly.

'Have something yourself,' he offered.

'Later, perhaps.'

'That was *my* thinking.'

A giggle. 'Now don't start all that again.'

'Then stop looking so damn sexy.'

'I do have other guests, you know.'

'Oh, sure,' he said before sipping his drink. 'But you gotta admit that I'm your favourite.' The grin became a leer. 'Come on, Sheil. Lighten up. Why not bow to the inevitable? We could really go places together.'

The giggle was tinged with reserve this time but she could still not bring herself to put him firmly in his place. She remembered the Korean at the bar.

'I must get back.'

'Until later.'

'Don't bank on it.'

'You won't let me down.'

As she went off to serve the other customer, the door

opened and Eric Fretton stepped in. He soon regretted it.

'Hey!' called Stone. 'Something for my pal.'

'Er, no thanks,' said Eric.

'Give the guy whatever he wants, Sheil.'

'Actually . . .'

'Now, don't run out on me, Eric. I got the lowdown on the American team for you. Inside information. The best. Pull up a chair for two minutes. What'll it be?'

Eric Fretton sighed, ordered a drink and went across to join Stone at the table. He concealed his dislike of the man beneath a bland smile. Stone was turning out to be the kind of aggressive bore that the editor had met in golf clubs all over America, and he usually took care to dodge them. At the same time, however, he was ready to collect any snippet of gossip that he could find about the Ryder Cup, and the old man might be able to provide that. The brandy which Sheila now brought over would help to anaesthetise him slightly.

'Thanks, Mrs Dowling.'

'You're welcome, Mr Fretton.'

'Stick it on my tab,' said Stone airily.

'I will, don't worry.'

'And remember your own drink.'

He watched her go back to the bar, then turned to his companion. Eric lifted his glass in acknowledgement.

'Cheers!'

'To an American win!' said Stone.

'Still confident?'

'Sure thing!'

'We have the home advantage.'

'Makes no difference, Eric. Our boys are here to kick some ass and they'll do just that. There's no way they can lose – even on that shithole of a course.'

'What's wrong with it?'

'Just about everything.'

'They've made big improvements since last time.'

70

'Ha!' Stone was scornful. 'They shoulda dropped a bomb on the place then started all over again.'

'Have you ever *played* the Brabazon course?'

'Don't need to, pal. I can use my eyes. Fairways as wide as Kentucky. Semi-rough that's neat as a new haircut. Sandtraps that couldn't catch a fly. Greens that even *I* could hit without any trouble. There's nothing out there to worry a hardened pro.'

'What about the water hazards?'

'Well, a coupla holes might be testing,' conceded the other, 'but not the rest of the course. The Belfry is about as flat and unexciting as an airport runway. You check the membership list. I bet you'll find that Mickey Mouse plays here every week.'

Eric was grateful for his brandy. Though he did not rate The Belfry very highly himself, he found himself defending it with patriotic vigour against the attack. Hubert Stone recited a whole litany of faults before summing up his feelings.

'That course? Got no teeth.'

'English weather is a good dentist.'

'I'll believe it when I see it.'

Eric had intended to finish his drink as quickly as possible before excusing himself and sloping off to his room, but something now detained him. Though Stone talked volubly about the Ryder Cup, his eyes kept flicking across to the bar and their message was quite candid. Sheila Dowling was a definite target. Ordinarily, Eric would not have bothered. Women who ran hotels met this kind of situation all the time and knew how to handle it, but there was something about Sheila Dowling that aroused his protective instinct. He felt that he could not abandon her to the attentions of this old vulture. Much against his wishes, therefore, he determined to sit it out and endure another round of drinks in the hopes of taking the edge off Stone's carnal appetite.

71

The editor probed away about the American team. In amongst the boasts and the sweeping assurances, there were some occasional nuggets and Eric pounced on them at once. Hubert Stone really did have confidential information and a second glass of whisky prised it out of him. He was in full flow about Tony Bianco for over half an hour. Eric then muddied the waters of their discussion.

'And what about all those rumours?' he said.

'What rumours?'

'The Bianco marriage.'

'Sound as a bell!'

'That's not what I heard.'

'Then you heard wrong, Eric.'

'There were stories in the American press. They suggested that Bianco's loss of form could be put down to his domestic problems.'

'He's got no domestic problems!' said Stone angrily.

'Then where did the stories come from?'

'Assholes!'

'So there's no foundation at all to them?'

Stone breathed heavily. 'Listen to me and listen good. Tony and Glenn are as happy as bugs in a rug. *I* should know. I see them together all the time. That marriage is a hundred per cent proof.'

'I'll take your word for it.'

Hubert Stone was so eager to ram the point home that he forgot all about Sheila Dowling and did not notice when she slipped away to be replaced by her son. Eric Fretton had clearly touched a raw nerve. The vehemence of the old man's denials were confirming all the rumours that the editor had heard. Stone insisted that his niece and her husband enjoyed complete marital bliss, then he ended on a note of chilling certainty.

'You have my personal guarantee!'

*

When Don Hawker opened an eye to take a first hazy look at his surroundings, he was convinced that he had died, gone to Hell and been locked up in the same room as Adolf Hitler. The Führer thrust his face in close and barked an order in German. Hawker quickly retreated into unconsciousness. It was twenty minutes before he ventured out again and he regretted it immediately. As he tried to move his head, he realised that it was held tight in an iron clamp while someone drove a spike into the base of the skull. Complete immobility was the only way to deaden the pain. Another five minutes slipped away. His eye opened more cautiously this time. He saw that he was lying in a bed in a bare, white, featureless room. His nose caught a faint whiff of disinfectant. He heard the distant echo of raised voices in long corridors.

Hitler came back into view, but he had changed his appearance and his nationality. When Hawker brought his other eye into play, he observed that only the moustache remained intact. The rest of the Führer's face resembled Detective Superintendent Frank Rayment. The voice, too, was uncannily like that of the detective. Hitler interrogated him in a Birmingham accent.

'Can you hear me?'

Hawker managed a dull grunt.

'Can you speak?'

He progressed to a painful croak.

'Don't rush it. We can wait. Take your time.'

Hawker did just that. As his brain slowly cleared, he began to remember what had happened and to work out where he must be. The presence of a nurse in white uniform acted as confirmation. She was standing behind Rayment and beside the baby-faced Detective Sergeant Mike Impey. The patient was in a side ward that seemed far too small for so many people. Hawker wanted to be left alone with the man who was now starting to drive the spike even deeper into his head. He closed his eyes once more until the agony subsided. Rayment was waiting for him when he risked another glimpse of the real world.

'What happened, Mr Hawker?'

'You tell me.' Each word was a separate ache.

'Someone hit you from behind.'

'Who was it?'

'That's what we intend to find out, sir. It was obviously someone who doesn't like you very much. Did his best to split your skull in two.' Offhand concern showed. 'How are you feeling now?'

'Terrible.'

'You were extremely lucky.'

'Lucky!' The exclamation made his brain clang.

'Your assailant could have done a lot more damage.'

'He did enough.'

'He could have finished you off.'

'Why didn't he?'

'We'll come to that, sir.'

Hawker brought a tentative hand up to touch the bandage that encircled his head. A burning sensation across his chest made him wince. Rayment explained.

'You've got twenty stitches in the back of your head and a dozen or so more in your chest where you fell on to the barbed wire.' The detective sighed. 'Just as well we drained most of that stuff out of the lagoon. If you'd fallen in there, you might have drowned.'

'Don't remind me.'

'You were indeed fortunate.'

Hawker groaned. '*This* is fortunate?'

'Relatively speaking.'

'Who found me?'

'*We'll* ask the questions, sir.'

'I'd like to know, Superintendent.'

'All in good time,' soothed the policeman.

'At least tell me where I am.'

74

'In hospital, sir. Safe and sound.'

The nurse stepped in to make a brief check on the patient's condition. Satisfied that he was well enough to continue the interview, she nodded to the two detectives, then left the room soundlessly. Impey loomed in the background in his ill-fitting suit, a bouncer on the alert.

'Now, sir,' said the superintendent with crisp relish, 'perhaps we can begin at the beginning.'

Hawker grimaced as a sharp pain lanced his chest.

'Where were you when it happened?'

'Standing beside the lagoon.'

'Why?'

'I fancied a swim.'

'Very amusing, sir. Now tell us the truth.'

'I was interested, that's all.'

'That field is out of bounds. Police orders.'

'Curiosity got the better of me.'

'What did you hope to find?'

'Nothing.'

'So why bother?'

'Who knows?' murmured Hawker. 'Who knows?'

Mike Impey spoke up. 'Half a mo. Are you saying that you were drawn back to that slurry lagoon?'

'That's what it felt like.'

'Returning to the scene of the crime, maybe.'

'Exactly, Sergeant.'

'Activated by some impulse of guilt.'

'You're a genius!' mocked the patient.

'Don't be sarcastic,' said Rayment testily. 'If we're to track down your attacker, we need your help.'

'Then tell your sergeant here to stop accusing me of murder. I did not kill that poor devil.'

'We believe you, Mr Hawker.'

'That's something, anyway.'

'But we still think that you're holding out on us.'

'Give me a break.'

'You must learn to trust us.'

More sarcasm. 'Where have I heard *that* before?'

'We're on your side,' snapped Rayment.

'That's what worries me.'

The superintendent got up angrily from his chair and had a muttered conversation with Impey. The latter withdrew. His superior came to stand over the patient so that he could do his impersonation of Hitler again.

'Why did you visit that lagoon?' he barked.

'It looked so romantic in the moonlight.'

'You ignored a police warning.'

'Bad habit of mine.'

'I think you were looking for something.'

'It wasn't a bang on the head, I can tell you!'

'Don't try to do our job for us, sir.'

'I wouldn't dare, Superintendent.'

Rayment stroked his tribute to the Führer.

'Retrace your steps.'

'Eh?'

'From the moment you arrived back at Corley Hall earlier tonight. Take me through it in stages.'

'I'm not sure that I can . . .'

'Try, sir. To please me.'

Hawker shrugged and set off the man on spike duty. He waited until the blows lost some of their venom, then did his best to assemble thoughts in his clanging brain.

'I got back well after eleven,' he recalled.

'And?'

'Parked the car halfway down the drive.'

'Was anyone else around?'

'Not a soul.'

'So what did you do?' said the detective.

'I went for a stroll in the night air.'

'Towards the slurry lagoon.'

'Yes.' Hawker was artless. 'Quite by chance.'

76

'Tell me – precisely – what you did.'

'I mounted the bank and looked in over the fence.'

'For how long, sir?'

'It seemed like a matter of seconds.'

'And you heard nothing?'

'Not until it was far too late, Superintendent.'

'Did you try to turn round?'

'No time. I was knocked cold.'

'You have a very thick skull, Mr Hawker.'

'It feels like paper at the moment.'

'That blow could have killed another man!'

'Thanks for the reassurance!'

'Be grateful for the sympathy.'

'Is that what it is?'

'Some people might say it served you right.'

Rayment looked more like Hitler than ever now, his singsong accent a dagger that jabbed at the eardrums.

'Mr Starrett.'

'What about him?'

'He was the one who came to your rescue.'

'Oh?'

'Heard your car return and couldn't understand why you didn't come into the house. He gave you a few minutes, then went out to investigate.'

'And found me draped across the barbed wire.'

'Mr Starrett rang us immediately.'

'He would!'

'You should be grateful to him, sir.'

'I am.'

'Then sound it.'

Hawker could not make the effort. He still had grave reservations about his landlord. Norman Starrett already had a number of black marks against his name and a new one could now be added. He was the person to find the wounded man. Hawker wished that it could have been almost anybody else. Starrett would revel in what he would see as his moment of heroism, and his guest shuddered at the thought. Corley Hall became less appealing than ever.

Frank Rayment glanced at his watch.

'I need my beauty sleep,' he decided.

'What time is it?'

'Two in the morning.'

'How long do I have to stay here?'

'Ask the doctor.'

'I've got a job to do, Superintendent.'

'Haven't we all?' He moved away. 'Good night, sir.'

'Before you go . . .'

'Yes?'

'The murder victim. Have you identified him yet?'

'We think so.'

'What's his name?'

'It will be released in due course.'

'Why all the secrecy?'

'I could ask you the same question, sir.'

Hawker fought against a wave of drowsiness.

'Where am I?' he said.

'In hospital.'

'Which one?'

'The George Eliot in Nuneaton.'

'You having me on?'

'That's what it's called, sir, I promise you. George Eliot. Author of you-know-what.'

'Stop gloating.'

Frank Rayment gave a tired grin.

'You might say it was poetic justice.'

Golf had brought them together and it still remained a safe mode of communication when other channels had broken down. Glenn Bianco was not a typical golfer's wife. She was an accomplished player in her own right with a string of amateur titles to her name. It was the game which had introduced them in the first place. After one of her victories in her native Arizona, she

78

had received her trophy and winner's cheque from the hands of Tony Bianco himself, thereby setting a precedent for their married life. Tony continued to thrust trophies and cheques at her, the difference being that he had won them himself, though Glenn always claimed that she played a creative role in his triumphs. Golf was their element.

'How's it going?' she asked.

'Fine, fine.'

'Ironed out those swing problems?'

'More or less.'

'What about your mental attitude?'

'Just right.'

'That sounds good.'

'Bob Jaglom is delighted with me.'

'So he should be.'

The faint glimmer of a compliment made Tony Bianco look up from his breakfast. He was seated at a table in their hotel room with a tray and a morning paper in front of him. His wife had just emerged from the bathroom. She always dressed and undressed in private now. Glenn gave him a brisk smile and crossed to pick up her handbag from the bedside table.

'What are you doing today?' he asked.

'Oh, just stooging around.'

'Are you seeing any of the other girls?'

'Yeah, Alma Lapidus.'

'Why not come out and watch me play?'

'I'll have three days of that.'

'Appreciate your company.'

'You wouldn't even notice me,' she said tartly. 'When you get out on a golf course, nothing else exists for you. I'm not in a mood to play Mrs Anonymous.'

'Not even as a favour to me?'

It was the nearest he came to showing a sign of weakness. Glenn Bianco flicked his request aside with a dismissive gesture. His tone darkened.

'What about Uncle Huby?'

'What about him?'

'Do you have any plans to meet him today?'

'Maybe.'

'Then keep him well away from me.'

'But he's anxious to talk to you, Tony.'

'Too bad!'

'Uncle Huby only wants ten minutes.'

'We're closed to visitors.'

'Is it asking too much of you?'

'Yeah.'

'Why?'

'Because the guy's a jerk.'

'He's my uncle.'

'Makes no difference.'

'Tony —'

'Keep him away from me!'

She stifled a reply and walked over to confront him.

'You've never forgiven Uncle Huby, have you?'

'That's beside the point.'

'St Louis. Two years ago. Remember?'

'It's history now.'

'Only because he found out about her.'

'We have to get past that, Glenn.'

'So you keep telling me.'

'It's all over and done with now.'

'Not from where I stand.'

'How much longer you gonna punish me?'

'Till it begins to hurt.'

'It *does* fucking well hurt!' he snarled. 'It's never stopped hurting. Thanks to that goddam uncle of yours. And you expect me to be pals with that sleaze-ball. I'd sooner make friends with a viper. So get him outa my hair, will you? I hate the guy!'

Glenn Bianco saved her barb until the end.

'I'm glad you're teaming up with Hal Mayo.'

'Eh?'

'I like something sexy to look at.'

Before he could reply, she swept out of the room and slammed the door behind here. She did not see him jab the table with his knife. Tony Bianco was livid. Just when he felt they were making progress, they had another row and found themselves back where they started. It was soul-destroying. He simply had to put the whole thing out of his mind and concentrate on his golf.

His wife, meanwhile, came down the stairs and went over to the Reception counter. A smart young woman gave her a regulation smile.

'Can I help you, madam?'

'Yeah,' said Glenn. 'I'm Mrs Bianco. Room Fourteen. Any messages for me?'

The receptionist checked the pigeon-hole.

'Nothing at all, I'm afraid.'

'Are you sure?'

'The cupboard is bare.'

Glenn Bianco felt a surge of pain.

How much longer would she have to wait?

A disturbed night gave Don Hawker a modicum of rest and the determination to get out of the George Eliot Hospital as soon as possible. Against medical advice, he discharged himself next morning and walked into Nuneaton to get a taxi. He was back at Corley Hall by nine o'clock. He was still heavily bandaged and the pain was constant, but his head no longer felt as if it was about to drop off his shoulders at the slightest provocation. Most of the cars had left the drive and there was no sign of life in the farmyard. What he did notice, however, was a large shovel that stood up against one of the pens. The mere sight of it intensified his headache.

Norman Starrett was astonished to see him.

'They let you out like *that*?' he said.

'I'll be okay.'

'You need care and attention.'

'I need a cup of coffee and some answers.'

'Doesn't it *hurt*?'

'Only when people go on about it.'

'Sorry, Mr Hawker.'

'Try to ignore my head.'

'Right. Coffee, did you say?'

'Strong, black, no sugar.'

'On its way. Come into the kitchen.'

'Thanks.'

Hawker followed his landlord down the passageway and into a large low room that had been turned into the archetypal farmhouse kitchen. Stripped pine ran riot. A massive Welsh dresser dominated one wall and groaned beneath the weight of china and pewter. Copper and brass dangled from every beam. Two mullioned windows looked out on a garden that provided fruit and vegetables in season. Even the fitted units had a period feel. Ultra-modern equipment reached a compromise with the past.

When the men entered, a couple of local girls were loading the last of the breakfast things into the dishwasher. They reacted with mild alarm when they saw the thick bandage, then scurried out in response to a nod from their employer. Starrett reached for the coffee percolator and filled two cups before carrying them to the long pine table in the middle.

'Take a seat, Mr Hawker.'

'Right.'

'I can't tell you how upsetting all this is.'

'Then please don't try,' said Hawker pointedly.

They sat opposite each other at the table and Starrett added milk to his cup of coffee. Starrett held up the jug with a rueful smile.

'Another source of friction, I fear.'

'What do you mean?'

'Well, here we are, living right next door to a dairy farm and we have our daily pinta delivered by a milkman from Coventry. It doesn't go down well with Leech.'

'He can't expect to supply you, surely?'

'Yes, he can. He sold directly to my predecessor.'

'Straight from the cow?'

'More or less.'

'Is the milk safe to drink?'

'According to Leech. It's what they themselves live on and they seem to thrive. But my guests are a bit more discriminating. They want something cold and reliable out of a bottle, not something warm and murky out of a steel jug.'

'Did you say that to Leech?'

'Word for word. He didn't take it kindly.'

'Has he always been such an awkward neighbour?'

'I'm afraid so,' said Starrett. 'The fact of the matter is that he resents me because I'm not a true countryman. Farmers are very conservative. You have to live in the area for at least fifty years before they even begin to accept you.' He sipped his coffee. 'Right from the start, I tried my level best to get on with Leech and he was quite civil in those days. Not what you could call friendly, but polite in a gruff sort of way.'

'Why did he become more hostile?'

'Because of this.' Starrett waved a hand to indicate the whole house. 'Corley Hall was a success – in moderate terms. We've got a good location and provide a reasonable service. The hotel will never be a major money-spinner but we tick over very nicely. Brian Leech, by contrast, is struggling to survive. That farm barely pays its way.'

'Don't they run it properly?' said Hawker.

'That isn't the problem. They're tied hand and foot by EC regulations. Take the dairy side, for instance. It was the one part of the enterprise that brought in a regular profit. Next thing you know, there's a directive to say that the national milk yield has got to be cut back and herds have to be reduced in size.'

'Did that affect Leech?'

'Badly,' said Starrett as the accountant came through. 'He lost twelve cows. Over a whole year, that's an appreciable drop in gallonage and in income.'

Hawker got the picture. 'Meanwhile this place went from strength to strength. Every time Leech looked over the fence, he saw big expensive limousines on the drive.'

Starrett ventured a smile. 'Until you came.' He went on quickly as he collected a glare. 'I suppose that I only added fuel to the flames of his discontent. It was tactless of me, really, but it could actually have paid off if only he'd considered it properly.'

'What?'

'Farm holidays,' explained the other. 'We don't take children here at the moment. It broadens your clientele no end if you do. And if we could offer some amusement on the spot, we'd be a more attractive propositon. That's why I suggested a possible link up with Leech. We have the accommodation and he has the farm.' Starrett let his vision unfold. 'Ideal family holidays. The parents laze around the hotel while the kids have fun on the farm. They could watch the milking, help to feed the calves and collect the eggs from the chickens. They also keep a few pigs and occasionally rent out a couple of fields to a sheep farmer. There's something going on all the time. Besides which, you've got eighty acres of land to roam about in and a marvellous wood to explore.'

'I can guess what Leech said.'

'He was deeply insulted. Said that he was a farmer and not a sideshow for kids.' Starrett was contrite. 'It was the most stupid thing I could have done. I hurt his pride and he's never forgiven me.'

Hawker pondered while he finished his coffee.

'How many of them live in the farmhouse?'

'Three. Leech, his wife, and their son Roy. Mrs Leech is quite nice but she gets dragged down by the two men. Oh, then there's Malcolm.'

'Is he that youth with the straw-coloured hair?'

'The resident labourer. They made him a room in one of the outbuildings. Malcolm is a real oddball. To use a local expression, he's a bit yampy.'

'That was my impression.' Hawker's wound throbbed. 'Is Leech a vindictive man?'

'Very.'

'How far would he go?'

Starrett glanced up at the bandaged head and pursed his lips. Hawker felt the clash of steel against bone. His host weighed in quickly with his story.

'I heard your car,' he said. 'I was in my study when I heard you slam the car door and walk back down the drive. Couldn't understand it. I mean, what could you want out there at that time of night?'

'So you came looking for me?'

'I was worried.'

'With cause,' conceded Hawker.

'I went down the drive, looked up and down the lane, then crossed to the field. It must have been instinct. Anyway, there you were.'

'Alone?'

'Yes,' said Starrett. 'Nobody else about, though I did hear a car start up just round the corner. It shot off down Bennetts Road.'

'What did you do next?'

'I climbed into the field and came across to the lagoon. I could only pick out this shape in outline. Until I got there, I wasn't even sure it was you.'

'Was I hanging over the barbed wire?'

'Like a rag doll. I saw the state you were in, lifted you off then ran to call the police.' Irritation showed. 'I got

85

blood all over my sleeve. My wife was angry about that. It was my best sports coat.'

Hawker listened intently as his companion went over the story again, embellishing it with a few details and apologising profusely for everything that his guest had endured.

'It wasn't your fault, Mr Starrett.'

'I feel responsible. You were on my property.'

'Leech's property.'

'Yes. That's the nub of it all.'

Hawker thought of the dead body in the lagoon.

'Do you ever have Americans staying here?'

'Occasionally.'

'When was the last time?'

'The police asked me that. It was about three months ago. An elderly couple.'

'Was the husband interested in golf?'

'I don't think so,' said Starrett. 'Apart from anything else, he suffered from arthritis. He was a retired engineer from Nebraska. This was their first visit to Britain. They loved it here. Nice couple.'

'Did they sign the book?'

'Of course.'

'Could I possibly see it?'

'If you wish, but I can't see what use it will be. The police have already been through it with a fine-tooth comb. They found nothing.'

'Let me try.'

Starrett hauled himself up and vanished for a few seconds before returning with a visitors book that was bound in real leather. He handed it over and Hawker flicked through the pages. The guests from Nebraska soon surfaced.

'They stayed for a whole week,' he noted.

'We're a good base from which to explore the area.'

'Did they bring anyone else back here?'

'Not that I can recall.'

'No friends? No fellow Americans?'

'None.'

Hawker fired off more questions, but they failed to unearth anything significant. Evidently the couple from Nebraska were not connected in any way with the murder victim. Hawker needed to look elsewhere. As he chatted to Starrett, he kept turning over the pages of the book and going steadily back in time. American guests were his special interest, but he soon stubbed his toe against a name that took him completely by surprise.

He recognised the looping signature at once.

It belonged to Tom Pickard.

Fitness was the essence of her job. Karen Maxwell trotted a hundred yards or so until she had a good view of the eighteenth green then she paused to watch the end of another practice round. The morning was still young, yet she had already travelled extensively around The Belfry as well as handling dozens of enquiries in the press tent. There would be more miles to scurry before the end of the day. Karen watched as the tall figure of Tom Pickard stood over his ball, made the last checks on direction and distance, then played his shot with perfect weight. The ball went as straight as a die and dropped into the cup. Rolf Kohlmar sank his putt with his usual taciturn efficiency to complete a decisive win over Ian Roslin and Claudio Mundi. Angus Cameron moved in to give the four players his advice.

When they headed towards the clubhouse, Karen fell in with the group, walking between Pickard and Kohlmar. She congratulated the victorious pairing. Rolf Kohlmar nodded with lugubrious sagacity.

'Good that Germany and Britain can work together.'

'Make that Britain and Germany,' said Pickard then he grinned at Karen. 'How's my favourite press officer?'

'Starved of player comment.'

'Take that up with Angus.'

'I did, Tom. He almost court-martialled me.'

'You should hear him when he really loses that Scots temper of his, Karen. It's the verbal equivalent of being shot at dawn.'

'I hear you,' warned Cameron, a few paces in front.

Pickard nudged her. 'He'll dock my pocket-money for insubordination.'

'What is this?' asked Kohlmar seriously. 'I hear nothing about pocket-money.'

'It's a joke, Rolf.'

'Oh. I see.' He obliged with a short laugh.

Angus Cameron was setting his usual brisk pace, so the three people ahead soon drew away out of earshot. Karen fished for information.

'How was it out there today?'

'Chilly,' said Pickard.

'I wasn't talking about the weather.'

'I am.'

'Okay, Tom. Message received. You're gagged.'

'Sorry. Captain's orders. Right. Rolf?'

'*Ja, ja,*' said the German. 'He is very strict.'

'There's your answer, Karen.'

'Can't you speak to me off the record?'

'That's what I am doing.' Pickard gave a lazy grin. 'Anyway, you don't need to pump me. You can get all the info you need from our mutual friend.'

'I'm not with you.'

'Don Hawker.'

'Ah.'

'A little bird tells me you two are good pals.' He feigned innocence. 'Don always keeps his finger on the pulse. He must have a private source of intelligence.' Pickard chuckled at her discomfort. 'Don't be coy about it. I love Don. Great bloke. You couldn't be in safer hands.'

'It's not like that, Tom.'

'That's your business.' Another chuckle. 'Hey, I'll tell you this much. Things are going well. There's a mood of cautious optimism in our camp.'

'Good.'

'Angus actually smiled on the fourteenth green.'

'We'll have to put up a plaque.'

'There's still some fine-tuning to be done, but we seem to be in form at the right time. Especially Rolf.'

'Me? I just play my normal game.'

'Well, I'm glad you're on my side, mate.'

'The Americans are confident as well,' said Karen.

'They always are.'

'Patriotic bravado?'

'It goes deeper than that,' argued Pickard. 'They think they have the right to win. They work on the assumption that they're intrinsically better than anyone else in the world.'

'Except the Germans,' said Kohlmar loyally.

'The Americans have a chance to prove their point,' said Karen. 'Maybe they still are number one.'

'Not if I can help it!' said Pickard with sudden intensity. 'Angus is right. This is war. And I'll do everything in my power to make sure that we win. If you really want a comment off the record, I'll give you one.'

'Go on,' she urged.

'This is not for public consumption, mind.'

'You know me, Tom.'

Real venom peeped out. 'I hate bloody Yanks!'

Hubert Stone came downstairs from his room on his way out to The Belfry. He had a small favour to ask first. Sheila Dowling was at her desk in the office, totting up the bar takings from the previous night. Stone rapped on the open door with his knuckles and stepped boldly in.

'You work too hard, Sheila.'

'The hotel won't run itself.'

'Delegate,' he said expansively. 'Leave yourself free to make administrative decisions and to have fun.'

'Work *is* fun to me,' she replied. 'Mostly, anyway.'

'You deserve better than this, honey.'

She giggled. 'Is that a proposal?'

'Why don't we discuss it later on tonight?'

'That would be very improper, Mr Stone, as you know.'

'The good things in life are always improper.'

'Stop trying to lead me astray.' She made an effort to be businesslike. 'Was there something you wanted?'

'And how, baby!'

'Be serious.'

'Sorry,' he said with a disarming grin. 'Actually, I came to ask you another favour. Is there any chance I could use the phone just once more?'

'What's wrong with the one in the hall?'

'It's so much cosier in here. Besides, I have to make a transatlantic call this time and I don't want to stand there shoving coins into the slot.' He touched her arm lightly. 'It would mean a lot to me, Sheil. You've no idea how grateful a guy like me can be.'

'Are you going to ring America?'

'Yeah, I need to talk business.'

'Won't it be the middle of the night there?'

'My partner is an insomniac. He's at his best in the small hours. It's the one time I can be certain of getting him straight away.'

Sheila was reluctant to let him take over her office again but she was unable to deny him, somehow. Stone had a way of bulldozing aside any objections.

'So you want to ring a business partner?' she said.

'That's the idea.'

'I thought you'd retired?'

'Old soldiers like me never give up completely. I like to keep some irons in the fire.' He winked at her. 'You never know when some extra dough might come in useful. So I always have a few projects in hand.'

Sheila stood up. 'Well, okay . . .'

'I'll time the call and pay you the exact rate.'

'You'll have to, Mr Stone. I can't afford to pick up the tabs for a call to Arizona.'

'This is somewhere else in the States.'

'Well, try not to be too long. I need my office.'

'Be as quick as I can, sweetie.'

Before she could say anything else, Sheila Dowling found herself ushered out and groped in the process. She did not know whether to protest or giggle, but found she had no time to do either. The door closed firmly and she was shut out of her own office. Telling herself that the needs of the guests always came first, she went off to the next job on her long list.

Hubert Stone, meanwhile, dialled a number that he knew by heart. His affability had evaporated and his face now wore an expression of stern concentration. As soon as the receiver was picked up at the other end, he jumped in.

'Jake, it's me.'

'For Chrissake, Huby!' said a weary voice. 'Do you know what time it is here? I was fast asleep.'

'This is important. I kept leaving messages on your answerphone but I couldn't be too explicit. I had to speak to you direct.'

'How's it all going over there?'

'Oh, we're still on course for the big one.'

'So why drag me outa my bed?'

'We hit a slight snag.'

'I don't like the sound of that, Huby.'

'Neither do I. It's not terminal and we may still get away with it but we ought to brace ourselves.' He took a deep breath. 'Stage One of the operation was not quite as clean as we'd hoped, Jake.'

'Shit!'

'There may be repercussions . . .'

Whatever his faults, Malcolm was not afraid of work. Up at his usual time of five-thirty in the morning, he took the cow dogs up into the field to get the herd in for the first milking. When Brian Leech joined him at six, the first batch had already had the clusters fitted and the remainder of the animals were lowing in the standing pen. After a quick breakfast at eight, Malcolm went on his rounds to feed the young stock before taking charge of the tractor with the front-loader so that he could clean out some loose boxes. He worked hard until eleven when the three of them adjourned to the farmhouse. Olive Leech had coffee and biscuits waiting for them. She was not happy about that morning's visit by the police.

'I hope you had nothing to do with it, Brian.'

'Be quiet, woman,' said her husband.

'Someone nearly killed that Mr Hawker.'

'That's his lookout.'

'But it was on our land. I feel guilty.'

'We got nothing to fear.'

'Are you sure?'

'Drop it, Mum,' said Roy irritably as he looked up from his copy of the *Sun*. 'I'm trying to read this.'

His mother shot all three of them a look of alarm then went back into the house. Leech filled his pipe and puffed away at it, Roy was mesmerised by the girl on page three, and Malcolm sat there happily drinking his coffee. When he had finished, the labourer slipped off to use the outside lavatory then he popped into his room which was near by. He wanted another peep at his latest trophy. It hung in the middle of the largest wall and Malcolm had polished it to a high sheen.

Using it as a mirror, he combed his hair with his hands, then grinned at himself. He was looking at the hub-cap from the wheel of a car. It bore the insignia of the Vauxhall Motor Company.

Chapter Six

When Don Hawker first removed the bandage he felt as if his head was about to fall into two halves. He held them together with his hands, and the insistent throb at the base of his skull slowly lost its venom. He was in the bathroom at Corley Hall, taking stock of his injuries and wondering how he came by them. The mirror showed him a man whose face looked surprisingly normal, although his matted hair could clearly do with a wash. He angled his head to inspect it more comprehensively but all he could make out was the contour of a sizeable lump at the rear. His fingers explored it gingerly and found swollen flesh that was knitted together with a line of stitches.

Hawker removed his shirt and saw another tramway snaking across his chest on the yellowing embankment of a bruise. He ran a bath, stripped off and got in. The pain and discomfort were quickly offset by the curative effects of the warm water, and he was soon able to reach for the shampoo and gently wash his hair. Dried, dressed and restored, he went back up to his room to collect a few things and to glance out of the front window. Two magpies were skipping about on the front lawn. A tabby cat came prowling out of the rhododendrons. A wheelbarrow stood unattended on the gravel path that bisected the garden.

Norman Starrett appeared with a roll of wire fencing and a couple of stout posts. He wore old clothes, a pair of gumboots and a battered felt hat. Putting his cargo into the wheelbarrow, he transported it to the very front of the garden and stopped beside a wide gap in the hedge that bordered the lane. He selected a spot for the first post and used a spade to dig a hole. There was nothing unremarkable in what Hawker had seen so far. His landlord was exactly the sort of man who would economise on a gardener by doing some of the chores himself. What caused the watching journalist to shudder, however, was what happened next. Placing the post in the hole, Starrett used the back of the spade to hammer it viciously into the ground, swinging the implement with power and fluency to hit his target bang on each time. Here was no retired accountant, pottering amiably in his garden. Here was an irate man who was expressing his anger in a display of controlled violence that was quite spine-chilling.

Hawker's head wound ached anew.

Hubert Stone strutted around the course as if it belonged to him, beaming with proprietary glee at any golfers from the American team. He waved to Hal Mayo, he gave a victory sign to Vance Dressler, he shouted his encouragement to Gary Lapidus and he managed a short chat with Bob Jaglom. It all served to lift his spirits and to freshen his arrogance. Walking beside him, Glenn Bianco was morose and preoc- cupied. She only half-heard his comments.

'We're gonna be okay,' he said. 'I feel it.'

'Good.'

'That cup is going right back home where it belongs. Bob and the guys have got this match sewn up.'

'Yeah.'

'Tony will blaze the trail for them. Wait till the other team gets a load of that old Bianco magic. It'll destroy 'em! Say, honey, where is he, anyway?'

'Mm?'

'Tony. Your husband.'

'Oh, yes. Sorry, Uncle Huby . . .'

'You were miles away.'

'Tony's out on the course somewhere,' she said. 'But maybe it wouldn't be a good idea to crowd him.'

'I wanna let him know I'm here.'

'He gets easily distracted.'

'Not by me.'

'Uncle Huby . . .'

'Tony is my pal. Hell, he married my favourite niece, didn't he? Lemme see the guy.'

'He may have finished his practice round.'

'Then let's track him down in the clubhouse.'

'Another time.'

'What *is* this? You hiding him from me?'

'Of course not.'

'I wanna see my boy.'

Glenn guided him over a little stone bridge and steered him back in the direction of the hotel. She also attempted to move the conversation away from the vexed subject of her husband.

'How are you enjoying your stay in England?'

'Great!'

'Nice hotel?'

'Kinda small but I like it. Sheila gives me four-star treatment all the way down the line.'

'Sheila?'

'Lady who owns the hotel. Sheila Dowling.'

'What's she like?'

'Terrific. I may marry her.'

Glenn gulped. 'Marry!'

'Only for a night or two.'

'Uncle Huby!'

Her protest was drowned beneath his loud chuckle. He went on to list the attractions of his landlady and to outline his plans to get more closely acquainted with them. Glenn was torn between amusement and disgust: yet one more example of the ambivalent relationship she had with her uncle. There were times when Hubert Stone was a real embarrassment to her. His monologue came to an abrupt end as he spotted someone in the middle distance.

'Hey, there's Tony!'

'I see him,' she said dully.

'Then what are we waiting for, honey? Come on.'

'He hates to be interrupted out on the course.'

'By me?'

'By anyone.'

'But I'm family, Glenn.'

'It makes no difference.'

'The guy is my hero. I gotta talk to him.'

'That may not be wise, Uncle Huby.'

'Stop holding me back,' he complained. 'Anybody'd think I got no right to meet Tony Bianco, but I got every right in the world. You forgetting that?'

Glenn considered his statement then shook her head. As she looked across at her husband, a sly smile touched her lips. Tony Bianco had no time for her uncle and had warned her to keep him well away. Events in St Louis all that time ago still weighed very heavily with the golfer. She saw that she had a strong weapon in her hands and she felt a sudden urge to use it to the full.

'You really wanna talk to him?' she said.

'Sure thing!'

'Then let's get over there right away. If I know him, Tony will be real delighted. I can just see the look on his face.' She beamed. 'Let's go, Uncle Huby.'

Glenn would be getting her revenge on both of them.

They were standing near the golf shop when Don Hawker came up to them. Eric Fretton was his usual dapper self in faded denim with enough badges on his jacket to start a retail outlet. He threw the immaculate designer outfit of Alma Lapidus into sharp relief. She was a short dark vivacious young woman with a breathy laugh and a habit of tossing her curls. Rings, bangles, earrings and a gold necklace gave a rather obtrusive sense of prosperity. Hawker tried to hide his revulsion. Dangling from the woman's right hand was a charm bracelet that would have cost the bulk of his annual salary. He steeled himself.

'Good morning,' he said.

'Ah, there you are!' greeted Eric. 'And about time.'

'Traffic problems.'

'Don't give me that.'

'I made it, didn't I?'

'Hours late. Now let me introduce you . . .'

Hawker shook hands with Alma Lapidus and the charm bracelet jingled. She looked even more attractive close up and he could see why Gary Lapidus was so protective towards her. Alma had a way of simultaneously exciting a man and appealing to his paternal instinct. Hawker could not make out if her manner was natural or affected. At the very least, he decided, she was a clever actress.

'Are you enjoying the golf?' he asked.

'Frankly, no.'

'Why not?'

'Because I despise the game.'

'Isn't that a bit of a problem for the wife of a professional golfer?'

'I don't think so,' she said airily. 'Seems like a crazy way to make a living, anyway. Hitting that ball into a series of little holes. Still, if that's what Gary wants to do, good luck to him. As long as it keeps him happy and brings in the money.'

Hawker got a clear indication that the money meant far more to her than her husband's happiness, yet he could not bring himself to dislike Alma Lapidus. There was an engaging candour about her that smothered his

98

prejudices. At the same time, however, she seemed an unlikely choice for the comedian of the American team. He could not imagine them having too many laughs when they were on their own together.

'Is this your first visit to England?' he asked.

'Yeah,' she said. 'I just love it here.'

'Sorry about the weather.'

'You can't have everything.'

'I hope it picks up for the match.'

'Well, *I* don't,' said Eric. 'It's one of the few real advantages we've got. Being accustomed to the vagaries of the English climate. If I was pulling the switches up there, I'd make it rain cats and dogs tomorrow.'

'That's all we need.' Hawker turned back to Alma. 'Have you managed to do any sightseeing?'

'Quite a bit.'

'Where have you been?'

'Oh, all the usual places, I guess.'

'Warwick, Stratford?'

'Yes, and Kenilworth. Gary's been a real sweetie to me. We've spent a fortune in the antique shops here.'

'Have you been anywhere else?' asked Hawker.

'No. Except Coventry, that is.'

'What did you see there?'

'Two cathedrals. One beautiful old one in ruins and one hideous modern thing. Why didn't they just rebuild the original? That's what I'd have done!' She recalled something else. 'Coventry was pretty dull but it was a lot better than that last place we visited.'

'Where was that?'

'Some little village about five miles away.'

'What was it called?'

'I didn't really want to go but Gary insisted. It was a sort of pilgrimage, you see. On account of Zelda.'

'Zelda?'

'My husband's first wife.'

'Ah.'

'She was killed in a car accident in Memphis. It was tragic.' A tasteless giggle emerged. 'For her, that is. Not for me. Zelda's loss was my gain, as you might say. I met up with Gary a year later and my whole life changed.'

'What did you do before then?' wondered Eric.

'I was an exotic dancer.'

'I can believe it.'

'Coming back to this village,' said Hawker. 'In what way was it a pilgrimage?'

'Zelda's father was born there.'

'In Warwickshire?'

'Sixty odd years ago. He was only a kid when his family emigrated to the States. They farmed in Oklahoma and made a real success of it. Zelda's father inherited the spread and that's where she was brought up.'

'How did she meet Gary?'

'At college in Boston. She was a student. A friend of hers fixed her this blind date with a guy she said played a little golf. Can you imagine it? Gary was just starting to make a name for himself then.'

'So they got married?'

'Not for a few years,' said Alma. 'He never rushes these things. It took *me* eighteen months to get a proposal out of him but I won through in the end.'

'You still haven't told us about this pilgrimage,' said Eric. 'Where did you actually go?'

'To the Roberts's house. That was the family name. Zelda Roberts.' She tossed her curls. 'I didn't want to go to that hole in the hedge but Gary insisted. Showed me this tiny little cottage where Zelda's father was born. Gary is a tough cookie most of the time but he also has a sentimental streak. It really got to him.'

'What was it called?' said Hawker.

'Rock Cottage.'

'Not the house. The village.'

'Corley.'

A feeling of excitement shot through Hawker. He had established a link in a way he could not possibly have foreseen. Rock Cottage was the property adjacent to the cattery. The journalist had noticed it on the previous day when he ran to the end of Burrow Hill Lane. The cottage was in the lee of Corley Rocks. If Gary Lapidus had visited the house, he would have had an excellent view of the slurry lagoon in the field down below.

Before she could be questioned further, Alma Lapidus saw someone walking away from the driving range and she waved a jingling bracelet.

'Hi, Glenn! Over here, honey!' She smiled at the two men. 'Look, fellas, you'll have to excuse me. Me and Glenn are gonna drive in to Birmingham this morning. Nice meeting you both . . .'

Hawker and his editor added their farewells as she trotted off, then they watched the little pantomime that was going on near the driving range. Glenn Bianco was strolling beside two figures who seemed to be locked in argument. One was an American golfer and he was holding up his hands to keep an old man at bay. The latter was gesticulating wildly and getting more worked up with each second. Even from that distance, Hawker could see the malign pleasure that Glenn was getting from the situation.

Eric Fretton identified the combatants.

'It's Tony Bianco with Hubert Stone.'

'Stone? Isn't he staying at your hotel?'

'That's him. The madman of Phoenix, Arizona.'

'I thought he was a friend of Bianco's.'

'So did I.'

'Not any more.'

Hawker took a few paces forward and watched the altercation with growing interest. Eric noticed the lump and the stitches on the back of his friend's skull.

'My God, man! What happened to your head?'

'I got hit by a golf ball.'

It was a version of the truth.

Jenny Dowling was a pale plump young woman in her early twenties with permanent furrows of anxiety on her brow. Working sixteen hours a day at the Whitehall Hotel was bad enough, but to do so under the nominal control of her mother made it almost purgatorial. Whenever she tried to leave, however, she was racked by guilt and beaten into submission by Sheila's notion of familial duty. It made for a stressful life. Jenny was at the mercy of her mother's galloping optimism, like a small child caught up in the reins of a runaway horse and unable to free herself, as she was dragged along in front of a gaping public. Money made the horse go hell for leather.

'It looks like being another bad month, Mum.'

'Rubbish!' said Sheila. 'We've done quite well.'

'Have you seen the bills?'

'They can wait a bit.'

'Most of them are final demands.'

'We'll pay them soon enough, Jenny.'

'Only if you take my advice.'

Sheila folded her arms. 'No. That's just not on.'

'It's the only way.'

'We are not going to raise our charges.'

'But we have to increase our income somehow.'

'Then we attract more custom,' said Sheila simply. 'We advertise more widely for weddings and parties.'

Jenny sighed. 'Advertising is expensive and we have to take on extra staff for functions.'

'It brings the money in.'

'But not enough of it.'

Jenny gave up. They were in the little office by the entrance hall, cashing up after the departure of four of their guests. Sheila noted the details in her register, then put the cheques into the metal cash box before

102

moving to the small safe that was cemented into an alcove and concealed behind a curtain.

'What about the VAT?' asked her daughter.

'It's not due till the end of next month.'

'How are we going to pay it?'

'We'll manage somehow.'

'You always say that, Mum.'

'It's true. Try looking on the bright side.'

'*What* bright side?'

Sheila laughed merrily and bent down to pull back the curtain. She put the cash box back into the open safe then noticed the parcel that had been left there by one of her guests. It was about a foot square, six inches deep and wrapped in thick brown paper. The owner's name was scrawled importantly across the front in big letters.

'Hubert P. Stone,' she read.

'Oh! Not him!'

'I wonder what the "P" stands for?'

'Pain in the neck!'

'Jenny!'

'Well, that's what he is, Mum. Mr Stone has the whole lot of us at his beck and call. He's very demanding and very rude.' She coloured slightly and shifted her feet. 'Then there's all the rest of it.'

'What do you mean?'

'Those remarks he keeps passing.'

'Oh, that's just his way, Jenny.'

'I don't like it.'

'Ignore him. He means no harm.'

'What about those looks he gives you?'

'*I* can handle Mr Stone,' said Sheila with blithe confidence. 'When you deal with the public, you have to learn to find the good in people.'

She locked the safe and pulled the curtain across. As she stood up, she found her daughter staring at her with a mixture of fear and warning.

'Mum . . .'

'Yes, dear?'

'You won't . . .?'

'Of course not!' A sudden laugh. 'What an idea!'

'He looks the type, that's all.'

'Leave him to me.'

'I'd hate to see you get into another –'

'That's quite out of the question,' said Sheila briskly. 'I run this hotel in a professional manner and there's no chance of anything like that happening.' A wistful smile settled. 'On the other hand . . .'

'Well?'

'I've always wanted to go to America.'

Jenny's sigh of despair was the deepest so far.

'Oh, Mum!'

Hawker managed ten minutes alone in the coffee lounge with Tom Pickard and caught up on some of the latest gossip from the home camp. The Yorkshireman was as relaxed and cheerful as ever, but Don Hawker detected early signs of strain as the big event drew nearer. Since the room was quite full they had to keep their voices down and their exchange of confidences limited to essentials. Hawker lied about his head wound and tried to pass it off as an accident. His friend was not fooled. When Pickard was completely off guard, the journalist sprang the question on him.

'Why didn't you tell me about Corley Hall?'

'Eh?'

'You stayed there some months ago.'

'Did I?'

'May the sixteenth, to be exact. A Tuesday.'

'What *is* this, Don?' said Pickard with a defensive chuckle. 'The Spanish Bloody Inquisition?'

'I wondered why you never mentioned it, that's all.'

'Why should I?'

'Because you know that I'm staying there.'

'It just didn't register, mate.'

'Corley Hall is not a place you forget.'

'I know,' agreed Pickard. 'I remember it only too well, believe me. They gave me the front room in the attic with birds nesting under the bargeboarding. Kept me awake all night with their scratching.'

'What were you doing there?'

'Trying to bloody well sleep.'

'At that particular hotel, I mean.'

'What? Oh, it was only for a night. There's a driving range a couple of miles up the road in Sandpits Lane. Big new extension to their golf shop. I was there to cut the ribbon and open it. All I had to do was to smile at the camera and collect my cheque. Lot easier than playing.'

'And that's the only time you've been there?'

'Where? Sandpits Lane?'

'Corley Hall.'

'Can you imagine me wanting to go back?'

'Take your point,' said Hawker. 'Still seems a little strange, though. A murder happening more or less on the premises and you say nothing about staying there.'

Tom Pickard was blandly reassuring. 'I stay at lots of hotels in the course of a year. You know that, Don. A pro golfer lives out of a suitcase.'

'I'm in the same room.'

'Eh?'

'Front one in the attic.'

'Those damn birds still there?'

'Not any more. Of course, what you do get from that window is a perfect view of the slurry lagoon. Where the murder took place.'

'I'm sure you're right, mate.'

Pickard was giving nothing away and Hawker was at once puzzled and disappointed. He could not understand why one of the most open men he knew was being so evasive, and he was upset that their supposed friendship had developed a hairline fracture. Hawker turned to a more neutral topic, then lost his companion altogether when Angus Cameron glowered his way into the lounge. Pickard responded to the signal from his team captain and excused himself from the table. They left the room together.

Hawker made for the press tent. Although the match did not start until the next day, there were hundreds of people milling about. He made his way through the melée until he caught sight of a hunched figure on a wooden bench. Hubert Stone looked both angry and forlorn, an irascible old man with a pathos about him. Hawker went across to join him.

'Mr Stone?' he said.

'Who wants to know?'

'My name is Don Hawker. I'm a journalist. I believe you know my boss, Eric Fretton.'

'Eric who?'

'Fretton. He's staying at the same hotel.'

Hubert Stone shook himself properly awake and heard what was being said. A grin resurfaced and some of his jauntiness came back into play.

'Oh, sure. I know Eric. Pleased to meet you, er . . .'

'Hawker. Don Hawker.'

The old man's handshake was firm and inviting.

'Sit yourself down, Don.'

'Thanks.'

'Hope you're not rooting for the wrong team.'

'I try to be impartial,' said Hawker as he lowered himself on to the bench. 'But Eric tells me you're quite an authority on the American players. Contacts in high places and up-to-the-minute information.'

'Yeah, I been around golf all my life.'

'It shows, Mr Stone.'

'Hubert. Call me Hubert.'

'You have the look of a golfing man.'

'I'd sure hope so after all this time.' Stone was

106

rallying quickly and shrugging off his earlier mood. 'Haven't missed a Ryder Cup match since I don't know when. Matter of pride with me. I take it serious.'

'Eric says you're from Arizona.'

'Finest state in the whole damn country.'

'And you have some connection with Tony Bianco.'

Stone's face clouded slightly. 'He's married to my niece, Glenn. Heck of a good golfer herself, thanks to her Uncle Huby. I taught that girl good.' His spirits picked up rapidly. 'Tony is pretty tense at the moment, as you'd expect before something as big as this, but he'll come out fighting tomorrow. Talked to him this morning and gave him some last advice. He's one of the best golfers in the business yet he's still ready to listen to me.'

Hawker let the old man ramble on as the latter tried to convert what had evidently been a heated argument into a discussion of tactics for the morrow. Hubert Stone talked himself back into a good humour and boasted about the certain success of the American team. Hawker quizzed him about each of the players and found him forthright in opinion and rich in anecdote. It was an education to listen to someone as obsessed with golf as the old man.

'What about Gary Lapidus?'

'The guy's a genius out on the course.'

'Why does he clown around so much?'

'Who cares? It works.'

'He looks to be in form.'

'Gary is the ultimate pro,' explained Stone. 'Knows how to pace himself. Like a boxer. That man only steps into the ring when he's at his peak. It's a lesson to some of the younger kids. They think you can drink all day, screw all night and still break the course record every time you enter a tournament. No chance, brother. Golf at the top level is about discipline. You gotta practise self-denial.'

'Then why did Lapidus bring his wife?'

Stone chuckled. 'Good point, Don. That Alma is the cutest thing I seen in a long time. What more could a man want when he comes off the eighteenth green? No wonder Gary gets a bit uptight about her sometimes.'

'Uptight?'

'Restive.'

'In what way?'

'Well – look, this is not for publication, mind you. Strictly off the record, though everyone in the States knows about it.'

'About what?'

'Gary Lapidus has a jealous streak. Who doesn't, for Chrissake? I did when my wife was alive. But it goes deep with Gary. Maybe it was losing Zelda in that car crash. Made him much more insecure in his second marriage. I don't know but one thing is certain. He sure doesn't like it when guys get horny over Alma.' He winked at Hawker. 'Though how can you help it with a woman like that?'

'What happened?'

'Fight in a bar.'

'A fight?'

'Not even that, really. This guy started making up to Alma, and Gary took exception. Slugged the fella there and then. Broke his jaw.'

'Gary Lapidus?' said Hawker in surprise.

'Don't be fooled by all that Steve Martin stuff he puts on for show. Gary is not laughing underneath. He's a mean sonofagun and he'll go in hard when it matters.'

'And he really broke the man's jaw?'

'Listen,' said Stone confidentially. 'That guy was lucky to get off so lightly. Gary Lapidus is not just in love with that wife of his. He'd *kill* for her.'

Glenn Bianco stood at the perfume counter with Alma Lapidus and tried one more scent. They had spent two hours shopping in Rackhams and they had both spent

108

freely. Large plastic bags with the store logo on them rested against the foot of the counter. Glenn Bianco inhaled the new odour without enthusiasm.

'No. I don't think so.'

'Gimme a sniff,' said Alma.

'Too cheap for me.' She held up the bottle for her friend. 'What do you think?'

Alma sniffed. 'I kinda like it. But it's not you.'

'That's what I thought.'

'Still, that's not the only consideration.'

'What do you mean?'

'Well, you don't only buy a perfume that turns *you* on. It's got to do the trick for your husband as well. Reckon Tony would come running for this?'

'He won't get the chance,' said Glenn, passing the bottle of perfume back to the salesgirl. 'Come on, Alma. Time we were heading back.'

'But I'm enjoying this.'

'We mustn't be too late.'

'Anything is better than watching golf.'

'You promised Gary.'

The reminder drew a click of the tongue from Alma and a reluctant agreement to leave, though she did contrive to buy a pair of earrings *en route* to the main exit. Carrying a few bags apiece, they came out into Corporation Street and headed down towards the taxi rank outside the railway station. They were chattering happily away when they came to a news-stand that was piled high with the early edition of the *Birmingham Evening Mail*. Clipped into the front of the stand was a white sheet of paper with the crude headline – MURDER VICTIM NAMED.

Glenn Bianco obeyed instinct. Without even realising what she was doing, she bought a copy of the paper and glanced at the story on the front page. The man whose body had been hauled out of the sludge in Corley was at last identified. His name hit her like a thunderbolt and she reeled. Alma Lapidus was far too slow to catch her. Newspaper and shopping bags were just dropped on to the pavement. Glenn went down after them in a dead faint.

Intense work pressure was mounting on Karen Maxwell but she still found time to fit in a brief chat with Don Hawker. Seated at her desk and coping with two simultaneous telephone calls, she somehow contrived to lend some of her attention and all of her sympathy to her friend. Hawker had told her the truth about his head injury and they had both speculated on who his assailant might be. Inevitably they wondered if it might be the same person who had committed the murder at the farm in Corley, and they sifted the new details that had now emerged about the case. Hawker was holding a copy of the lunchtime edition of the *Coventry Evening Telegraph* which carried a much fuller report of the latest developments in the police investigation than the rival Birmingham paper. He had read it a dozen times already.

Their fractured conversation was fitted in around the two phone calls. Hawker toyed with a name.

'Larry Newmark . . .'

'Means nothing to me, Don.'

'Rings a bell somehow.'

'You were the one who found the poor man.'

'It's more than that. I've heard that name before. Or seen it in print. Newmark. Larry Newmark.'

'Where did you say he was from?'

'Denver, Colorado.'

'And what was he doing in Britain?'

'Hoping to watch the Ryder Cup.'

'For pleasure?'

'And business, it seems. Larry Newmark ran a company that manufactures golf wear.'

'Do they have a stand at the exhibition here?'

'No mention of it.'

One of the phone calls came to an end so Karen was able to offer him more concentration. Hawker looked once more at a key paragraph in the newspaper article.

'How did Newmark get to Corley?' she asked.

'The police are working on the theory that he was killed elsewhere and brought to the slurry lagoon to be tipped in. Time of death is put around the early hours of that same morning.'

'But why take him *there*?'

'Ideal place to hide a corpse.'

'Only if you knew that lagoon was there.'

'Exactly.'

The second caller rang off but Karen was soon picking up the receiver again as someone else needed to speak to her. Hawker waited and pondered. The name of Larry Newmark flitted around his brain. It was five minutes before the press officer came back to him.

'Sorry about that, Don.'

'Caught you at a busy time.'

Karen blanched. 'Oh dear!'

'What's wrong?'

'I just heard what you said. About this Mr Newmark. If his company *is* exhibiting here, we'll have the police crawling all over The Belfry. That's the last kind of publicity we want on the eve of the Ryder Cup.' She looked over at the paper. 'How many boys in blue have they got involved?'

'Over sixty Murder Squad detectives under the command of Superintendent Frank Rayment. He'll love that. One of those men who get their kicks out of power.'

'Are there any other kind?' Her cynicism softened at once. 'Present company excepted, that is.' Concern showed again. 'Oh, I do hope this is not going to upset the apple cart. They've been planning this event for two years. So much sheer hard work has gone into it. I'd hate to see it jeopardised in any way.'

'It may not come to that,' said Hawker. 'But we have to take on board one possibility.'

'What's that?'

'The murder of Larry Newmark is linked with the game of golf somehow. Not necessarily with this particular match, but there is a definite connection.'

'How can you be so sure?'

'Morse code.'

'I'm not with you.'

'This lump on my head is throbbing out a message.'

Karen reached out a consoling hand then diverted it at once to pick up a telephone as it rang. She despatched the caller with a few crisp sentences, then compassion put a worried frown on her face.

'Take care, Don.'

'I always do.'

'You know what I mean.'

He touched his head. 'I survived the attack.'

'This one, maybe.'

'I'll be looking next time, Karen.'

'That's what alarms me,' she admitted. 'Wouldn't it be better to check out of that hotel altogether? I mean, it's brought you nothing but trouble so far.'

'I never run away from trouble.'

'Perhaps it's time you learned how.'

'You can't teach an old dog new tricks.'

'This is no trick, Don. It's common sense. Don't hang around any more. Get out of Corley Hall today.'

'No chance.'

'Not even to please me?'

He was touched enough to hesitate, but it did not change his mind. There was a redoubtable quality in his make-up that could not be extinguished. Hawker thrived on confrontation. Retreat was simply never an option.

112

'I have to stay,' he said. 'Besides, you can't just pick up accommodation like that. Everywhere else in the area is booked solid. Where could I go?'

Both telephones rang. Karen ignored them.

'I'll find you somewhere,' she said quietly.

Norman Starrett was putting a plastic sack of refuse into the bin when she came out of the milking parlour. He gave her a polite nod. Flustered for a moment, Olive Leech recovered quickly and came to the fence. She was anxious to show that there was some conscience in the family.

'We were very sorry to hear about Mr Hawker.'

'A bad business,' said Starrett. 'Somebody did their best to decapitate the poor chap.'

'Well, it wasn't anyone from here.'

'I never claimed that it was, Mrs Leech.'

'You must have thought it, though,' she said. 'Brian and Roy can be a bit aggressive at times but they'd never stoop to anything like that. They're good men at heart.'

'I'm sure they are.'

She emphasised the point by telling him about some domestic incidents that showed them in a good light and he kept a straight face as he heard her out. This was more than just a chat about an injury sustained by one of his guests. It was an attempt to renew some kind of dialogue between warring factions. She was well-named. Olive Leech was trying, albeit clumsily, to offer an olive branch. Starrett had always liked her, not least because she had an innate deference for anyone she perceived as a gentleman. He also pitied her for having to share a household with such uncouth company, and her litany of anecdotes only confirmed his worst suspicions. At the same time, however, he warmed to her overtures of peace. The break in hostilities was only temporary, however.

Brian Leech came out of the parlour in a rage.

'What you talking to him for, woman?'

'I was just –'

'Get back to the house.'

'Your wife and I were having a chat,' said Starrett.

'And you can shut up as well.'

'Brian!' chided his wife.

'Back to the house.'

'I'm doing no harm.'

'On the contrary,' agreed Starrett. 'Your wife is doing a great deal of good. We were discussing the –'

'I don't care!' snarled Leech. 'We got no time to exchange tittle-tattle with you over the fence.'

He glared at his wife until Olive Leech buckled visibly. Shooting her neighbour a look of despair, she turned on her heel and scurried off through the farm buildings. Leech himself aimed a glare at Starrett then went angrily back into the milking parlour.

The olive branch lay snapped on the ground.

Another full afternoon saw Don Hawker circling The Belfry at random and picking up opinion and information wherever he could find them. He was in good spirits. There was no sweeter balm for the wound on his head than the invitation from Karen Maxwell, and he savoured it in retrospect. An idea which had been slowly forming in his own mind had been put into words and action by her. It was the best thing that had happened to him since he had arrived in the Midlands. His luck had at last turned.

He was heading back towards the hotel when he saw an old man come stomping out into the car park with his eyes blazing. Hubert Stone was no longer the beaming know-all with endless time on his hands to talk golf. Holding a crumpled newspaper, he was now a restless and embittered creature who could not get away from The Belfry fast enough. Hawker unwisely stepped in to delay him.

'Mr Stone?'

'Yeah. Who are you?'

'Don Hawker. We met earlier.'

'Did we? Maybe, young fella. I forget.'

'We had a long talk about the Ryder Cup,' reminded the journalist. 'You seemed to know just about everything that's worth knowing about the event.'

'Golf is my life.'

'So you're well up with the current American scene.'

'Of course,' said Stone. 'I just got no time to chat about it now. Find someone else.'

He pushed past Hawker and continued towards his car, but the journalist was not shaken off as easily as that. Falling in beside the old man, he continued questioning.

'Didn't you say you'd been a backroom boy of golf?'

'Maybe.'

'Does that mean you know about the merchandising side of the game?' pressed the other. 'There's someone I'd like to ask you about.'

'Not now, Mr Hawker. I got other fish to fry.'

'This won't take a second. His name is Newmark.'

Hubert Stone came to a dead halt and turned to face his interrogator. Fury which was already barely contained now started to bubble and froth. Hawker was undeterred.

'Larry Newmark. Have you ever heard of him?'

'You trying to be funny, mister?'

'Not at all.'

'Then scram while you still can.'

'Does that mean you know this Newmark character?'

'No, I do not!' hissed the old man.

'He was involved with a company making golf wear.'

'I don't care who he was or is. I never heard of the guy and I don't want to hear about him now.'

'There's no need to be so stroppy about it.'

115

'You looking for trouble?' threatened Stone.

'I asked a simple question, that's all.'

'Then here's a simple answer.'

The punch caught Hawker on the side of his face and it made his head ring. It was so unexpected that it had taken him by surprise. Before he could even think of retaliation, he saw the old man get into his hired car and drive swiftly away. It had not been one of his more enjoyable interviews but it had been extremely productive in its own way. Something had changed Hubert Stone. The journalist had somehow caught him at a vulnerable moment.

There had been a witness to the brief encounter. He was standing in the shade of a tree and pulling at his beard. The argument between the two men had been of profound interest to him and he was able to supply a caption to the picture. It brought him no pleasure.

Chapter Seven

Hubert Stone was in a strange mood when he returned to the Whitehall Hotel that evening. There was no vestige of the usual ferocious attention-seeking or of the reflex lechery. He was subdued and withdrawn. A more perceptive woman than Sheila Dowling would have noticed the deep rage that was being carefully held in check but she saw only the surface calm. When she tried to jolly him out of his sombre state, he remained determinedly serious and asked for the package which was locked away in the hotel safe. Stone then retreated to his room for ten minutes or more.

He came back with the package reduced to half its size and with the brown paper carefully sellotaped. It was only when Sheila had shut it securely away that he was able to relax. He ran an expert eye over the slope of her buttocks as she bent over the safe. Some of the old sparkle had trickled back when she turned to face him. He spread his arms wide.

'You look just great tonight, Sheil!' he said. 'Why didn't you tell me you were coming?'

'Where?'

'Into my life.'

She chortled happily. 'The things you say!'

'I'd have waited for you.'

'Stop teasing me.'

'You ever been to Arizona?'

'Mr Stone!'

117

'Hubert. Now, answer me. Have you?'

'I've never even been to America,' she sighed.

'You'd love it there.'

'I'm sure.'

'Maybe I'll invite you over some time.'

'I'll believe that when it happens.'

'It will. You're sort of growing on me.'

'That's what they all say.'

She chortled again but he suddenly lapsed back into seriousness. He checked his watch and made plans.

'I gotta go up to my room for an hour or so.'

'Will you be dining here tonight?'

'Supper around ten. Okay?'

'All part of the service.'

'Meanwhile I don't want to be disturbed up there.'

'You won't be, I promise.'

'Good.' He brightened. 'Later on, maybe I'll buy you a drink or two. As a kind of celebration.'

'Of what?'

'Your trip to Arizona.'

She pouted provocatively. 'You haven't asked me yet.'

'That comes later.'

'I think you're pulling my leg.'

'Wait and see,' he suggested. 'Who knows? If things pan out the way I hope, you might even get a proposal. I can't guarantee it'll be a proposal of marriage but it'll certainly be an offer you can't refuse.'

'Try me,' she teased.

'That's the general idea, honey.'

'You Americans are all the same!'

'We aim to please, ma'am.' He leered at her. 'If I was a younger man, I'd offer you my hand and heart, then carry you straight back home to Phoenix. Things are different now and I gotta be real careful. Because I'm so sexy and irresistible, some women spend all their time trying to trick me into marriage, but they're wasting their breath.'

'Why?'

'Because I'm the *gigolo* type.'

'Oh, I bet that *I* could coax a proposal out of you.'

'Impossible, honey.'

'Is it?'

'Like getting blood out of a Stone!'

His harsh laughter took him out of the office.

It had been a bad day for Norman Starrett. Murder on his doorstep had cost him three of his guests and a fourth had announced a premature departure on the morrow. Don Hawker was also uneasy about his accommodation. Though Starrett had bought the property for his retirement, he expected it to pay its way and his profit margins were not high. A sudden loss of business caused by adverse publicity about the murder was a severe blow. A quiet country hotel looked vastly less appealing when police cars were parked in the lane outside.

Fading light brought him in from some last chores in the garden and he washed his hands in the downstairs cloakroom. Seeing a line of empty milk bottles on the drainer, he looked in the refrigerator to see how many full bottles were left. He wrote a short note for the milkman then took it to the front door with the empties. As he put them down on the step, outrage beckoned.

Skip, one of the farm dogs, was halfway down the drive. He had climbed through the railings and was spreading his legs before relieving himself on the gravel. Starrett was fuming. Keeping the cow dogs at bay was a difficult job and he had invested heavily in wire fencing. Skip had breached his defences and left a dramatic reminder of his illegal visit. Starrett flew into action at once, stooping down to gather up some stones and hurling them wildly at the animal. The dog yelped

119

as one of the missiles grazed him, then he raced down the drive and around into the farmyard.

Brian Leech had seen it all from one of the pens. He ambled out with a pitchfork in his hands and the two neighbours traded an ugly scowl. Starrett was still so angry that he was not frightened by the farmer's physical presence. He pointed after the dog.

'Keep him off my drive!'

'Free country.'

'Did you see what he did?'

'Yes,' said Leech. 'He speaks for both of us.'

Starrett snorted and turned towards the house.

'I'll get a dog of my own,' he said. 'A guard dog!'

Leech sniggered. 'Then you'll have two lots of shit on your drive.'

'Learn to control your animals.'

'They do exactly what I tell them.'

Pomposity took over. 'You do realise that I could report you to the police over this? If that dog is a persistent nuisance, I'd be within my rights.'

'Just try,' warned Leech. 'You be awkward and we'll be even more awkward. Right, Malc?'

'Yeah!' said the youth with enthusiasm.

'You might wake up one morning and find a whole herd of cows crapping in your drive!'

'And the pigs,' said Malc. 'Pig shit stinks worst of all.'

Norman Starrett found himself being drawn forward into a row that he could never win. He went into reverse gear and tried to salvage some of his dignity.

'There's no need to be vindictive about this,' he said quietly. 'Let's just forget the whole incident. I'd just be grateful if it didn't happen again. Is that too much to ask?'

Brian Leech gave a noncommittal shrug and watched his neighbour go back into the house. Malcolm wanted to press their advantage home.

'Hey, we ought to teach Skip to crap on his car!'

The drive back to Sutton Coldfield took them less than ten minutes, but it was long enough to convince Eric Fretton that his chauffeur's car needed an overhaul.

'What's that rattle, Hawker?'

'Which rattle?'

'Every time we hit a bump in the road.'

'Dunno. Had it for ages.'

'There's something wrong with your suspension.'

'The car goes. That's all that concerns me.'

'It's a death-trap on four wheels.'

Hawker grinned. 'I always drive this way.'

The press tent back at The Belfry was still very crowded and Hawker was fed up with joking enquiries about the injury to his head. When his editor had invited him back to the Whitehall Hotel for dinner, therefore, he was only too glad to escape the bustle and the veiled hostility. On the way they discussed prospects for the first day of the Ryder Cup, then Hawker shifted the conversation back to the subject which preyed on his mind.

'Larry Newmark.'

'What about him?'

'He was the murder victim.'

'I know that.'

'The name keeps bugging me.'

'It would bug *me* if it was mine,' admitted Eric. 'I'd have it changed by deed poll.'

'Newmark. Larry Newmark.'

'I hear you, I hear you.'

'Where have I come across that name before?'

'Search me.'

'I keep seeing a photograph.'

'Watch the road ahead instead.'

'It was fairly recent. In a magazine.'

'The only magazine you need to worry about is ours,'

said the editor. 'Find the facts, chase the stories.'

'That's what I am doing.'

'Forget this Newmark character.'

'But he's all part of it, Eric.'

'Just stick to your job for once.'

'It will come to me in a moment.'

They hit a pothole and set off the rattle again.

'There it is!' shouted Eric. 'This bloody car is falling to pieces. We're disintegrating!'

Hawker drove up the Tamworth Road and stopped at the traffic lights. When they turned green, he went straight across into Anchorage Road. He could see the hotel on the right, a big white house with a drive that dipped sharply as it ran alongside the building. Parked just beyond the hotel was a blue Volvo Estate and a tall bearded man was getting out. He trotted to the hotel and let himself in through the front door. As the Cavalier bounced its way down the drive, Hawker wondered why the Volvo had not used the car park at the rear of the house.

Sheila Dowling gave them both a cordial welcome and hustled them to a table in the dining room. Jenny was the waitress for the night and she soon supplied them with their needs. Over a light salad, Hawker worried away at the name of the murder victim. Eric's patience finally ran out and the talk turned back to the Ryder Cup. The journalist appeased his editor by revealing some of the snippets he had picked up from Tom Pickard. With his own trained ears, Eric himself had collected a lot of useful information to toss into the common pot of knowledge. They were enmeshed in discussion when Sheila sidled over.

'Excuse me, gentlemen . . .'

'What is it, Mrs Dowling?' asked Eric.

'I thought I ought to tip you the wink. Mr Stone will be down for his supper soon.'

'Thanks for the warning.'

'We could serve coffee in the lounge, if you like. That way you'd miss him.' She smiled fondly. 'I know that he can be a bit trying at times.'

'The man's a social menace!'

'I wouldn't say that, Mr Fretton.'

'Then what would you say?'

'Mr Stone is . . . very American, that's all.'

Having found an excuse for his bad behaviour, she withdrew from their table and headed for the stairs. It was well after ten o'clock now and the supper was ready for Hubert Stone. She decided on a personal call for him. Down below in the dining room, Hawker and Eric Fretton finished their pudding and sneaked off quietly into the lounge, feeling that they had had more than enough Anglo-American relations for one day. Jennye pursued them loyally with a tray of coffee.

Sheila, meanwhile, ascended the stairs to a room on the second floor. It was the largest in the establishment and it had been given to Stone when he had complained bitterly about the original room he was assigned. As it was, he still reserved the right to moan about the absence of any lift in the hotel. Sheila paused outside the door then tapped hard with her knuckles.

'Mr Stone . . .'

No answer and no sound of movement from within.

'Are you there?' she called.

Lack of response moved her volume control upwards.

'Can you hear me, Mr Stone! Your supper is ready. Are you going to come down and have it now?'

Sheila Dowling pounded on the door then looked down. It was a mistake. She saw something which made her lose all control and scream hysterically until the whole building echoed with her terror.

A pool of blood was oozing under the door.

Don Hawker was the first to sprint up the stairs and he

caught the sagging figure of the landlady. He managed to calm her slightly by the time the others arrived, then he handed her over gently to her daughter. Borrowing the pass key, he cleared the landing of everyone but Eric Fretton and himself, then he opened the door. It met an obstruction after a mere eighteen inches. Hawker put his head into the room and saw the problem. Hubert Stone was lying just the other side of the door, bleeding profusely from a throat that had been slit right open. Sightless eyes stared up at the ceiling. The trail of blood on the carpet suggested that the American had made a desperate bid to crawl to the door before his strength gave out completely.

Hawker knelt to make a cursory examination. He shook his head sadly. The man was beyond help now.

Eric lunged uncontrollably for the gruesome pun.

'Stone dead.'

While the editor went off to ring the police, Hawker glanced around the room. Signs of a struggle were clear. A small table had been overturned and golf magazines were scattered on the floor. Stone's jacket lay where it had been thrown. Robbed of its money, his open wallet floated in a small estuary of blood. Hawker went to the bedside table to pick up the thick folder of press cuttings. There were dozens of articles and news items, scissored from their original sources and photostated with care, all relating to two golfers. Tony Bianco and Gary Lapidus. A biographer of the two men could not have been more thorough in his research. Colour photographs abounded.

Hawker felt the need to get out quickly. He took one last look, then he closed the door on the grisly scene. He was grateful that Sheila Dowling had been spared the full horror of what had occurred in her best room. He crossed to the window on the landing and opened it wide so that he could fill his lungs with fresh air, then he spotted the gap in the line of parked cars.

The blue Volvo Estate had vanished.

Closing the window, he went downstairs to find Sheila Dowling in a state of near-collapse. Brandy helped her to stop trembling but she was in no condition to answer any questions. Hawker left Eric Fretton to minister to her and turned instead to the daughter.

'When did Mr Stone come back to the hotel?'

'Earlier this evening,' she said.

'Eight? Nine?'

'About eight-thirty, I suppose.'

'Alone?'

'Oh, yes.'

'Did he have any visitors in his room?'

'Not that I know of,' said Jenny.

'Has anyone ever come here to see him?'

'Never.' She shivered involuntarily. 'Mr Stone was not a very nice man. It's hard to see why anyone should want to visit him.'

'What about phone calls?' asked Hawker.

'No one rang him, as far as I know.'

'But he made some calls himself,' blubbed Sheila. 'He used the phone in the office. Two local calls and one to America. He said it was to a business partner.'

'I got the impression he was retired,' said Eric.

'Maybe that was deliberate,' mused Hawker.

'The safe,' croaked Sheila. 'Tell them about the package, Jenny. He took it out tonight.'

Hawker looked quizzical and the daughter explained. When she told how the package had been locked away in the safe again, he asked if he could possibly see it. Jenny was reluctant but her mother gave the signal that the journalist could be trusted. The four of them repaired to the little office and the curtain was pulled back in the alcove. Jenny knew the combination and soon opened the heavy door. The package was taken out and handed over to Hawker.

He studied it carefully, then looked for more approval from the hotelier. She nodded her assent. He used strong fingers to tear at the brown paper and open the parcel up. What he found made them gape with wonder. Wads of used notes were stacked neatly together. Denominations were low but there was still a substantial amount of money in Hawker's grasp. He flicked through it.

Sheila Dowling was jerked out of her state of shock for a few moments. She could simply not reconcile the sight of so much money with someone who stayed at a hotel with such modest prices as her own. Jenny felt a more mercenary impulse. She wanted to reach out and claim the cash as theirs, feeling that they had earned it by putting up with Hubert Stone. It would solve all their financial anxieties in a flash.

Hawker was still trying to assess the amount.

'How much?' asked Eric.

'Difficult to say.'

'Rough guess?'

'A hundred thousand dollars.'

When Dr Philip Tate was appointed as Honorary Physician to the Ryder Cup, he expected to have to cope with all kinds of contingencies during its three days' duration, but he could not have foreseen that his first patient would be a young American woman who had fainted at the sight of a newspaper headline. What made it worse was the fact that Glenn Bianco concealed the true nature of her malady from him and left the doctor treating vague symptoms of stress. His rather hearty bedside manner did not seem to help and he came out of the room in some confusion. The anxious husband followed him.

'What's wrong with her, Doc?' said Tony Bianco.

'Oh, nothing serious.'

'Are you sure?'

'Your wife is a little over-strained, that's all.'

'Glenn keeps herself in great shape.'

'Maybe jet-lag has finally caught up with her.'

'There's more to it than that.'

'I wouldn't get unnecessarily alarmed.'

'She goes off on a shopping trip, bursting with health, and she comes back a nervous wreck.'

Philip Tate grinned. '*I'm* always like that after an afternoon in Rackhams.'

'This is no joke, Doc.'

'No, no, of course not,' said the other quickly. 'Your wife obviously has something wrong with her, but I don't think it's anything worse than exhaustion. Those pills I prescribed should do the trick.'

'And if they don't?'

'Call me back any time you like, Mr Bianco.'

The doctor gave him a reassuring pat on the arm, then he went off down the corridor. Bob Jaglom was waiting to move in. News that Glenn Bianco was feeling unwell had caused him some concern because it could affect the way that her husband played golf the next day. Aware of their marital difficulties, he did not want any additional problems in the Bianco bedroom.

'How's she looking, Tony?' he asked.

'Better. Much better.'

'Good. Tough kid you got there.'

'That's what I can't figure out, Bob. I mean, she's almost never ill. Shrugs off the kind of things that drag the rest of us down. I can't ever remember her taking to her bed like that.'

'Maybe the tension's getting to her.'

'Never has before. Glenn's cool as they come.'

'What exactly happened in Birmingham?'

'According to Alma, she just keeled over in the main street. That's not natural, Bob. Dammit, she's in her prime. Why did she hit the deck like that?'

'Have you tried asking her?'

127

'She clammed up on me.'

'Maybe Alma Lapidus can shed some light.'

'No, nothing. Just repeats the same story. The two of them are walking down the street when Glenn feels giddy and goes down like a sack of potatoes.'

'Don't worry about it,' said Bob confidently. 'I'm sure she'll be fine after a good night's sleep. Then we can put the whole incident behind us.'

Tony Bianco nodded. He let his team captain soothe him with wise words and urge him not to let his wife's condition unsettle him on the eve of such a vital event. To ram his point home, Bob Jaglom floated the idea that he could always pull the player out of the opening foursomes if the latter did not feel that he would be at his best.

'You can forget that, Bob,' said the other firmly.

'Can I?'

'Come hell or high water, I play tomorrow!'

'That's what I like to hear.'

'Didn't come all this way to miss the action.'

'You're a real pro, Tony.'

Having achieved his object, Bob Jaglom took his leave and went off on a round of the other players. Tony Bianco let himself back into his room and got a thin smile from his wife. Glenn was propped up in bed, making a desultory attempt to watch a sitcom on television.

'So how you feeling now, honey?'

'Not too bad, I guess.'

'Have you taken those pills?'

'Yeah.'

'They should help.'

'Hope so.'

He approached her tentatively and sat beside her on the bed. Prepared for rejection, he was pleased when she let him take her hand. He stroked it softly.

'I'll take care of you.'

'Will you?'

'If you let me.'

Glenn Bianco stared at the screen without seeing anything. Her mind was still on a name that she had read in a provincial newspaper. She felt quite numb. As her husband continued to stroke and comfort her, she was in a world of her own and it was impossibly bleak. Making a conscious effort to escape it, she came to her senses and saw where she was and with whom. Her first instinct was to pull away, but there was nowhere to go now. Despair made her shiver all over.

'Tony . . .'

'I'm here.'

'Will you do something for me?'

'Just name it, honey.'

'Put your arms around me.'

It was nearly midnight by the time he finally arrived, but Karen Maxwell still gave him a warm welcome. She was staying at a small hotel in Coleshill within easy reach of The Belfry. His telephone call had alerted her to the possibility of delay and she would happily have waited even longer for him. Hawker was contrite as she brought him into her room and locked the door quietly behind her.

'Sorry.'

'It's not your fault, Don.'

'The police kept grilling me.'

'Must've been a nightmare.'

'It was.'

'Poor you!'

'Save your sympathy for Sheila Dowling.'

'Who?'

'The woman who runs the hotel. She was completely pole-axed by it all. Stone was an awkward customer in every way, but she actually liked him. Then someone calmly walks upstairs and slits the old man's throat. No wonder she went to pieces.'

'Is Eric Fretton still there?'

'Yes. Good man in an emergency like this.'

'It must have been dreadful.'

'I've had better nights, Karen.'

'What's the situation now?'

'It's in the hands of the police.'

'Do they have any leads?'

'Not yet.'

'On the phone, you mentioned some money.'

'Yes,' said Hawker. 'It was stashed away in the safe in a brown paper parcel. Apparently, Stone had taken some of it out earlier in the evening.'

'How much was there?'

'Lots. He must have been a very wealthy man.'

'Then why stay at a modest hotel like that?'

'Rich people are often quite mean.'

'There must be another explanation.'

'I'll let you know.' He sat down and stifled a yawn. 'One way and another, I'm beginning to regret I ever came to the Ryder Cup. Every time I turn around, I seem to find a dead body.' He gave a wry smile. 'Or maybe they find *me*.'

Karen perched on the edge of the chair and put an affectionate hand on his shoulder. They sat in silence for a few minutes as he tried to make sense of what had happened and she did her best to assess both his mood and his needs. Hawker wanted time to unwind. He was still coming to terms with the shock of what he had encountered in the Whitehall Hotel. Karen Maxwell was soon able to read his mind.

'Did it make you think of Elaine?' she said.

'Yes.'

'Why?'

'All that blood. All that waste.'

'Elaine took her own life.'

'So?'

130

'This was murder.'

'The result is the same,' he said. 'Whether you cut your wrists like her or have your throat slit. There's one God-awful mess left behind.'

'Do you want to talk about it?' she invited softly.

He looked up at her. 'Another time.'

As their eyes met properly for the first time, they found the strength to put away the horrors of the night for a while and remember why they had come together. They got up, kissed, crossed to the bed and undressed each other very slowly. It was gentle, languid, unforced. When they got into bed together, the excitement of novelty was tempered by a wonderful sense of familiarity as if they were old lovers enjoying a reunion. They knew that they could rely on each other and so they could afford to relax. An hour or so slipped by with magical ease. Karen was given release from the rigours of a sixteen-hour day while Hawker was thrown a lifeline of hope.

When it was all over, they lay entwined among the rumpled sheets and listened to the sound of each other's breathing. His mind eventually returned to the problems that were taxing him and he ran a hand through her hair.

'Did you find out anything for me?'

'About what?'

'Larry Newmark.'

'Oh.' Disappointment made her tense slightly. The golden moment was over. 'As a matter of fact, I did.'

'Well?'

'His company are not part of the exhibition here.'

'That blows one theory of mine.'

'But he does have a business connection here.'

'With whom?'

'One of the American team. I heard on the grapevine that Newmark had just signed him up to promote a range of golf wear for men. The name took

131

me by surprise.'
 'Out with it.'
 'Gary Lapidus.'

The Vauxhall Cavalier wheezed in protest when the
ignition key was switched on. Having found what it
thought was a safe haven for the night, it was very
loath to start up again. Hawker spent some time
coaxing life into the engine. When he drove away from
Coleshill, the car moved with mutinous reluctance.
The rattle of which Eric Fretton had complained was
now a resounding bang.

He reached the M6 in minutes and found it
relatively empty at that late hour, allowing him to hug
the inside lane at a steady fifty. His mind was confused.
It did not make sense. Why had he left a gorgeous
woman in a warm bed in order to go back to a house
that held such painful memories for him? Karen had
been deeply hurt and he could see that he had
offended her. It was a poor show of gratitude on his
part for the most glorious hour he had spent with
anyone for months. Karen Maxwell had been a
marvellous tonic and they had shared something very
special, but she had one irremediable defect. She was
not Elaine. To get so close to someone who had known
and understood his wife very well was a blessing that
was not unmixed with a curse.

Karen was at once a supreme distraction and a cruel
reminder. She helped him to forget the pain of a
traumatic event at the same time as she was deepening
it. Hawker simply had to leave her that night. There
were three of them in the bed.

He was still trying to rationalise it all when the
enemy struck. Blithely unaware of the headlights that
trailed him, he saw no danger when the vehicle surged
out into the middle lane to overtake. He was climbing
the long steep hill and trying to rehearse the apology

he would have to make to Karen at their next meeting. Without warning, the car alongside him went straight past, then cut diagonally across his path. All at once, survival was the name of the game. Hawker swung on the steering-wheel and veered crazily off to the left, mounting an embankment and cutting deep swathes through the grass before skidding back down to the hard shoulder and spinning to a halt. It all happened in a split second.

The Vauxhall Cavalier was now facing the wrong way. When Hawker looked over his shoulder, he saw that the raised embankment had given way to a deep slope that was protected by a crash barrier. The object of the exercise now became clear. Having chosen his spot well, the other driver had attempted to force him off the motorway and down into oblivion. It was not only the car which would have been a complete write-off. Hawker got out to check his vehicle and noticed for the first time that one of his rear hub-caps was missing. He did not bother to look after the other car, which was already well out of sight. Hawker could guess its make and its driver. It was a blue Volvo Estate with a bearded man at the wheel.

As he stood there in the darkness, he realised that he had once seen that same vehicle in the sunshine of an early morning. It had been parked in Burrow Hill Lane when Hawker went for his run. He was now certain that its driver had been inside. He had met the man at Corley, at the Whitehall Hotel and on the M6. The nature of their relationship had been made all too evident. Hawker's head ached and he wondered if they had had another meeting beside the slurry lagoon.

He was shaken but unhurt and he was able to take a kind of perverse comfort from what had happened. If he had become a target himself, it could mean only one thing. His investigations were slowly bearing fruit. He was getting warm. Miraculously, the much-abused

Vauxhall Cavalier started first time and he did an illegal U-turn on the motorway before trundling off up the hill. He could even afford a dry laugh. His callous indifference to his car had probably saved him. Had he been in a faster and sleeker car, the two of them would now be lying in a mangled heap at the bottom of the slope. The banging which had slowed him down had been a gentle tap from the hand of God.

Hawker nursed the Cavalier all the way back to Corley Hall. As he parked on the drive, he noted how few cars were now there. Evidently the owner of the hotel was having the sort of problems that Sheila Dowling could now expect to face. Murder killed off business. Guests preferred clean sheets without bloodstains.

The moment he got out of the car, he knew that he was being watched. If the incident on the motorway had done nothing else for him, it had at least put him on full alert. His nerve ends were positively tingling. Somewhere in the dark a hostile pair of eyes was keeping him under surveillance and there was an even chance that those eyes had a beard beneath them. It was an unpleasant feeling, and Hawker schooled himself to remain calm and show no awareness of his discovery. As casually as he could, he reached back into the car to pick up the heavy rubber-cased torch that lay under the dashboard. Armed and ready, he locked the door then sauntered down the drive as if savouring the cool night air.

Though he sensed a threat, he could not work out from which direction it would come. The farmyard was a black jumble of shapes to his left, while the high garden wall with its rambler roses was on his right. He reached the lane itself and looked up and down it. There was nobody in sight and the only sound he could hear was the dull blur of traffic from the motorway. Hawker dismissed his fears as the result of

134

an over-active imagination and strode back up the drive. The pounding at the base of his skull eased off.

It was when he approached the garden gate that his warning system came back into play. He heard the rustle of leaves on the lilac tree and knew that somebody was tucked in behind it. Without checking his stride, he walked on until he drew level with the gate, then swung the torch abruptly up as a weapon and switched on its beam to identify his target. A man in a dressing-gown gave a sickly grin and blinked.

'Don't shine that in my eyes,' said Norman Starrett.

'Then don't creep up on me.'

'The sound of your car woke me up.'

'So? I can let myself into the house.'

'But you didn't,' said the other. 'I listened for the door. It was the same as last night.'

'Where did you think I'd gone? Across to the field for another bang on the head?'

Starrett coughed to hide his embarrassment. When he was unable to assume his lordly posture or to fall back on oily ingratiation, he was lost for words. He fiddled with the belt around his dressing-gown.

'Why don't we go in?' suggested Hawker.

The hotelier led the way into the garden and along the gravel path to the front door of the house. Once inside, he took his guest to the kitchen and moved to pick up the electric kettle.

'Can I make you a drink of any kind?' he offered.

'No thanks.'

'How about a nightcap from the bar?'

'Far too late.'

'What kept you out so long?'

'I was debating whether or not to come back.'

'Yes,' gabbled Starrett, launching into what was patently a rehearsed speech. 'My wife and I have been talking about that. We feel that we ought to offer you some sort of discount in view of what's happened to

135

you since you've been with us. I know that it's not strictly our fault, in that sense, but we feel we'd like to make amends in some way.' He put the kettle down and spoke honestly. 'We've invested a lot of ourselves as well as our money in this enterprise and we don't want it to fail. We may have occasional problems with Leech, but it never really affects the way we run our business here. Corley Hall has been a going concern until now. We'd very much like to keep it that way.'

It was a direct appeal and Hawker paid heed to it. When Starrett forgot about the architectural merits of his house and stopped delivering his lecture about the author of *Adam Bede*, he was almost human. Hawker could not bring himself to warm to the man, but his coldness did thaw out somewhat. He changed the tack completely.

'Tom Pickard.'

'I beg your pardon?'

'Tom Pickard. He's a golfer. He stayed here.'

'Heavens, *I* know who he is,' said Starrett, regaining some of his self-importance. 'Our secret weapon against the Yanks in the Ryder Cup. I've seen Tom Pickard play dozens of times. On telly, that is.'

'Tell me about his visit here.'

'It was a fair while ago.'

'Just for the one night?'

'Yes,' confirmed the other. 'He was here to open the golf shop in Sandpits Lane. They wanted a big name to pull in the crowds, and Tom was ideal. Normally he would have been booked in at the De Vere or the Leofric in Coventry, but it was the conference season and both were full. So Corley Hall got another celebrity.'

'Did you see much of him while he was here?'

'Very little – though he enjoyed his stay with us.'

'Oh? He told me the birds had kept him awake.'

'Tom must have been teasing you,' said Starrett. 'He

had an excellent night. I remember how cheerful he was over breakfast. In fact he was so grateful for the way we looked after him that he gave us a memento.'

'Memento?'

'Yes, he's a keen photographer. He always takes his camera with him on his travels. Sent us the most marvellous picture of the house. Well, you've seen it.'

'Have I?'

'It's the one hanging in the dining room.' Starrett took him through. 'You must have noticed it.'

'Not really.'

'Here it is. We had it enlarged.'

The framed photograph of Corley Hall was hanging on the wall above the reproduction Jacobean court cupboard. Starrett beamed complacently. It was not the work of an amateur. Shot from the perfect angle with the sun falling across it, the house looked superb, a blaze of white in a bright green setting, an ideal country property. The proud owner added a subtitle.

'*Some* of our guests have been happy here.'

'It's a great photo.'

'Tom experimented with angles for hours.'

'Where was this taken from?'

'An elevated position in the field opposite.'

'Elevated.'

'Yes,' said Starrett. 'The slurry lagoon?'

Hawker was glad that he had asked.

Chapter Eight

Heavy rain fell on The Belfry that morning, but it did not dampen the spirits of the large crowds who converged on the course from seven o'clock onwards. The main car park was a multi-coloured sea of golf umbrellas as spectators left their vehicles and made their way over the makeshift road bridge to the turnstiles. Programme-sellers did brisk business and everyone scanned a copy of the pink drawsheet which gave them details of the order of play for the day. On the back of the sheet was a brief message from Angus Cameron, forecasting an exciting contest and exhorting the fans to uphold the high standards of behaviour which had dignified the event in the past.

A major golfing tournament is one of the few sporting occasions where the devotee can dress exactly like the players, and many people – women just as much as men – had yielded to the impulse to wear their Pringle sweaters, their Farrah trousers, their two-tone waterproofs, their spiked shoes and their natty headgear. Battle-hardened veterans also brought something on which to stand, so that they could get a view of the action on a course that still tended to obscure most of the prime moments from most of the spectators most of the time. Small periscopes were also pressed into service, and more than one child was hoisted on to fatherly shoulders. Half an hour before the start of play, the ropes down each side of the first fairway were thronged with buzzing support. In the hospitality tents that overlooked the scene, the business community were warming themselves up with a continental breakfast.

Excitement built when the crowd got their first glimpse of the distinctive outfits worn by their players. European and American fans alike raised a cheer as their heroes came out to commence hostilities. The visitors had won the honour and it was the chunky figure of their key player who stepped forward.

'On the tee – Tony Bianco!'

Generous applause came from the galleries, and it was repeated with extra gusto when the opening drive explored the air in a graceful arc before landing in the middle of the fairway some hundred and twenty yards from the pin. Play had begun at eight o'clock precisely. The Johnny Walker Ryder Cup was under way.

'On the tee – Rolf Kohlmar!'

The German was plainly nervous as he addressed his ball and it transmitted itself to his shot. Though it had length and height, its direction was wayward and it ended up just outside the ropes to the right of the fairway. His partner could see the green from that position, but he was left with a tricky shot as his opening contribution to the event.

Don Hawker watched it all with interest. Not for him the relative comfort of the press tent with its serried ranks of desks and its televised pictures. He wanted to be where the action was and to enjoy the atmosphere that was unique to the Ryder Cup. At the same time he had a more personal reason for keeping an eye on one of the players in each team. Tony Bianco and Tom Pickard might be involved in a game of golf, but they were also factors in two parallel murder investigations. What was really significant about the American was the absence of his wife. Hal Mayo's latest girlfriend was in the back of the golf buggy being driven down the fairway by Bob Jaglom, but there was no sign of Glenn Bianco. The death of her uncle had apparently sapped her enthusiasm for watching the game. Tom Pickard was another matter. Relaxed and confident, he was sizing up his shot as he walked towards his ball, unaware of the fact that his biographer was harbouring suspicions about him. When Hawker had agreed to work with his friend on the book, he had no idea of the latter's acquaintance with a field opposite Corley Hall. He was fervently hoping that he would not have to include the word 'murder' in the index.

Hal Mayo lived up to his glamour-boy image with a flashy shot that rolled to the heart of the green. Tom Pickard matched it with a stunner that stopped only a yard from the cup. Both teams collected their first encouraging birdie and the hole was halved. Lifted up by the applause, the four players headed for the second tee.

Hawker stayed to watch the other foursomes go off at fifteen-minute intervals, then he walked diagonally to the fourth hole to catch the closing stages of the leading battle. The Americans were into their stride but their opponents were giving nothing away. They were still all square as they moved on to the next theatre of war. The galleries had now come up hard against the limitations of the viewing facilities, but Hawker's press badge gained him privileged access to the path that ran down the side of each fairway between double ropes. It meant proximity to the general public, and he was recognised by dozens of people who spoke to him with the familiarity of lifelong friends. Fame was a lingering burden.

The opening foursome had reached the short seventh hole when Hawker's interest in the match was terminated. He just had time to see Kohlmar use a medium iron from the tee and put his ball into the deep solid-faced bunker at the front of the green, before feeling a tap on the shoulder. He was less than pleased to turn around and be confronted by the face of Detective Sergeant Mike Impey.

'Good morning, sir.'

'It was until now.'

'How are we doing?'

'Even-stevens in this match.'

'Sorry to interrupt you,' said Impey with one eye on Bianco's tee shot. 'The Super wants a word with you.'

'*Now?*'

'That's the general idea.'

'But I'm working.'

'So are we, sir.'

There was a grim intensity about the man which told Hawker he had no room for manoeuvre. He let Impey duck under the ropes, then followed him as he bullocked his way through the thickening crowd. They reached clear grass and quickened their pace. The rain eased slightly.

Superintendent Frank Rayment was waiting for them back at the hotel and he looked impatient. It was clear that he thought the whole idea of a golf tournament was an irrelevance beside the important job of tracking down the killer of a visiting American. He stood in the lounge and radiated contempt for everything around him. His moustache twitched as they bore down on him.

'What kept you?' he snapped.

'Sorry, sir,' said Impey.

'Where did you find him?'

'I was trying to watch the golf,' said Hawker. 'Oddly enough, that's why I came to the Midlands in the first place, Superintendent.'

'Oh, I think it has other attractions for you.'

'Like a bang on the head?'

'Or a night with the press officer.' He all but sniggered at Hawker's discomfort. 'We like to keep ourselves well-informed on these matters. Sometimes has a bearing on the case in hand.' He cleared his throat with extravagant discretion. 'I trust that you and the lady had a pleasant time together.'

'What do you want?' said Hawker coldly.

'How about some cooperation, sir?'

'I've given you all I can.'

'That's not how we see it.'

'Come again?'

'Tell him, Sergeant.'

Impey stepped forward. 'We've found out a little more about Larry Newmark, sir. He was building up quite a flourishing business in the golf world and on the verge of hitting the big time. According to his partner back in Denver, he was here to see the Ryder Cup and to negotiate some important deals. Getting the picture, sir? Mr Newmark was a coming man. Handsome, educated, early thirties. Very ambitious by the sound of it.'

'So why did he take a dive in the slurry lagoon?'

'Someone wanted him out of the way.'

'Brilliant deduction, Sergeant.'

'For a long time.'

'Yes,' added Rayment. 'He wasn't supposed to be found as quickly as that. The plan was that he would rot quietly under the brown stuff while the cows were grazing all around him. A rural idyll.' He gave a shrewd glance. 'By the way, how are you getting on with *Adam Bede*?'

'I gave it up.'

'Mistake, sir. Gets better as it goes on.'

'Take your word for it.'

'Especially the chapter about the murder.'

'Tell me more about Larry Newmark.'

'He was staying at a place in Meriden.'

'Is that far from Corley?'

'Mere ten minutes by car,' said Rayment easily. 'Not

142

that our friend had much time to enjoy the hospitality of the Manor Hotel. Seems he checked in one morning, went out alone that afternoon and was not seen again until you spotted him bobbing about in the lagoon.'

'Why was he naked?'

'To hinder identification. And for another reason.'

'Which was?'

'I'm not at liberty to disclose that, sir.'

Mike Impey resumed. 'Larry Newmark was quite an interesting character. Kept a high profile back home in Denver with a marketing operation that was nation-wide. His partner was the man in the back room. Mr Newmark stole all the publicity. He loved to get his photo in the papers. Something of a hustler.'

'What are you saying, Sergeant?'

'He was the sort of man who makes enemies.'

'Would they follow him all the way here?'

'If they hated him enough.'

'Why not just bump him off in the States?'

'Maybe the killer lives over here.'

'Have you got any clue who he might be?'

'No,' said Rayment. 'But we think that you do.'

'Me?'

'You're still holding out on us, sir.'

'Here we go again!'

'Why not let us in on it?'

'Because I don't know what it is myself.'

'Then why go in for all the Sherlock Holmes stuff?' said the Superintendent. 'We've kept an eye on you, sir. We know that you've been snooping around. Now, what have you found out?'

'Nothing.'

'We'll keep asking.'

'Several times a day,' warned Impey.

Hawker weighed up the situation. They were tenacious men who could disrupt his work completely.

The only way to get them off his back was to concede a few snippets of information to them while keeping essentials to himself.

'Okay,' he said. 'Gary Lapidus was about to clinch a deal to promote golf wear for Newmark.'

'Give us more than that,' said Rayment.

'Lapidus has a connection with Corley.'

'We know that, sir. His late wife was a member of the Roberts family who hailed from the village. They used to live in Rock Cottage in the days of the outside privy. Talk to the vicar if you ever want to know local gossip. He told us all about the American connection. Ted Roberts visited Corley himself ten years ago – he's the former father-in-law of Lapidus. Ted presented a bible to the church to honour his link with the village. He even read the first lesson from it at Morning Service.'

'Ephesians two. Verses one to ten,' confirmed Impey.

'Gary Lapidus has a genuine reason to visit Corley. Nothing sinister in that.' He searched Hawker's face. 'Unless you have something to add.'

'You seem to have been admirably thorough.'

'We know about Tom Pickard as well.'

'I see.'

'Leave it to the professionals, sir.'

'I always do, Superintendent.'

'That's not our experience. Nor is it the experience of our colleagues in Sutton Coldfield.' He fingered his moustache. 'You have quite a record with Warwickshire hotels. Every time you visit one, a body turns up. Even last night in Coleshill – though that particular body happened to be alive, of course.'

'My private life is my own, Superintendent.'

'Not when it touches on a murder enquiry.'

'Two,' reminded Impey.

'Yes, Mike. Two. Larry Newmark and Hubert Stone.' He subjected Hawker to the Hitler stare. 'We're

144

treating them as unrelated incidents at the moment, but that could soon change. I mean, there is one obvious common factor.'

'What is it?' said Hawker.

'You, sir.' There was a sting of accusation in his voice. 'By the way, how's the head?'

'Still on my shoulders.'

'Then use it.'

Frank Rayment got up and motioned for his assistant to leave with him. They paused long enough for the senior detective to give Hawker some finger-wagging advice.

'Don't go too far away, sir.'

'I've done nothing illegal, Superintendent.'

'Matter of opinion. One last thing . . .'

'Well?'

'Something you should know about Karen Maxwell.'

'Leave her out of it,' said Hawker defensively. 'She has nothing whatsoever to do with this business.'

'Then you shouldn't have dragged her in, sir, should you? Besides, she's another element in what you might call the Yank factor.'

'I don't follow.'

'Remember where Larry Newmark is from?'

'Denver, Colorado.'

'Karen Maxwell lived there for six months.'

They left Hawker in absolute turmoil.

Glenn Bianco lay sprawled in an armchair with a fashion magazine unopened across her lap. One death had rocked her, but the second, ironically, had come to her aid. The murder of Hubert Stone gave her a legitimate cause for mourning. She had always had reservations about her uncle and discovered now that they were quite severe. Although horrified to learn of his murder, she was not stricken down by grief on his behalf. She felt curiously untouched by his loss because it paled beside the greater blow she had already suffered. A name in a Birmingham newspaper had devastated her. The untimely end of Hubert Stone was a convenient way of explaining her depression.

She brooded for a while longer, then got up to switch on the television, changing channels until the Ryder Cup match came on. The first game had just been completed and the victorious Americans were being interviewed on the eighteenth green. Hal Mayo basked in the attention and grinned happily at the world. Tony Bianco, by contrast, was cold and impassive. Instead of savouring his moment of glory, he wanted to talk about the fourballs due to be played that afternoon. Glenn stared at him for some time and tried hard to believe that she had married him for his charm. She could not bear to listen to him and used the remote control to switch off the programme.

She flopped down into her seat. Before she could lapse back into despair, however, the telephone rang. She stared blankly at it for a few seconds before picking the receiver up and speaking into it in a whisper.

'Hello . . .?'

'Is that Mrs Bianco?' asked a man's voice.

'Yeah. Who am I talking to?'

'That doesn't matter, lady. Just listen. You and me got some unfinished business to discuss.'

'Look, who are you?'

'A friend.'

The accent placed him in the American Midwest and she judged him to be in his thirties, but that was all she could divine. Eager to put down the receiver, she yet clung to it and listened with gathering fear as he spelled out what he wanted.

'We need to talk, Glenn. Real soon.'

'What about?'

'Larry Newmark.'

146

'You *knew* him?'

'Very well. Saw him recently as a matter of fact.'

'When was this?'

'I'll tell you when I see you.'

'Why should I see you?'

'Because you have no choice.'

'Get off this line!' she ordered.

'I know about Larry – but your husband doesn't.'

'Go away, will you!'

'When we've sorted this out.'

'There's nothing to sort out.'

'Oh, but there is, baby. Lots and lots.'

'Just leave me alone.'

'I'll be in touch. Soon.'

She put down the receiver and sought to work out the implications of what she had just heard. On top of what she had suffered already, it was intolerable. Her whole body shook and she began to weep uncontrollably. Behind the tears, however, she confronted an ugly thought.

There might be worse to come.

Eric Fretton loved his golf. The brutality of the English weather was a bonus to him because it made the course more difficult to play and thus produced more interesting situations. A true disciple of the game, he was always ready to trade off the scenic attraction of a beautiful course in bright sunshine for the excitement of watching golfers struggle to master adverse conditions. Honours were still even at the end of the morning. The foursomes had been consistently fascinating, with the advantage swinging to and fro like a pendulum. At the lunchtime interval the 2-2 scoreline was a fair reflection of the play so far, though it was viewed differently by the respective team captains. Angus Cameron, who had seen his strongest pairing beaten 3 and 2, was disappointed and snapped

147

at the heels of his men. Bob Jaglom, however, was quietly satisfied. He had seen Tony Bianco in superb form and knew that the American challenge would be toughened even more. Bianco had an amazing effect on the general morale. When he played well, the whole team improved.

Over a guzzled snack, Eric Fretton made the same point to Don Hawker. The editor felt that if any one man would dominate the event, it would be Tony Bianco.

'What about his wife?' said Hawker.

'Eh?'

'She didn't turn up this morning.'

'So?'

'Can you imagine a woman like Glenn Bianco flying six thousand miles in order to miss the very thing she came to see? Her place was beside her husband, cheering him on. In any case, she's a golfer in her own right with a real commitment to the game.'

'Aren't you forgetting Uncle Hubert?'

'Not at all. And I'm sure she was knocked for six when she learned about the murder. Who wouldn't be?'

'Then there's your answer,' said Eric. 'She's up in her room, piping her eye and grieving over Stone's death.'

Hawker was sceptical. 'Maybe. But I'm not convinced that she was all that fond of her uncle. I'm only going on what I saw but I got the impression that she was not exactly a dutiful niece.' He bit into a sandwich and chewed away. 'Besides, there's another element.'

'Is there?'

'Glenn Bianco is like Alma Lapidus. She loves to dress up and strut around in public like a peacock.' He indicated the crowds. 'Is she going to miss a chance like this to show off? Frankly, I don't think even the death of an uncle would stop her.'

'So what's the explanation?'

'Love to know.'

'How about just concentrating on the golf?'

'Eric, I've got a much better story here.'

'You think.'

'I know. And it's all tied in with the Ryder Cup.'

'In what way?'

'That's the bit I haven't worked out.'

'Don't invite trouble.'

'But I feel I'm almost there.'

'Stick to sportswriting, Hawker,' said his editor firmly. 'The next clonk on your head may be the last.'

He moved away to join some friends and take part in a discussion of what had been the finest shot of the morning. Hawker had no time to consider the warning he had been given because he caught sight of Karen Maxwell. Surrounded by people, she was able to give him no more than a brief wave but the gesture was eloquent. There was a hurt quality about it, a what-did-I-do-wrong, the muted distress of a woman who gave herself wholly to a lover and who does not deserve to be abandoned by him in the middle of the night without explanation. Hawker was not good at apologies but one was patently in order.

He shouldered his way across the room and found her handling questions from two senior golf correspondents at the same time as she was being consulted by her assistant and chatted up by a Spanish journalist. Karen saw him coming and detached herself from the quartet long enough to have a snatched conversation with him in a corner. She hid her wounded feelings behind a pleasant smile.

'Who said being a press officer was easy?'

'You could do it on your head, Karen.'

'I'm frazzled and this is only the first morning.'

'Stay with it,' he encouraged.

'One consolation, anyway,' she said. 'No ruinous publicity from the murder at the Whitehall Hotel. It didn't make waves in any of the nationals.'

'What about the local papers?'

'They went to town, as you might expect, but they didn't over-emphasise the Ryder Cup angle. They just say that Hubert Stone was in the area to watch the golf.'

'Have the police been in touch at all?'

'Not so far.'

'They must've contacted Glenn Bianco, surely. It was her uncle who was killed. She has a right to know.'

'Oh, she knows,' said Karen. 'It's the reason she hasn't stirred from her room today. That, and the fact that she's been a bit off colour.'

'Since when?'

'Yesterday. Dr Tate, our resident quack, was called in to give her the once-over. Apparently she fainted in the street in the middle of Birmingham.'

'Did he say what was wrong with her?'

'Strain, probably. He couldn't find anything.'

'Sounds odd.'

'She was shopping with Alma Lapidus. They came out of a store, bought a copy of the *Birmingham Mail* and then it happened – Glenn Bianco keeled over.'

Hawker was still trying to assimilate this new detail when Karen was hailed simultaneously from both sides of the room. People started bearing down on her. Hawker's time was running out and he used it clumsily.

'About last night . . .'

'That was history.'

'It wasn't that I didn't enjoy it, Karen.'

'Forget the whole thing.'

'All I'm trying to say is –'

'What's the point?' she cut in abruptly.

Hawker was hurt and felt a stupid urge to retaliate. Before he could control himself, the words tumbled out.

'Why didn't you mention you'd lived in Denver?'

He had never seen her blush before. It began at her neck and rose right up her cheeks. Karen shot him a pained look, then went off to talk to the two men who converged on her. Hawker chided himself bitterly. In trying to resolve an awkward situation, he had contrived to make it far worse, perhaps even to put it beyond repair. He stalked out of the room and went straight to the car park, needing to be alone for a while to take stock and to make plans.

It was a fortuitous choice of venue. As he stood quietly among the parked cars, he saw the jaunty figure of Gary Lapidus come out of the hotel. The golfer went across to his hired car, unlocked the door and took something out from beneath the dashboard before going quickly back into the building. What arrested Hawker's gaze was not the American himself but the vehicle that he chose. It was a blue Volvo Estate.

Hawker thought of two initials on a golf ball.

Oblivious to the rain, Malcolm sat in the tractor as it chugged its way along Burrow Hill Lane. This was his favourite and most productive hunting ground, especially at night when courting couples came to park along the ridge and enjoy furtive moments in the dark. Not only did Malcolm give himself the pleasure of watching them at it, but he sometimes collected a little souvenir at the same time. Two people in the throes of uninhibited passion would not hear if their fog lamp disappeared or if their rear windscreen wiper was severed from its base. Malcolm knew how to work quickly and quietly. During the summer months when bolder spirits shunned their vehicles and went off into the long grass to express their urges in more dramatic fashion, he was able to take more time and claim richer spoils. His little hobby was endlessly satisfying to him. It combined the thrill of voyeurism with the exhilaration of theft and his chances of being caught were minimal. He looked upon it as the greatest bonus of work on the farm.

Today was a disappointment. There were only two cars backed off the road in the shade of the rocks. One of them was plainly occupied by a man on his own, eating a sandwich with one hand and reading through some sales invoices with the other. The nearby Jaguar was far more promising. It had trade plates to show that it came from the factory in Brown's Lane and had no right to be where it was. Though the driver was staring ahead through the windscreen as if lost in contemplation, his baser needs were being attended to by a woman whose head was out of sight in his lap. From his raised position, Malcolm could just make out the back of her neck as it bobbed bravely up and down. He sniggered aloud as he felt his own blood race, then accepted there were no easy pickings to be had that day. Swinging right past Rock Cottage, he changed gear and let the tractor rumble down the lane at a fair speed.

The nose of a Citroën BX poked out of the drive of Corley Hall. Norman Starrett was going out somewhere. Malcolm saw a chance to strike a small blow for the cause of agriculture. Accelerating sharply, he took the tractor towards the rippling puddles in front of the car and sent up a small tidal wave to wash over Starrett's windscreen. The latter hooted his horn in annoyance but Malcolm only laughed even more wildly. It was all a game to him and he had scored another point for the farm. When he thought about it, he saw that it had so far been an excellent week for him and the fun was certainly not over yet.

Sheila Dowling had got over the initial shock and she was adjusting to it with typical resilience. Viewed from one perspective, Hubert Stone had done what nearly

152

all the men in her life had done. Having sedulously wooed her, he had made a dramatic departure at the worst possible time and left her to pick up the pieces. It was the same old story of misplaced trust. The only thing that made him different was the manner of his exit. Sheila did not blame him in any way. She would not speak ill of the dead.

'What was he like, Mrs Dowling?'

'A nice man. A very nice man.'

'Where was he from?'

'Phoenix – that's in Arizona, you know.'

'Was there any hint that he might be in danger?'

'None at all.'

'Did you get the feeling he was under pressure?'

'Quite the opposite,' she said. 'Mr Stone was open and friendly. He was the ideal guest, really. Everyone loved him. He brought so much life and laughter into the hotel.' She sighed. 'I wish they were all like him.'

Jenny Dowling did not. What she wished was that her mother had a better memory and a tighter grasp on reality. Hubert Stone had been a troublemaker from the start, and he had caused a disaster by the way that he had checked out of the establishment. It was unlikely that the Whitehall Hotel would ever recover from the blow, yet its owner was talking to the reporter from the local weekly newspaper as if she did not have a care in the world. Jenny winced at each syllable.

'Mr Stone was a proper gentleman,' insisted Sheila. 'He knew how to pay a compliment to a lady.'

'How long was he here?' asked the young man.

'Only a few days.'

'Yet he dug himself in?'

'He was that sort of person. Truly cosmopolitan. At home anywhere – Arizona, New York, Sutton Coldfield.' She almost simpered. 'He was extremely kind to me.'

'Can you give me an example of that, Mrs Dowling?'

'Several.'

The biro hovered over the pad. 'One will do.'

'Well . . .' She became quite wistful. 'Hubert – that's Mr Stone – invited me to visit him.'

'In America?'

'Of course.'

'That's not strictly true, Mum,' said Jenny.

'Yes it is.'

'He only meant it in fun.'

'*I* know what he meant, Jenny.'

'You mustn't give the wrong impression.'

'How can I? He was a gentleman.' She turned to the reporter. 'Mr Stone and I had . . . an understanding.'

'Oh, Mum . . .'

Jenny Dowling backed off in alarm. Her mother had an idiosyncratic version of the truth and nothing could budge her from that. It was her way of coping with the tragedy that had befallen them. In Sheila's eyes, Hubert Stone had been a harmless visitor who had shown her affection and who did not deserve the terrible fate that had been meted out to him. It never even occurred to her that the violence of his end might have been foreshadowed by some more sinister elements in the man himself. Her memories remained unassailably fond.

'He was a stickler for English marmalade,' she said.

'Was he?'

'And coffee. Hot black coffee.'

The biro was given an entire day's menu to record.

'He was a keen golfer, I believe?' said the reporter.

'That's right,' she replied confidentially. 'He told me that his life's ambition was to be a professional but he never quite made it. A shame, really. It obviously got to him.' She smiled sweetly. 'Still, there was one big compensation. His niece turned out to be a very good player, thanks to him. She married a top golfer.'

'Tony Bianco.'

154

'Mr Stone worshipped him.'

'Did he ever talk about his niece to you?'

'All the time. He said that he coached her on the golf course. They were very close, you see. I do feel sorry for the poor girl.' A motherly sigh. 'What a state she must be in now! This must have shattered her. Glenn thought the world of her uncle.'

Tony Bianco kissed her gently on the forehead and went across to the door. His wife gave him a wan smile.

'Good luck!' she said.

'Thanks, baby.'

'Show them who's champ.'

'Leave it to me.'

He blew her another kiss and slipped out of the room. Though he was naturally concerned about her, it did not dampen his high spirits. He had played exceptionally well that morning and was pleased to see that the opposing team captain had been forced to shuffle the pack for the afternoon fourballs. With Hal Mayo alongside him, he would now be taking on Tom Pickard and Ian Roslin, a golfer known for his supreme reliability rather than for any flights of brilliance. The Americans had a definite edge.

Bianco sympathised with his wife's apparent show of grief, but he did not share it. Seen in cold terms, the death of Hubert Stone was an unqualified boon to him and he did not want to dwell on its nature or implications. All that he needed to know was that he was relieved for ever of the tedium of the old man's attentions and of the latter's rather unhealthy relationship with Glenn. Putting it all behind him, Bianco went out to represent his country in exactly the right frame of mind.

Back in the hotel room, his wife had another fit of weeping as she read a letter that she kept hidden away in her purse. So much promise had been destroyed by one act of sadistic madness, so much happiness had been blighted. She felt that she would never get over the experience and had no urge to go on alone. The ringing of the telephone cut into her maudlin reminiscences. She shrunk away at first, but it would not let her escape. Its relentless sound could only be stilled one way. Fearing the same caller as before, she grabbed at the receiver.

'Well?'

'Mrs Bianco?'

'Yes.'

'My name is Don Hawker. I'm a journalist.'

'What do you want?' she snapped.

'Well, I know this is hardly the best moment but I wondered if I could possibly have a word with you?'

'It's not convenient.'

'Perhaps I should tell you what it's about,' he said with quiet persistence. 'I was at the Whitehall Hotel in Sutton Coldfield last night. As a matter of fact, I was the person who found your uncle's body.'

Glenn Bianco shuddered involuntarily. Relief that it was not her earlier caller gave way to another kind of apprehension, but this in turn shaded into a kind of grudging curiosity. With all his faults – and she knew them better than anyone – Hubert Stone was her own kin and she would have to face family questions when she got back home. It would be sensible to find out as much as she could about his demise.

'What was the name?' she said.

'Hawker. Don Hawker.'

'You'd better come on up. Room Fourteen.'

She hung up, then put her letter away. Two minutes in front of the mirror with her make-up bag restored some of her colour and poise. The tap on the door was considerate and well-meaning. She admitted Hawker and sized him up and down, hearing a bell ring in her memory as she fitted his name to his face and distinctive build.

'Don Hawker. You wouldn't happen to be . . .'

'Yes, Mrs Bianco.'

'I guess I saw you on TV,' she said. 'I was really interested in athletics when I was a kid. Not that I'm trying to make you feel old. I mean . . . oh hell, what does it matter, anyway? Take a seat, Mr Hawker.'

'Thanks.'

He sat in a chair and refused the offer of a drink. Waiting patiently until she had poured herself a large vodka and tonic, he let her sit opposite him on the sofa before he began to probe.

'Your husband is playing very well, Mrs Bianco.'

'Tony is a great golfer.'

'He's been through a pretty lean patch recently.'

'It happens.'

'I'm surprised you're not out there with him.'

She lowered her eyes. 'My uncle was very dear to me. It would be an insult to his memory.'

'Are you sure?' he said. 'I'm told that he lived for the game of golf and that he idolised Tony Bianco. There was a sheaf of press cuttings about your husband on his bedside table. If it was left to your uncle, he'd want you out there rooting for the American team.'

She took a moment to appraise him properly.

'Who are you, Mr Hawker?'

'I work for a sports magazine.'

'Were you staying at Uncle Huby's hotel?'

'My editor was. We drove back there together last night. Mrs Dowling – she's the owner – went upstairs to call your uncle and . . . saw something that made her scream. I raced up there and let myself into the room.'

'Was it horrible?' She flinched as he nodded. 'Who could *do* such a thing to Uncle Huby?'

'You have no idea yourself?'

She shook her head. 'None. He could be a maddening old galoot at times and he had an eye for

157

the ladies, but that was all. He didn't deserve to be . . .'

Fresh tears threatened. Hawker leaned forward to console her but she waved him away and resorted to a handkerchief that was plucked from her sleeve. He studied her carefully until she was ready to resume.

'Was your uncle a rich man, Mrs Bianco?'

'He was very comfortably off.'

'Then why was he staying there?'

'In Sutton Coldfield?'

'It's a very small hotel. Rather basic, in fact. I would have thought Mr Stone would have insisted on something more luxurious.'

'He had a miserly streak,' she confessed, sipping her drink. 'Uncle Huby made plenty but he was determined to hang on to it. If you struggle to make your dough, he said, you don't give it away easy.'

'How much did you see of him?'

'I played a round of golf with him on Wednesday, then he came across here yesterday.'

'Did he have a row with your husband, by any chance?'

'No,' she retorted.

'That was the impression I got. I saw them talking.'

'You were quite mistaken.'

'But he was a very argumentative man, by all accounts. My editor had a few heated discussions with him, and Mr Stone did not mince his words.'

'Uncle Huby had strong opinions, that's all.'

'So he might easily have upset someone.'

'Not to *that* extent, Mr Hawker.'

The journalist sat back in his chair and gave her a moment's respite. She was far too tense and highly strung to yield information willingly, and he did not want to run the risk of offending her. The speed at which she was gulping down her vodka showed how jangled she was. He expressed genuine concern.

'I was sorry to hear about yesterday,' he said. 'I

believe that you were taken ill in Birmingham.'

'Oh, that?' She was evasive. 'It was nothing.'

'Yet the doctor was called in.'

'Purely as a precaution.'

'What did he say?'

'That's my business, Mr Hawker.'

'Of course.' He pretended to retreat. 'I was just worried about you, that's all. It's so easy to pick up a strange virus when you travel abroad.' He got to his feet. 'Well, I won't detain you any longer. I can see that you'd rather be alone and I do apologise for intruding at such an awkward time.'

'That's all right. I'll show you out.'

He let her shepherd him to the door before he spoke.

'One small detail,' he said casually. 'Did your uncle ever meet Gary Lapidus?'

'Several times. He met all the top players. Uncle Huby used to haunt the pro circuit.'

'How did he get on with Lapidus?'

'Like most people. He thought Gary was hilarious.'

'They had no . . . business dealings, I suppose.'

A fractional pause. 'Not to my knowledge.'

'What exactly was Mr Stone's line?'

'Look, you'll have to excuse me, I'm afraid,' she said briskly. 'I really would like to be –'

The telephone bisected her sentence and made her jump. She took another long drink from the glass before she had the courage to cross to the instrument. A glance at Hawker was enough to send him on his way. He waved his thanks and let himself into the passageway, standing there to muse on all that he had heard, wondering why she had gone to such lengths to lie about her uncle. Glenn Bianco was not just mourning the death of a relative. Something far more complex was going on. He was about to walk away when the door opened behind him. Trembling and white-faced, Glenn Bianco beckoned him to her.

'He wants to speak to you.'

'Who does?'

'I don't know his name.'

With a puzzled frown, Hawker went swiftly back into the room and picked up the receiver. She closed the door behind her and stayed flattened up against it. After a look at her, he spoke into the mouthpiece.

'This is Don Hawker.'

'We've met before,' said an American voice. 'You have a nasty habit of ignoring warnings, don't you? This is your last one. Disappear while you still can.'

'And if I don't?'

'Wait and see, brother.'

'Who are you?'

'A well-wisher.'

'How did you know that I was here?'

'I been keeping tabs on you, mister. That's why I'm always two jumps ahead of you. Pity you won't see sense. That kind of mistake is fatal.'

The line went dead and Hawker hung up the receiver. He could see from the deep panic in Glenn Bianco's eyes that she had no idea who the caller was either. One thing could now be safely assumed. The driver of the blue Volvo Estate had an American voice that sounded as if it was used to issuing dire threats. The warning could not have been more explicit. If Hawker stayed around, he could meet the same kind of death as Hubert Stone. Shaking off his fears, he felt a tingle of excitement. In making contact with him, the man had thrown down a challenge. It would be a head-to-head contest that was fraught with danger. America was taking on Britain in another life and death struggle, but there was more than golfing prowess at stake.

Hawker now had his own Ryder Cup match.

Chapter Nine

The afternoon belonged to Europe. Though Tony Bianco was on a roll that made him quite invincible, his team-mates could not emulate him and fell away badly in the fourballs. The Americans trailed 3-1, giving them a deficit at the end of the first day's play of 5-3. Even the normally scintillating Gary Lapidus was out of touch and his barrage of jokes waned steadily as the game wore on. Europe could take heart from their performance, but the dour Angus Cameron was permitting himself only a wee dram of cautious optimism. His one anxiety concerned Tom Pickard who had now been on the losing side twice in a row. To rest him from the foursomes on Saturday morning would wound his pride and might erode his confidence, but the fact was that others in the camp were playing better and with more purpose.

Angus Cameron was nothing if not direct. While his opposite number, Bob Jaglom, favoured a relaxed approach that rubbed off on his players, the little Scotsman liked to take the bull by the horns, even if that bull happened to be the senior member of his team. They were just leaving the locker room together.

'You've no' been up to scratch today, Tom.'

'I don't need to be told that.'

'We expect a lot more from a man of your calibre.'

'You're entitled to, Angus.'

'So what's the problem, man?'

'I couldn't seem to hold it together,' admitted Pickard. 'If I got a birdie at one hole, I'd play rubbish at the next. I just didn't seem to have any luck.'

'Ha!' sneered Cameron. 'That's a word that's no' in my vocabulary. Never rely on luck. Golf is about cause and effect. It's simply a matter of application and if you fail once, you have to try and try again.'

'Is that the Robert Bruce principle?'

'It's *my* system.'

'I'll be okay tomorrow,' said the other. 'You know me, Angus. I'm always a bit of a slow starter.'

'Some more practice would no' come amiss.'

'But I'm knackered, man.'

'Have you forgotten how many errors you made out there today? They need working on. Nothing can be taken for granted in this game. Even veterans like you and me have to keep plugging away at the basics.'

Tom Pickard tightened his jaw in irritation, but he made no protest because he knew that his captain was right. It was up to the senior golfer to set an example to others, but the Yorkshireman had failed badly so far and his philosophical calm was starting to crack at the edges. To appease Cameron and to vindicate himself, he agreed to a practice session that evening. When the Scotsman went off to snap at the heels of his other players, Pickard made straight for the bar. Two long rounds of uninspired golf had reminded him of the curative properties of a pint of beer.

Eric Fretton was in genial vein when they bumped into each other. He bought the first round and they drifted off to a quiet corner for a chat. The editor lifted his glass to propose a toast.

'To European victory!'

'I'll drink to that,' said Pickard. 'I just hope that I can do my full share towards it.'

'You had so many near misses today, Tom.'

'I never got out of first gear. As for my bunker play,

it was pathetic. I haven't shifted so much sand since I were a kid on holiday in Blackpool.'

'Europe is leading. What more do you want?'

'A personal victory under my belt.'

'It will come,' said the other. 'Who do you fancy in the singles on Saturday?'

'Who else?'

'Tony Bianco?'

'Aye,' said Pickard covetously. 'He's their kingpin and no question. Bob Jaglom took one hell of a risk when he selected him, but it's paid off. Bianco was pure magic today. We couldn't live with him.' He gritted his teeth. 'But singles is another matter and I'll be lying in wait for him. I want his scalp, Eric.'

They chuntered on about the day's play, then both waved as Karen Maxwell went past. She gave them a dazzling smile that belied the fact that she had been on her feet since six o'clock that morning. Her stamina was matched by her cheerfulness and her efficiency. Eric Fretton had been in the right place to notice.

'She's really brightened up the press tent.'

'Karen? Smashing girl.'

'I had my doubts when she got this job,' said the journalist. 'Frankly, I thought she was too young and too inexperienced, not to mention being too nice to cope with such a dreadful species as the golf writer, red in tooth and claw. She's kept the lot of us in our place.

'Ideal person for the post,' said Pickard, gazing fondly after her. 'I knew she would be.' He finished his drink and smacked his lips in appreciation. 'I needed that before my tee shot on the eighteenth! Another?'

'Not for me, thanks.'

'Then I'll love you and leave you, Eric. First on the agenda for me is a long hot bath while I reflect on all the silly bloody mistakes I made.' He got up from the table. 'By the way, what's this about another murder?'

'I blame Hawker.'

'In your hotel, wasn't it?'

'Only because I took him back there. Honestly, that man is jinxed, Tom. Wherever he goes, you can guarantee that something nasty will happen. Sometimes I wonder why I employ the man.'

'Because he gets stories that nobody else can.'

'Yes,' said Eric wearily. 'Horror stories.'

Expecting to glean very little from his interview, Hawker had in fact learned far too much to process all at once. He had discovered that Glenn Bianco's distress was not caused by her uncle's death and that she patently knew more about the old man's business activities than she was prepared to admit. He had picked up other intriguing vibrations from her, but they had all been relegated into second place behind the dramatic telephone call that he had received in her room. In finding a golf ball, he had gained himself a mortal enemy whose handiwork he had already seen in a hotel bedroom. Hawker was alarmed at the thought that he had been in the sights of the bearded American all the time, but that concern was softened by the fact that he had finally drawn his attacker out into the open. He might be a target himself but he had at least been given one of his own at which to aim.

Glenn Bianco denied all knowledge of the mystery caller and fell back on a burst of hysterics to dislodge Hawker from her room. As he left the hotel, he had food for thought that took him all the way to the tenth green where he caught up with the main golfing action of that afternoon. From time to time he was carried away by the drama of the contest, but always checked his emotions and looked over his shoulder. Somewhere in the same crowd was a man with a beard and a vengeful streak. It kept Hawker on his toes in every sense.

When the foursomes were completed he did not go

to the press tent to hear the rival captains giving their summaries of the day's play. His interest was in the second wife of a jaded comedian. Alma Lapidus provided the real glitter among the American ladies, the lurid brightness of the uniform bringing out her finest qualities. In the absence of Glenn Bianco she was without question the most attractive woman, and she revelled in the attention she was getting from all sides. Hawker noted that her husband was clearly uneasy with this situation and they exchanged a few marital words as they left the course. Quite unrepentant, Alma Lapidus was giving as good as she got. When her husband went off into the locker room, she slipped in through the rear entrance of the hotel and Hawker chose his moment to pounce.

'Hello, Mrs Lapidus. Remember me?'

'Oh, hi. Yeah, I remember. Mr Walker, was it?'

'Hawker. Don Hawker.'

'I'm not good with names,' she said, squeezing his arm by way of apology. 'Say, wasn't it dreary out there?'

'Typical English weather, I'm afraid.'

'I was talking about the golf, honey. It was like watching paint dry through a pair of dark glasses. Do all these people actually get a kick out of something as dull as that? Where was the real *action*?'

'I can see you're not a golf buff.'

'It was like force-feeding,' she complained. 'Stuck on the back of that golf cart and trailing around after Gary for four hours in that drizzle. Jesus! What a way to spend our holiday! I was promised fun.'

Hawker saw that he would get very little out of a bored woman with a chip on her shoulder. His only hope was to get her into more congenial surroundings where he might hope to catch her off guard. He invited her to have a drink in the bar and she perked up immediately, taking pleasure in mocking the dress

165

sense of the wives and girlfriends of the European team and opening like a flower as she collected approving male glances and the occasional compliment. Hawker praised her appearance himself and came as near as he dared to flirting with her, much to her evident enjoyment. It was only after treating her as a social butterfly for some time that he felt able to manoeuvre the conversation around to more pressing topics.

'I see that you've been driving a Volvo Estate.'

'Yeah,' she said. 'Gary hired it because it's so roomy. Me? I prefer something a little more sporty. Hell, why not let people know you're coming, for God's sake? Show some *style*.'

'Has anyone ever borrowed the car from you?'

'Borrowed it?'

'Some friend or associate of your husband, maybe?'

She gave a shrug. 'It's possible, I guess, but you'd have to ask Gary about that.'

'I was thinking specifically of last night.'

'We were both here,' she said. 'Bob Jaglom was giving the guys a team talk so I went up to spend some time with Glenn Bianco because she was feeling so low. The Volvo was parked outside, as far as I know, but Gary might just have loaned it to someone else. It's the kind of crazy thing he'd do. He never tells me anything.' She eyed him up and down. 'You married?'

'I was.'

'Did you confide in your wife?'

'Most of the time.'

She gave a brittle laugh. 'I bet you did!'

'Coming back to Glenn Bianco . . .'

'Yeah,' she said, 'I gotta go and see how the poor thing is getting on. She had one heck of a blow last night. You hear about it? Someone bumped off her uncle. Can you believe it? Godammit, this is *England*! We don't expect that kind of shit here.'

'Oh, we have our problems here, I fear.'

'Keep them well away from me, is all I say!'

He let her ventilate some steam for a while, then steered her back to the subject of Glenn Bianco and asked about the shopping expedition to Birmingham. She gave him a vivid description of the fainting and showed a flair for dramatising such incidents. Hawker picked out the salient fact that it was the front page of the midday edition of the *Birmingham Mail* which had sparked off the collapse. He knew what the banner headline had been.

'Have you ever heard of Larry Newmark?' he said.

'Sure. He was the other guy who got bumped off.'

'The name doesn't mean anything else to you.'

'No. Should it?'

'Newmark was involved with the game. His firm manufactured golf wear and they were just launching an expansion drive.' He watched her closely. 'Did your husband ever have any connection with him?'

'I don't think so, but then Gary is very funny about those things. He never lets me into his business secrets because he doesn't want me to know where the money comes from and exactly how much there is of it.'

'So he's never talked about Larry Newmark?'

'Not to me.'

'Think, Mrs Lapidus. This is important.'

'Why not ask my husband?'

'Yeah,' said an unfriendly voice. 'Why not?'

Hawker looked up to see Gary Lapidus standing over him, the celebrated grin replaced by an impassive glare. The journalist tried to retrieve the situation, but the American had seen and heard enough to be more than angry. He took his wife's hand to lift her from her seat.

'We're going up to our room, honey.'

'Mr Hawker was asking about the Volvo.'

The glare intensified. 'Seems to me that Mr Hawker

has been asking a lot more than he should.' He curled a lip. 'That's it for today, pal. Keep away from Alma in future, okay? I do my own interviews.'

'Oh, he was being real nice to me, Gary.'

'I'm sure he was.'

'Is there some time when we could talk, Mr Lapidus?' said Hawker. 'Just to clarify a few points.'

'Ask me when the match is over.'

'It may be too late by then.'

'Tough! Come on, Alma.'

'Just tell me this . . .'

Hawker's mistake was to get up to put a hand on the golfer's arm. It was shaken off with a vicious shrug that was reinforced with a menacing hiss. Gary Lapidus, the crown prince of the greens, could be a different man when there was friction. In that moment, Hawker knew that what Hubert Stone had said about his compatriot was true beyond a shadow of doubt. Lapidus was capable of murder.

The evening meal at the farm was a noisy affair in the kitchen with three men slouched around the table as they loaded food methodically into greedy mouths that did not always close as they chewed. Olive Leech had long abandoned the hope of instilling any notion of etiquette into the household. After a full day's work, the men simply wanted to flop and gormandise, not listen to lectures on good manners. The pattern was depressingly the same at each meal. By the time Olive had set out the first course and was ready to sit at the table herself, they had already made severe inroads into the food. She was constantly left with the scraps which had to be bolted down because they were waiting with impatience for the next course. It was a treadmill that she could not escape and, as her legs got older, the wheel moved faster.

Brian Leech introduced a political note.

'Bloody rubbish!' he sneered.

'What's that, Dad?' asked Roy, munching happily.

'Flaming EEC. We should never have gone into it in the first place. Done us farmers no good at all. It was a vote for bankruptcy.'

'Yeah.'

'And all the damn paperwork it's brought.'

'It's not too bad,' said Olive meekly.

'It's madness, woman!' rebuked her husband. 'How can a man milk his cows and plough his fields if he's filling in forms all day long. The EEC is a menace.'

Malc listened to it all with a bovine grin. The farm labourer's political education consisted in picking up his employer's prejudices, and the best time to do that was over the evening meal when they gobbled competitively as they watched the news on the portable television that was balanced on top of the upright piano. Malc watched the screen with one eye while keeping the other on the tureens of food being put on to the table.

The head of the house found new cause for complaint.

'Oh no! Not again!'

'Silly sodding game,' muttered Roy.

'It's on all the time,' said his father. 'Who wants to watch golf, anyway? It's not a real sport.'

'Some people like it,' ventured Olive unwisely.

'What do you know about it?' demanded Leech.

'I'm entitled to my opinion.'

'Not when it's plain stupid.'

'Look at those big crowds,' she said, pointing at the screen. 'A lot of people go to these things.'

'Only because they don't know what work is.'

She gave up. 'Finish your potatoes.'

'Don't rush me, woman.'

Protesting about the sports coverage, the three men were nevertheless riveted to the highlights of the day's play. They watched Tony Bianco drive the green on the tenth for the second time that day, they saw Gary Lapidus sink a putt from all over thirty yards and they jeered as Tom Pickard's misjudged approach shot found water at the eighteenth. As the highlights came to an end, theme music was played and the camera panned across the whole course. Brian Leech was mesmerised by the sight of the rich green acres and contempt stirred within him.

'That's criminal, that is!'

'What?' asked Olive.

'All that farmland going to waste. Look!'

'They wanted it for their golf,' she bleated.

He banged the table. 'And where do they think their milk and their bread and their meat comes from? Farmers ought to be first. We should come before these bloody leisure industries. If it was left to me, I'd plough up every golf course in Britain and turn them over to proper agricultural use.'

'Yes,' said Roy. 'Fantastic! Let me loose on The Belfry with the tractor. I'd soon knock it into shape. Didn't it used to be potato fields or something?'

'Prime arable land. Thrown away.'

Father and son fantasised on their revenge, while Malcolm listened with growing interest. The labourer believed in guilt by association.

'That Hawker bloke is here for the golf,' he said.

Leech snorted. 'Bastard needs sorting out.'

'Leave him alone, Brian,' said Olive. 'We've had enough trouble from the police as it is.'

'Thanks to him!'

'What shall we do to Hawker?' asked Roy.

'Another bang on the head for starters.'

Malcolm's laughter had a manic edge to it.

Glenn Bianco was so stunned that she just stood there with the telephone cupped in her hand long after he had rung off. The third conversation with the mystery caller had been the most chilling yet. He had given her an order that was impossible to obey, and yet equally impossible to ignore. The consequences of the latter course of action were unthinkable. Everything would be in ruins. Wednesday had been the worst day of her life and she had wallowed in utter despair. Thursday had brought the murder of her uncle to sharpen her pain and deepen her anxiety. Friday was now proving to be as traumatic and terrifying as both together, and she was plunged into a maelstrom of naked fear. Glenn was falling helplessly through hostile space with nobody to help her and nobody to care.

Mad panic sent her to her handbag to get the number that her uncle had given her. She dialled it at once and made a supreme effort to pull herself together. A warm and maternal voice came on at the other end of the line.

'Whitehall Hotel. Can I help you?'

'Is that Mrs Dowling, by any chance?'

'Speaking,' said Sheila. 'Who is this, please?'

'You won't know me. My name is Glenn Bianco. I was Mr Stone's niece.'

'Oh yes! He told me all about you.' Sympathy gushed freely. 'I'm dreadfully sorry about what happened. He was such a lovely person. We'll miss him something terrible.'

'I talked to a Mr Hawker . . .'

'Yes, we met him. A very nice man. He was a rock.'

'He mentioned that Uncle Huby left some money on deposit with you.'

'One hundred thousand dollars.'

Glenn cleared her throat. 'It's extremely kind of you to look after it for him, Mrs Dowling. As his nearest blood relative, I think I should take it back home so that the lawyers can include it in his estate. When would it be convenient for me to drive over?'

'It would be a wild goose chase, I'm afraid.'

'Why is that?'

'Because the money is not here,' said Sheila. 'The police took it away. They said it might be material evidence of some kind. Besides which, I didn't want to keep that sort of sum on the premises. I had no idea that Mr Stone had cash in that package of his.'

Glenn was quivering. There was more to unsettle her.

'Funny you should ring,' continued Sheila in gossipy vein. 'You're the second person asking after that money. Mr Stone's cousin rang this morning.'

'His *cousin*?'

'Yes, a Mr Avondale. Sounded like a charming man. He wanted the money as well. Apparently, he'd been told to take care of it in the event of an emergency – and you couldn't have more of an emergency than this, could you?' Sheila carried on blithely. 'I told Mr Avondale that the police had the money and that he should contact them directly. Maybe you and he could sort this out together?'

'Yes,' murmured Glenn.

'Wait a minute. I've just thought.' Sheila had at last spotted a discrepancy. 'Didn't you say that you were Mr Stone's nearest blood relative? What about his cousin?'

'I was forgetting him,' said Glenn quickly. 'Thanks for your help, Mrs Dowling. That's clarified things a lot. Sorry to have disturbed you. Goodbye.'

She slammed down the receiver and collapsed to her knees with grief. There was no cousin. The only relationship that the caller had to Hubert Stone was a geographical one. Avondale was a town that was just to the west of Phoenix, Arizona. She realised the sequence of events. Having drawn a blank at Sheila Dowling's safe, the man had contacted her. Her one faint hope of escape had been blocked off completely.

Glenn subsided to the floor in anguish and curled

herself up into a tight ball. The visit to England had been fringed with promise, but it had now become a continuing ordeal. Uncle Huby had left a grim legacy for his niece. It was crushing her mind to a pulp. One factor dominated all the others.

Mr Avondale would show no mercy.

Disappointment brings its own kind of fatigue and it was an exhausted Tom Pickard who finished his lonely practice session and trudged back towards the clubhouse with his golf cart. With much to reflect on, he found a secluded place under some trees from which he could view the first fairway and rue the sliced tee shot which had got him off to such a poor start in the fourballs. He took out his pipe, filled it with Golden Virginia and lit up. The tobacco soothed him at once. Wishing to be alone, he was not pleased to hear footsteps and even more unwelcoming when he saw to whom they belonged.

Don Hawker had watched the session from afar.

'You're a glutton for punishment, Tom,' he said.

'Angus thought I needed extra practice. It's a bit like being kept in after school to fill the inkwells.'

'How are you feeling now?'

'Pissed off.'

'I thought you played quite well today.'

'Come off it, Don. I was crap.'

'You had a tough match. Bianco was white hot.'

'I'll cool him down!' vowed Pickard quietly.

There was an awkward pause as each waited for the other to make the first move. Hawker had to force himself to make an apology about which he had reservations.

'Sorry about our last chat,' he began. 'I shouldn't have come on so strong like that. All I was after was a simple answer.'

'Then stop putting loaded questions to me.'

'I had to ask, Tom. Heavens, I saw your name in the Corley Hall Visitors Book.'

'So? Is it a crime to stay there?'

'You should have told me.'

'Why?' said Pickard bluntly. 'It was months ago and none of your damn business. I'd forgotten all about it. Or chosen to, anyway.' Exasperation came out. 'The truth is that I just can't afford to get dragged into it.'

'Into what?'

'This murder investigation.'

'*I* was dragged in.'

'That's your problem, mate.' He chewed on his pipe and let smoke drift out through his lips. 'See it from my point of view, will you? Representing Europe in the Ryder Cup means a lot to me and demands every ounce of my commitment and concentration. Even then – as you saw out there today – I can come horribly unstuck. Imagine how much worse I'd have been if I let myself get distracted by what happened in some potty little country hotel down the road.'

'Tom, a man was *killed* there!' reminded Hawker.

Pickard exploded. 'I don't care if they found a hundred dead bodies in that slurry lagoon! The more the merrier. My own concern is my game. It has to be, Don. It's called professionalism.'

'I'd use another word for it.'

The golfer bit back an angry rejoinder and took refuge in his pipe. They had never had an argument like this before and it was bringing out the bitterness in both of them. Hawker abandoned all the niceties and went straight in with his accusation.

'I believe that you knew Larry Newmark.'

The Yorkshireman's face was as craggy and unyielding as his native dales. He tapped his pipe out on the heel of his spiked golf shoe, then slipped it back into his pocket. His tone was casual and in no way offensive.

174

'What if I did?'

'Don't you think it's relevant information?'

'Not any more. He's dead.'

'You should have told the police.'

'Hark who's talking!' said Pickard with a grin. 'Don Hawker. Police informer supreme. My God! You wouldn't even tell them what day it was.'

'How well did you know Newmark?' pressed the other. 'I'm directly involved in all this. Every detail helps. You can't just keep it to yourself.'

'I'm here to play golf. Remember?'

'Don't you have any conscience?'

'Mine is quite clear.'

'Tom, I need to know all you can tell me.'

'Hard cheese!'

'Whatever happened to friendship?'

'Whatever happened to privacy?'

They glared at each other in the fading light, and a relationship which had been deep and lasting now trembled on the edge of destruction. Tom Pickard wanted to shut it out of his mind completely, but he knew that Hawker would never allow him to do that. The journalist was ready to sacrifice any friendship in pursuit of the truth. It was the golfer who took the decision to pull back from the brink.

'If I tell you, Don . . .'

'No more pestering, that's a promise.'

'And my name must be kept out of this altogether.'

'You have my word.'

'That's good enough for me.' He inhaled a lungful of air through his nose. 'I only met Larry Newmark once. It was last year at The Masters. He was introduced to me by a friend at a party. It was all very informal – or so I thought at the time.'

'The meeting was set up?'

'Aye. They stage-managed it very cleverly. Newmark caught me right off guard. He talked about his

175

company and the plans he had for lift-off. Then he put out feelers to see if I was interested in an advertising deal with them.'

'And were you?'

'We all need to eat, lad.'

'Was it a tempting offer?'

'Extremely,' recalled Pickard. 'Newmark knew how to talk big. It's one of the things I despise about the Yanks. They're all so bloody plausible!'

'You turned the offer down?'

Tom Pickard nodded and ran a thoughtful hand across his chin. Something which he had intended to keep to himself was now being prised out of him and it was causing a lot of discomfort.

'I smelled something fishy, Don.'

'About Larry Newmark?'

'About the friend who introduced me to him.'

'Who was that?'

'Gary Lapidus.'

Hawker was all ears. 'Go on.'

'He was another potential client,' said Pickard. 'They used his name to lure me in. At first, I was flattered. I mean, Gary is an institution on the American circuit and I'm a sort of father figure over here. You can see their marketing strategy.'

'So what was the catch?'

'I discovered that Newmark had a silent partner.'

'Yes. Back in Denver.'

'No,' said the other. 'I don't mean him. He was only the front man alongside Newmark. There was somebody else who stayed behind the scenes and pulled all the strings. One of those power-mad freaks who thinks that money can buy you, body and soul. Not me, Don! When I got a sniff of that, I was out of there like a bat out of hell!'

'Who was this silent partner?'

Pickard was stern. 'If I tell you, I walk straight away

176

from here without another word. No more questions from you until this match is over and done with. Okay?'

'Agreed.'

The Yorkshireman grabbed hold of the handle of his golf cart and moved slowly towards the clubhouse. He tossed the name over his shoulder.

'It was Hubert Stone.'

Tony Bianco was at his most exuberant that evening. As he dined with some of his colleagues, he kept them amused and boosted their morale by pointing out weaknesses that he had seen in the play of the Europeans which he felt could be exploited on the next day. Bob Jaglom was in total agreement with the Bianco diagnosis and deeply grateful for the way that the golfer was taking the lead. The American contingent were being welded together more closely and learning to put the setbacks of the first day behind them. They still had plenty of time to assert their superiority and carry off the coveted trophy.

One of the reasons that Bianco was in such bubbling form was that his wife was dining alongside him and he was very conscious of the tremendous effort she was making to lend her support. Even though she was subdued and preoccupied, Glenn's presence meant a great deal to him. It was like a ratification of his manhood. He felt whole again. Bob Jaglom was the first to note it.

'That's a helluva woman you got there, Tony.'

'So I keep telling her.'

'Never underestimate the importance of a wife at a time like this,' said Jaglom. 'Mine keeps me sane and soothed. I'd be lost without her.'

'That sums up my feelings about Glenn,' said Bianco, and he was rewarded with a brave smile from her. 'She's the best club in my bag. Thanks, honey.'

'Tell her in private,' whispered his captain.

The golfer had already planned on doing so. When they went back to their room later on, he was pleasantly flirtatious. Glenn allowed him to slip an arm around her waist and steal a kiss on the cheek. After recent tensions between them, this was marked progress, though he did not want to jeopardise his chances by rushing things. He was happy to go at her pace. She sat at the dressing table to remove her earrings and kept an eye on him in the mirror.

'Tony . . .'

'Yeah?'

'Do we have any money with us?' she said.

'Some, but I got all my plastics.'

'I was thinking of hard cash.'

'Coupla grand in traveller's cheques,' he said. 'Plus a few hundred pounds. Why?'

'I just needed some dough, that's all.'

'Use your Amex.'

'That's not always possible.'

'Something you wanna buy, sweetie?'

'Yes,' she said. 'I've . . . set my heart on it. Oh, I know it's wrong of me to bother you in the middle of the match, but this is something special. Today's been a nightmare for me. I need cheering up.'

'Say no more.' He added indulgently, 'We'll move heaven and earth to make sure you get what you want. What is it, anyway?'

'I'd rather keep it as a secret.'

He grinned. 'That's fine by me. You can take all the dough and I'll cash those cheques right here at the hotel for you. If you find an Amex dispenser, you can draw some more cash. With your own card or with mine, if need be.'

'Thanks, Tony. That's wonderful.'

'For you, honey – anything.'

'You're quite a guy,' she murmured. 'Know that?'

'I was starting to forget.'

Their eyes met in the mirror and his sparkled with hope. Crossing to her, he gave her a gentle kiss on the neck then brought his hands around to fondle the diamond necklace that she was wearing.'

'Who bought you all this glitz, Mrs Bianco?'

'You did.'

'Plenty more where that came from.'

'I know, Tony.'

'If you want it, that is . . .'

The offer hung in the air. She considered it for a moment then brought up a tentative hand to touch his arm. It was all the confirmation he needed of a breakthrough. Kissing her on the head, he moved swiftly to the bathroom.

'Gimme five minutes, doll.'

'I'll be waiting for you.'

As soon as he went out, her face crumpled into a mask of apprehension again. Glenn Bianco was cornered. The man she longed to escape was now the only person who could set her free from an even worse kind of incarceration. A person she hated would now have to be won over with a show of love. The price was unbearably high but she would have to pay it with apparent willingness. Even then, it was only a partial solution to her problem because she would be nowhere near the amount of money demanded. She would have to buy her salvation by other means.

Pensive fingers stroked the diamond necklace. It had been a present from her husband on their first wedding anniversary and it was one of her most cherished pieces. But this was a crisis situation and sentiment had to be thrown to the winds. Coming to a decision, she removed the necklace and put it beside the earrings before opening her jewellery box and laying out all the items she possessed in a long, glittering line. With a pounding heart, she tried to assess their combined value and wondered if it would be nearly enough. She was still surveying the haul when her husband came back into the room wearing nothing but a black kimono.

'Gloating over your trinkets?' he said amiably.

'Not really. It's just that they bring back happy memories of better times together.'

'You deserved every one of them, honey.'

'Thanks.'

'It was my way of saying I love you.'

He put hands on her shoulders to help her up then turned her around to face him. Glenn Bianco steeled herself to let him take the first real kiss he had had from her in several months. His hunger made it even more of a trial, but she did not resist.

Tony Bianco eased her slowly across to the bed.

'You're so beautiful,' he said. 'So beautiful . . .'

Remorse and recrimination were old friends of Don Hawker. All three of them sat in the Vauxhall Cavalier and stared out blankly into the darkness. Hawker had been far too hasty and inconsiderate. He could see that now, regretted it profoundly and was ready to go to almost any lengths to make amends. An intimate moment with Karen Maxwell had transformed his life, yet he had been too impulsive even to take note of it, let alone to pursue it to its proper conclusion, and he was now left with that familiar feeling of emptiness and loss. Karen was not Elaine, nor could she ever become her. In confusing the two, Hawker had been unjust to both and finished up without either. His wife was beyond recall, but he now entertained the vague hope that his relationship with Karen might be salvaged.

It was almost midnight as he sat in the car park at the rear of her hotel and awaited her return. As press officer at such a mammoth event, her workload was quite daunting and he knew that it took her well into the evening, but he would have expected her back by now. A hint of jealousy seeped in. Karen was not short of other admirers; indeed, she spent a fair amount of time fending them off with a combination of charm and firmness. Hawker had been the preferred choice over all the others, yet he had squandered her favours. As he faced the possibility that she might now have looked elsewhere, and might even be spending the night in another bed, Hawker's guilt sharpened and his sense of betrayal deepened. The sound of an approaching car put both into abeyance.

As soon as the headlights raked the Cavalier, he knew that it was Karen and that she was returning alone. He watched her park, get out and lock her vehicle before he went across to meet her. She tensed automatically when she saw the burly figure coming out of the gloom at her, then she relaxed slightly when she recognised him. Karen was astonished when he produced a large bunch of flowers from behind his back and proffered them.

'For you,' he said. 'By way of an apology.'

'There was no need, Don.'

'Take them, anyway.'

She accepted the flowers with mixed feelings, then inhaled their fragrance before rewarding him with a half-smile. Hawker could see how weary she was looking at the end of a punishing day. He could also see that she would not be won over by a bunch of roses and a few mumbled words from him. The rift between them would not be healed quite as simply as that. He changed the topic.

'I've stumbled on to a missing link,' he said.

'Between whom?'

'Larry Newmark and Hubert Stone. It turns out that they had business connections.'

'How did you discover that?'

'It was something of a fluke.'

'Don't you think you should tell the police?' she said

with concern. 'You're withholding evidence.'

'I've got good reason.'

'You can't solve these murders all on your own.'

'Don't worry about me,' he said. 'I'll just do what I have to do as quietly as possible. One promise – I won't rock the boat and ruin the Ryder Cup. I know how vital it is to keep scandal away from the event itself. The press officer told me and she's the sort of person that I'd hate to offend in any way.'

Karen nodded gratefully. 'Thanks, Don. I suppose that one good turn deserves another. If you help to safeguard *my* job over the next two days, I ought to help *you*.'

'What have you got?'

'Only a small item, I'm afraid.'

'Everything counts.'

'It's about Larry Newmark,' she said. 'Remember the name rang a bell for you? I think I know why. Because of the Denver LPGA Classic.'

'Ladies' golf?'

'Newmark sponsored the event.'

'And presented the cheque to the winner!' said Hawker with a snap of the fingers. 'There was a picture in one of the mags. Larry Newmark was grabbing a kiss from some attractive young woman golfer.'

'*Golf Monthly*. June issue.'

'You're fantastic, Karen!'

'It's not much.'

'Who knows?'

She sniffed the flowers again and her resolution slowly wilted. Twenty-four hours earlier, they had found a commitment and closeness that had made a deep impression on her, until it was shattered by his departure. Karen had not particularly wanted to see him again, let alone get drawn into any form of intimacy with him. Hawker only let you in so that he could shut you out more completely, and she could never tolerate that. Yet here she was, alone with him once more in the moonlight, holding his roses and touched by his gesture, oozing forgiveness and feeling the old tug of desire, wondering if a second night together might obliterate the shortcomings of the first, ready at least to meet him halfway.

Hawker wanted a reconciliation as much as she did, but there was a fatal self-destruct in his wooing. He heard the name of the tournament she had mentioned.

'The Denver LPGA Classic?' he repeated.

'That's right.'

'Of course, that's a place you'd know.'

His chances were sabotaged in that single sentence.

'I'm tired, Don,' she said. 'You'll have to excuse me. I have to be up at the crack of dawn tomorrow.' She brushed his cheek with her lips. 'Thanks for the flowers. It was a lovely thought. Good night.'

'Karen . . .'

But she had flitted into the hotel before he could even try to mount another recovery. Blaming himself for his tactlessness, he stormed back to his car and drove off noisily. He had only contrived to make the situation worse.

His remorse eased off the moment he hit the M6 and gave way to the survival instinct. It was during his last trip on the southbound carriageway that he had been forced off the road by a car he could now identify as the blue Volvo Estate, and he had been given a blunt warning by the driver to expect a further visit. Staying in the middle lane, he kept one eye on his rear-view mirror and braced himself every time that headlights zoomed up behind him at speed. But no attack came and it was not long before he was turning off at Corley Services and looping back over the motorway bridge. A nostalgic ache in his head reinforced the policy of caution.

Instead of swinging into Rock Lane, he went a little further along the main road and stopped at the kerb. Twice in a row now he had come back to the hotel to be met by an unscheduled welcome, and it made him slip off his coat, change into his running shoes and take the rubber-cased torch with him. Farmyards in the dark were full of hidden perils. Hawker was ready for them.

He loped fifty yards up the lane to the hotel drive, then he crouched down beside the clump of sycamores and waited. Ten minutes or more passed without any sound of movement or any sign of danger. Hawker raised himself up to take stock of his surroundings with eyes that had now become more accustomed to the night. The garden wall struck off towards the house on his left and sheltered the cars that were parked up against it. On his right, the farmyard was full of amorphous shapes. Fresh rolls of barbed wire were stacked nearby, a harrow was left in a corner, and a huge steel wheelbarrow stood on its end near the milking parlour. Various implements were scattered about and a tarpaulin covered something tall and bulky.

The main item of interest was the tractor that stood parallel to the dividing fence. It was hitched up to a trailer that was stacked with a few dozen bundles of hay. Hawker saw nothing unusual and made his way up the drive. When he drew level with the trailer, however, his antennae picked up clear danger signals and he reacted just in time. A figure suddenly popped up like a jack-in-the-box from the middle of the trailer and hurled one of the bales of hay straight at him. Hawker was able to parry the heavy missile, though the torch was knocked out of his hand. Leaping over the fence, he went straight on the attack and clambered up on to the trailer, only to roll back as the sole of a boot jabbed him in the chest.

He recovered at once to hurl himself back into the

fray, but his attacker was retreating at full pelt. A tall thin ungainly figure in overalls and a balaclava was racing down the yard towards the lane. Hawker gave chase with a vengeance and tackled his man into the side of a shed, winding them both in the process. They grappled fiercely. Though Hawker had the greater strength, the other had more guile and he slashed the journalist's feet from under him with a well-aimed kick. As Hawker fell on the muddy ground, he heard a shovel being picked up and knew at once that he had been introduced to it before. He had no intention of renewing his acquaintance. When the shovel came scything through the air, he cleverly dodged it so that it spent its venom on the door of a loose box.

Up on his feet again, Hawker grabbed a pitchfork to defend himself against a second murderous swing. The implements met with a jarring clang that made both men stumble. They were not just adversaries now but two gladiators involved in mortal combat, knowing that they had to kill or be killed. The shovel whistled through the air time and again to be checked or diverted by the pitchfork. Both of them began to grunt and gasp for breath as the struggle took its toll. Sweat ran down faces and bodies. Hawker made the first mistake. In backing away from his assailant, he tripped over a coiled chain and fell to the ground again. The shovel was lifted high to complete the execution, but the journalist was not finished yet. Throwing the pitchfork at the other man's feet, he elicited a scream of pain and was able to roll out of the way of the shovel's final vicious descent.

The implement was abandoned as the attacker conceded defeat and sought to leave the arena, but his hopes of escape were ill founded. Spiked in the leg, he was only able to hobble down the lane, and he was no match for an athlete who kept himself in condition. Hawker vaulted the gate and sprinted off in pursuit, catching his man by the corner and flinging himself on to his back with such force that the two of them tumbled into a ditch that was filled with nettles and weeds. They punched and grappled as best they could in the confined space, then Hawker stood up and yanked his opponent to his feet. A knee in the crutch made the journalist double up in agony for a few seconds and gave him even more reason to exact his revenge. The other man was running away again but his injured leg was impeding him badly. Hawker ignored the pains that were coursing through his body and took to his heels again, finding a burst of speed that brought him up alongside his attacker as the latter was about to cross the motorway bridge.

Diving sideways, Hawker got an arm around his neck and pulled him to a halt. He applied maximum pressure and the resistance weakened with every second. When he felt that he had overpowered his man, he used his other hand to pull off the balaclava and reveal the pale panting face of Malcolm, the farm labourer. Making one last desperate effort to get away, the youth tried to bite the arm that was holding him, but he met swift retribution. Hawker was in no mood for half-measures. He swung Malcolm around and tipped him over the motorway bridge, holding him by the ankles and leaving him to dangle in mid-air above the passing vehicles that he coveted so much.

'No!' screeched the youth. 'Don't let go!'

'Why did you hit me with that shovel?'

'Pull me up!'

'*Why?*' yelled Hawker, shaking him about.

'It was only a sort of joke.'

'So is this!' Another shake produced wilder cries. 'Who put you up to it?'

'Nobody!'

'Tell the truth or I let go.'

'Please!' howled the other. 'Pull me back up.'

'Give me one good reason.'

'I know about the murder.'

Hawker relented enough to haul him back up so that he could grab hold of the struts in the fencing on the bridge. He made Malcolm pay for this minor concession.

'What do you know?' he demanded.

'Where he got into the field.'

'The police have worked that out.'

'I got something they haven't!' shouted Malcolm. 'Lemme show it to you. It's all yours.'

'What is?'

'I know what car the murderer drives.'

Taking him by the scruff of the neck, Hawker pulled him back over the fence and held him against it for a second, warning him that he would be dropped over the bridge without compunction if he was found to be lying. Malcolm's surrender, however, was complete, and he was now in a mood of repentance. Battered and bleeding, he led Hawker along Bennetts Road North to the grass verge where the police had been concentrating their attentions.

'He come in here,' said Malcolm.

'Yes. The barbed wire was cut.'

'That's not all. I collects things, see. Night before it happens, I'm coming back late from the pub. This car is parked right here so I creeps up, like, only there's nobody in there.' A hand wiped a trickle of blood from his nose. 'So I thinks they must have climbed into the field to do it. I got myself a souvenir for my collection. I cut it off with my Stanley knife.'

He pulled the weapon from his pocket, but made no attempt to use it. Instead, treating Hawker with great respect, he took him back towards the farm and let him in through the gate of the rickyard. They went along the side of the barn and through a maze of outbuildings until they came to the labourer's mean accommodation. He paused at the door and bargained for mercy.

Malcolm was gibbering. 'If I let you see it, you won't throw me off that bridge, will you?'

'That depends.'

'I didn't mean no harm, honest.'

'Show me!'

The youth opened the door and switched on the light. Hawker was struck by the crude simplicity of the room, and he coughed in the fetid atmosphere. Malcolm crossed to the wall where his trophy hung and he lifted it off its hook. He handed it to Hawker by way of tribute.

'It was from the back wheel,' he said proudly. 'I sliced it off in a split second.'

The souvenir meant a lot to the curator of the museum, but it had far greater value to Hawker. It was proof positive that the man who had killed Hubert Stone had also been responsible for the murder of Larry Newmark. What he was now holding was a black mud-flap which bore the name VOLVO in large silver letters. It had been stolen from a blue Volvo Estate which had parked on the grass verge while its driver was reconnoitring the slurry lagoon to assess its suitability as a last resting place for an American businessman. Hawker had seen and spoken to the driver of that car. A scuffle in a farmyard had provided him with a vital scrap of evidence.

Malcolm was now cowering before him.

'Don't turn me over to the police,' he whined.

'It's the least I should do.'

'They'd find out about this,' said the youth as he waved a grubby hand at his collection. 'They'd take it all back. Even that mud-flap.'

It was the one item that Hawker was not going to relinquish to Frank Rayment. Though the labourer deserved to be charged with assault and grievous

188

bodily harm, there were drawbacks in handing him over to the police. Hawker eyed him sternly. The youth's face was plastered in mud and streaked with blood. His hands were a mass of grazes and bruises. His overalls had been ripped and he was bleeding profusely from the gash made by the pitchfork. Expediency and a nudging sympathy influenced Hawker.

'Get that leg seen to,' he advised.

'I'll be okay.'

'You need stitches and a tetanus injection. Can you get yourself to the nearest hospital?'

'Yeah. The Manor over in Nuneaton.'

'What will you tell them?'

A vacuous grin. 'Had an accident, didn't I?'

'As for the police . . .'

'Don't report me, mister. *Please.*'

'I'll sleep on it . . .'

Hawker now had a weapon that the youth feared almost as much as a dive from the motorway bridge. Malcolm was anxious to ingratiate himself, and he limped across to the wall again to take down another object. He looked rather shamefaced as he handed over the hub-cap of the Cavalier.

'I only borrowed it,' he whimpered.

Chapter Ten

Saturday morning brought fine weather to The Belfry and sweetened the dawn chorus. Bright sunshine soon lit up the course, and a gentle breeze pulled at the corporate pennants over the hospitality lounges. Golf started early for some players. Waking from dreams of glory or from nightmares of humiliation, they were out with their clubs by six o'clock to work on particular shots or tinker with their swings or simply to warm up their engines for the long day ahead. It was a treat to savour the improved conditions and to practise before the crowd invasion began again. The team captains set both the tone and the pace. Angus Cameron had all his players out, supervising their work with the puritanical severity that had pushed the Europeans into an early lead. Bob Jaglom affected a more laid-back approach, leaving it to each individual to decide if he needed a pre-match outing, moving quietly among those who did opt for practice with his easy blend of wit and wisdom, relieving tension and instilling new confidence.

One of the earliest risers was Gary Lapidus, who was famous for his painstaking preparations. Unhappy with his performance on the opening day, he gave himself a solid hour to eliminate the error that had bedevilled some of his putting. Only when he felt he had found his touch and steadied his nerve did he head back towards the locker rooms. When he got back to his hotel room, his wife was sitting up in bed with a breakfast tray across her lap and a red chiffon wrap around her shoulders. She bit her way into another croissant and waved to him.

'How was it, honey?' she said.

'It's coming, it's coming.'

'I don't know how you do it, always worrying, always practising, day after day. It would kill me.'

'I like it, Alma.'

'So long as it keeps the dough rolling.'

Lapidus sighed. 'Look, I told you. The Ryder Cup is not a money-spinner for us. We play for status and for honour. There's no financial gain involved.'

'Then why bother?'

'Because we're Americans and that means we have to remind these Europeans that we can always lick them when we really put our minds to it.'

'But you can't, Gary. They're beating you hollow.'

'It's a three-day match,' he said testily. 'We got plenty of time to catch up. Just wait until the singles tomorrow. That's where we'll clean up.' Lapidus sat on the edge of the bed. 'The Ryder Cup is a great showcase. Perfect place to display your wares and let 'em see what you can do. World's golfing press is out there watching.'

'Wish *I* didn't have to,' said Alma with a pout.

'It's not much to ask, lover.'

'It is if you can't bear the game.'

'That's only because you don't understand it.'

'I don't *want* to understand it, Gary.' She poured more coffee into her cup. 'Do I have to be there?'

'Of course!'

'Nobody would notice if I wasn't.'

'*I* would and so would the rest of the team.'

'It's such an ordeal.'

'Alma, it's vital,' urged her husband. 'You just gotta stick it out. Weather's beautiful today and you'll have

191

the other girls to talk to out there. You don't even need to look at the golf as long as you're seen to be in support. This is important to me.'

She pouted again. 'Glenn Bianco stayed away.'

'That's different. Her uncle died.'

'Maybe she'd like company. Someone to console her.'

'I need you out there, Alma,' he insisted.

'But it's so pointless, Gary,' she argued. 'It's like me dragging you along to a fashion show three days in a row. You'd be bored rigid, like I am. As for Glenn, I just don't buy all this stuff about her being in mourning for that old gimp. Uncle Huby may have taught her all she knew about golf, but I never heard her say a good word about him. Why can *she* get excused when I can't?'

Lapidus jumped up and went off into such a tirade that she backed down at once. Without even trying, she had ignited all his neuroses and they crackled angrily for a long time. Her soothing sounds gradually dampened down the blaze and only the smoke remained. Alma moved on to toast, marmalade and an ill-considered question.

'Who was this Newmark guy, anyway?'

He bristled again. 'What?'

'That journalist was asking,' she said innocently. 'The one I spoke to yesterday. Hawker. Don Hawker, that was him. He asked me if you knew Larry Newmark.'

'Never heard of him.'

'That's what I told Mr Hawker.'

'You give that guy a wide berth from now on,' said Lapidus vehemently. 'Got it, Alma? Don't speak to any journalists. Most of all Hawker.'

'What's wrong with him?'

'Never you mind. Just do as I say.'

'But I'm entitled to have a reason, honey.'

'The reason is I'm ordering you not to, okay? Is that

plain enough for you? I got all the problems I can handle as it is, so I don't need Don Hawker on my back.'

'Don't shout at me,' she said in hurt tones. 'This was supposed to be a holiday for me, remember? And what do I get out of it? I'm forced to watch this crap game, then yelled at because some journalist speaks to me.'

'Alma, Alma . . .'

Lapidus controlled his temper enough to be able to calm her down with kisses and blandishments. Perching on the bed again, he put an arm around her and actually managed to forget golf for five minutes. Her naive enquiry ruined everything.

'Did you ever loan that Volvo to anyone?'

Gary Lapidus became an inferno of denial.

It was the best night he had spent at Corley Hall. He slept soundly and woke to the symphony of birdsong. Sunlight slanted in through the gap in the curtains and he drew them back to admit the day in all its glory. Don Hawker felt restored and refreshed. The cuts and bruises he had collected on the previous night were no more than a distant irritation, and he was even able to think less vengefully about Malcolm. As he gazed out of the front window he saw the herd in the top pasture, adjacent to the field with the lagoon. It was a tranquil scene with a timeless quality that appealed to him, contented cows ambling lazily about, dropping their heads to tear up rich green grass, then looking all around with inquisitive eyes as they chewed the cud and flicked the flies away with their tails. Farm life suddenly began to make a lot of sense to Hawker. Fertile land was being put to its proper use instead of being landscaped into a golf course to satisfy the sporting inclinations of the few. For the first time, he began to see Brian Leech's point of view.

A long luxurious bath revived him even more and gave him the chance to reflect on the events of the night. It was a tale of loss and gain. Karen Maxwell had signalled the end of their brief affair and he could only blame himself for that. The nocturnal attack had been a further annoyance at first, but it had yielded positive evidence that gave him the keen thrill of being one step ahead of the police. Things could only get more fraught with danger from now on, but he was ready to take that risk and press on with his investigation. Corley Hall was no longer a source of friction and hostility. He had the strange feeling that the house was now on his side.

Needing an early start, he cancelled his morning run and went straight down to have a continental breakfast in the dining room. He chose the table directly beneath the framed photograph of the house. It brought an immediate reward. He was able to take a closer look at the picture, which was much clearer in the daylight, and he noticed something that he had missed before. There was a figure in the attic room which he himself was now occupying. It was a shadowy presence that could only be seen in the barest outline, but he thought he saw a hand being waved at the photographer.

'Good morning!' said Norman Starrett as he breezed into the room. 'Everything okay?'

'Fine, thanks.'

'Good, good. That's what we like to hear.'

'Listen,' said Hawker. 'I thought that Tom Pickard stayed here on his own.'

'He did, no question of that. His wife wasn't able to come for some reason. Why do you ask?'

'Idle curiosity, Mr Starrett.'

'Have you been admiring that photo again?'

'Yes. I wondered if I could have a second look at your Visitors Book as well?'

'If you wish,' said Starrett fussily.

'I do.'

'Follow me.'

194

Hawker was taken out to the hall, then left alone with the leather-bound volume. He flicked to the page he wanted and saw Pickard's looped signature. Seven other guests were staying at Corley Hall that night in May, two couples, two men in single rooms and a lone woman. When he saw the name of 'Miss A Smith' alongside a London address that carried little conviction, he began to understand why Tom Pickard had been so reluctant to discuss his stay at the hotel. The golfer had not been alone. It had not been the birds that had kept him awake, but a female companion, so the gratitude he showed to his host was justified. The photograph of Corley Hall was no casual snapshot. Pickard stayed at countless hotels in the course of a year and probably did not lift a camera at any of them. This place was different. The photograph was a treasured memento of a night of bliss in the arms of a lover. Miss Smith was still up in his bedroom when the camera clicked.

Excited by his discovery, Hawker went off past the bemused Starrett and let himself out into the drive. A swollen and anxious face was watching him from the farmyard as Malcolm waited to know his fate. The merest glance showed that Malcolm had come off worse in the encounter in the dark. He had stitches in his lip and his temple to highlight the vivid bruises and the black eye. Hawker suspected that the youth was resting on one foot because the other leg was stitched and heavily bandaged. More bandaging was wrapped around the labourer's right hand. His torn soiled overalls flapped in the wind.

'Ah,' said Malcolm deferentially. 'I put it back.'

'What?'

'The hub-cap.'

Hawker looked to the place where he had parked his car when the fight was over and was startled to see that it had vanished. In its place was a brand new Vauxhall

Cavalier with its bodywork gleaming and its chrome a dazzle of silver. It was some moments before he realised that this was, in fact, his own car. Malcolm had evidently cleaned it with the pressure hose as part of his penance, then waxed and polished it in a way it had not known since it was standing in the showroom. Hawker was quite stupefied. He shrugged his thanks to the youth and suspended his judgement. Malcolm grinned sheepishly and limped hurriedly away behind the milk parlour.

Closer inspection of the car revealed dents and grazes that had lain hidden beneath months of accumulated filth, and the wounds from his trip up the motorway embankment could also be seen now. But it still looked like a new vehicle, and Hawker got into it with a sense of pride that he had never bestowed on a motor car before. He was still enjoying this novel experience when he spotted the sign which had been stuck on his dashboard. Written on a piece of gummed paper was a word that caused a ripple of fear to go right through him – TODAY. A farm labourer with a limp had been responsible for the improvements to the outside of the car, but it was an American with a beard who had gained access to the interior. The warning could not have been more precise. Larry Newmark and Hubert Stone had already fallen to the murderer's hand.

The date of Hawker's execution had now been set.

Tony Bianco was one of the few members of the American team who did not feel the need for an extended practice session that morning. Instead of honing his game, he was berating the receptionist at the hotel because she was refusing to cash his traveller's cheques in their entirety. To pay out as much as two thousands pounds to one customer was highly irregular and the girl stuck bravely to the established policy, but she was no match for Bianco, a man of bulldozer confidence who was buoyed up by his excellent performance on the previous day and by the fact that he had made love to his wife for the first time in several months. For her sake he was in a mood to take on anyone and he demanded to see the manager. Five minutes with the person in charge removed the difficulty at a stroke. Bianco got his money. He turned on the charm, thanked the manager, flicked away the receptionist's apology and showed that there were no hard feelings on his side by flirting with her. It felt good.

He took the money back to his room and laid it in a long line on the coverlet. His wife, just coming out of her slumbers, saw the trail of notes. It was a lifeline.

'All for you, honeybun,' he said.

'Thanks, Tony.'

'How're you feeling today?'

'A little better,' she said weakly.

'Feel like watching any golf?'

'I may do.'

'Me and Hal are first away in the foursomes.'

'I'm sure you'll do well.'

'Just let me at 'em!' he whooped then sat beside her. 'I can face *anything* when we get it together like last night, Glenn. Can't you?'

'Yes,' she lied.

'It's gonna be okay. I feel it. Now that we've broken the deadlock, the show is back on the road.'

'Let's hope so, Tony.'

'All our problems are behind us, honey. It'll be just like old times. You and me and lots of fun like last night. Hell, that's what life is all about, isn't it!'

She chewed on her lip to hold back tears. The effort of submitting to him had almost crushed her, and her control was now very ragged. While her husband was welcoming a new dawn in their marriage, she was struggling hard to cling on to the wreckage. He kissed her on the cheek then went to appraise himself in the mirror. Bianco was wearing the official garb of the American team.

'How do I look?' he asked.

'Fine.'

'Snazzy outfit, huh?'

'Better than the Europeans.'

'They never have any sense of style,' he said airily as he produced a comb to slick his hair. 'We always make them look shabby in that department. Time they got smart – in every way.'

'Shouldn't you be going?'

'What?' He checked his watch. 'Oh, yeah. Bob Jaglom wants to give us all a pep talk before sending us out, but I don't need it. You gave me my pep talk in bed. That fired me up good and proper. I'm-a-coming!'

'Good luck, Tony.'

'Thanks, hon.'

'My first shot will be for you,' he said. 'Love you to be there, if you feel up to it.'

'I'll see.'

'Why not give Alma a call? Come together.'

'Maybe . . .'

Tony Bianco paced the room in the hyperactive mood he always fell into before an important game. When he ran out of excuses to linger, he gave her another wet kiss and went happily out. Glenn flopped back into the pillows with relief, then let the tears moisten her cheeks. She looked down at the money that lay before her. It was not much, but it was a start, and it reminded her just how much there was to do. Leaping out of bed, she ran straight to the bathroom and turned on the shower. Her first priority was clear. She had to wash off the loathsome touch of her husband, though she knew that it would not be so easy to sponge the memory of what had happened from her mind.

Play began promptly on the second day of the Johnny Walker Ryder Cup, and the galleries were soon spellbound by the cut and thrust of exquisite golf. In such beautiful weather the Brabazon course lost much of its threat, allowing the number of birdies and eagles to grow steadily. Tony Bianco and Hal Mayo attacked the greens from the start, but they were given no quarter by Tom Pickard and Rolf Kohlmar. After the front nine it was the European duo who had edged slightly ahead and earned the loudest cheers. It was a titanic contest that inevitably attracted the largest and most vocal of the galleries.

Don Hawker mingled with the crowd to get the full flavour of the event, but he did not follow the match beyond the first few holes. The high drama out on the course did not detract him from the perils of his own position. Some time that day an attempt was going to be made on his life, and it served to focus his attention. When he saw the warning note in the car his immediate thought was that the vehicle itself would be the murder weapon, but a thorough search inside and beneath it had yielded no bombs or explosive devices. A nervous journey to The Belfry had ensued as he scanned windscreen and mirrors for any sign of attack. It was ironic. The Cavalier was clean and presentable for the first time since he had bought it, but he was not allowed to enjoy the fact. Malcolm's work had been in vain. He gave the farm labourer a moment's thought and realised that the fight in the farmyard had performed another function. It had identified his attacker at the slurry lagoon and taken the name of Norman Starrett off his list of suspects. He should have known that the hotelier would not resort to a shovel. His mode of attack was George Eliot and he had already given Hawker a headache by taking a swipe at him with *Adam Bede*. Buffeted by literature and felled by agriculture, he now faced a more sinister and daunting enemy. Caution was imperative.

He went into the Press Tent with his mind racing. A small man in denim swooped on him with heavy sarcasm.

'Hello, stranger,' said Eric Fretton.

'I've been here all along.'

'Doing what, though?'

'Absorbing the atmosphere.'

'Big deal!' said the editor. 'When you come to write your article about the Ryder Cup, that will give you all of two sentences. Atmosphere's only background. Where will the rest of your copy come from?'

'Have faith. It moves mountains.'

'But can it get a day's work out of Don Hawker?'

'Probably not.'

They traded gossip for a while and Eric chided him for constantly looking over his shoulder. Hawker relaxed somewhat. He was relatively safe in the press tent, to which admission was strictly controlled. All around him were rows of shirt-sleeved golf writers, staring up at the big television screens and tapping away at the keyboards of their computers or talking into telephones. His editor came up with some intriguing information that he had picked up over breakfast at the Whitehall Hotel.

'Glenn Bianco rang about that money,' he said.

'What money?'

'That hundred thousand dollars or so that Stone left in the safe. Mrs Bianco announced that she was his nearest relative and that it was her duty to take the cash back to America.'

Hawker was puzzled. 'Why should she do that?'

'Search me. All I know is that she was out of luck. Mrs Dowling told her that the money had been handed over to the police.' He paused to watch a ball hit sand up on the nearest screen. 'Besides which, someone else had beaten her to the draw.'

'What do you mean?'

'There was another caller. A supposed cousin . . .'

Hawker listened to the story and saw the bearded American at work again. It helped him to make a string of further connections and opened out the range of potential explanations. Eric was more concerned with Glenn Bianco's eagerness to get her hands on her uncle's legacy.

'It's not as if she needs the money,' he said.

'Exactly.'

'Even in a bad year, Bianco notches up over a quarter of a million dollars. That should be enough to keep her in hair lacquer and designer dresses. Why should she try to grab Uncle Hubert's loot?'

'I don't know.'

'Unless she's planning to split and needs capital.'

'Is their marriage really on the rocks?'

'Do you know anyone's that isn't?'

It was a flippant remark and Eric wished he had not said it with such cheerful cynicim because it produced the usual reaction in Hawker. The journalist always took such comments personally and saw them as an attack on a relationship which had been – and would always somehow remain – at the core of his life. Eric tried to talk his way out of the dilemma, then he was saved by television.

Wild applause went up from the British contingent as Tom Pickard sank a lengthy putt for another birdie. The press tent had its moments of chauvinism. Eric Fretton wanted to be involved in the real thing and scurried out to join the match, but Hawker went over to the desk that had been assigned to him. Dropping into the chair, he gazed up at the nearby monitor in time to see Hal Mayo fail with his putt from about seven feet. It was when he looked down that he saw the large brown envelope.

Karen Maxwell's writing was neat, distinctive and oddly familiar. He opened the package and took out a copy of the June issue of *Golf Monthly*. Hawker leafed through it until he came to the photograph that he remembered. It was a revelation. Larry Newmark was essentially a ladies' man and he contrived to share the picture with no less than ten gorgeous young women. He was handing a cheque to the winner of the Denver WPGA Classic and exercising his right to a privileged kiss. Newmark was handsome enough, but there was a flashiness to him that suggested a lack of stability. The winning golfer was a handsome girl in her twenties who could easily have made a career as a pin-up girl, but Hawker wasted no time on her. His eye went straight to the lady at Newmark's elbow.

It was Glenn Bianco, here referred to by her maiden name. She had been the only amateur ever to win that open event and her course record was unassailable. Hawker sat up when he read about 'the former Glenn Lukins from Phoenix, Arizona'. She was standing beside a Wilson golf bag which bore her name and which implied that she would almost certainly use golf balls with the same brand. Whether or not they were identical to the one in his pocket was another matter but it was an even possibility that she would personalise them in some way.

Glenn Lukins – G.L. He had to see her again.

It was a better morning for the Americans and they played the more attractive golf to shorten the gap between the two teams to one point. The significant event was that Tony Bianco suffered his first defeat as he was put in the galling position of seeing his excellent shots wasted by the erratic form of Hal Mayo. They were pipped at the post by the wizardry of Tom

Pickard who finally rose to the occasion like a true champion and stroked in the winning putt with ice-cool control. While the Yorkshireman went off to bask in Angus Cameron's praise – 'you were bloody great, mun!' – Bianco was piqued at the loss of his hundred per cent success rate. After the merest snack, he was out on the driving range to work on what he felt might be a potential defect. Tempted to blame his playing partner for the defeat, he was realistic enough to know that the faults were not entirely with Mayo and that his own game needed attention.

Bob Jaglom rang the changes for the afternoon fourballs. Three new players were brought into the reckoning and the pairings were changed around. Tony Bianco found himself teamed up with Gary Lapidus for the last of the four matches, and he was happy with this new dispensation. Their opponents were Ian Roslin and the ever-ebullient Claudio Mundi of Italy. It promised to be a lively encounter in every sense, and the one certain prediction that could be made was that all four golfers would enjoy themselves hugely.

Glenn Bianco timed her exit well. With her husband totally engrossed in his game, she slipped away from The Belfry not long after one, and calculated that she had at least three hours before he came off the course. It had been a trying morning for her, locked in her room as she wrestled with fear and tried to overcome sentiment. There was a moment of terror when the telephone rang again, but it was not her mystery caller with yet another demand. It was Don Hawker in search of a further chat that she categorically refused even to consider. He was a source of danger at a time when she was least able to cope with it, and Glenn had no compunction about being brusque with him over the telephone.

The hired Ford Granada had no difficulty leaving

the hotel. All the traffic was heading towards the Ryder Cup and the exit roads were surprisingly clear. She headed towards Coleshill then joined the M42 for a while, using the sight of the triple lanes as an excuse to put her foot down hard on the accelerator. Beside her on the passenger seat, her handbag bulged with its precious contents. Glenn was being forced to part with items that she prized enormously but she was given no alternative.

She drove on at an aggressive pace. Fifty metres behind her, a Vauxhall Cavalier with a purposive gleam was staying on her tail. It never even occurred to her that she might be followed.

Warwick on a Saturday afternoon was not the wisest place to visit. Filled with tourists and clogged with traffic, it was a confusing maze of narrow streets that seemed to wind back on themselves and it took her twenty minutes to find a parking place. The quaint charm of the half-timbered buildings only served to increase her deepening hatred of England and things English. Her trip had so far been a recurring disaster, and she wished that she had never agreed to come to the Ryder Cup. The risk she had taken had led to catastrophe.

She began her round of the jewellery shops but met with little encouragement at first. Polite rejection and covert suspicion greeted her when she produced the haul from her handbag. Her pieces were much admired but the dealers would buy nothing from her without seeing the proper receipts for the purchases. Each disappointment made her desperation more open, and she surged on to the next shop with greater urgency. Eventually she found an elderly woman who was more amenable to the bargains that were being offered, though a great deal of haggling was involved. Values were finally agreed upon and Glenn Bianco left the shop with a substantial amount of cash in her purse. She did not dare to ask herself what would happen if her husband ever discovered that all the expensive jewellery he had given her had been unloaded for less than half its original price.

Hawker watched it all as closely as he could, soon working out the purpose of her visit and trying to fit it into the pattern that was now emerging in his mind. He was hampered by having to look in two directions at the same time, dogging her footsteps while making sure that he himself was not being tracked. It was in Castle Street that his vigilance wavered for a second. Glenn Bianco was going down the hill on her way back to her car and he walked after her on the opposite pavement. She paused to gaze wistfully at the window of another jewellery shop and he made to cross the road. Only the squeal of tyres saved his life. As the blue Volvo Estate came hurtling down the street, it made enough noise to alert him to the attack and he dived head first for the pavement, turning a somersault and ending up in the doorway of a butcher's shop as the car mounted the kerb in an attempt to run him down. By the time he had regained his feet, the vehicle was vanishing around a bend but he did glimpse a telling detail. One of its rear mud-flaps was missing.

The frightening speed of the attack had confounded the great British public. Though the street was busy, it was bereft of reliable witnesses. He was showered with sympathy and sprayed with advice, but nobody gave him any hard facts about the car, its number-plate or its driver. To dispel the small crowd which had gathered anxiously around him, Hawker dismissed it all as a freak accident and ignored those who told him to report the incident to the police. That was the last thing he wished to do. He had escaped by the skin of his teeth and now felt almost exhilarated. In his personal Ryder Cup match, he was still marginally ahead of America.

205

One major consolation emerged. As the crowd drifted slowly away, an attractive young woman with a valuable handbag lingered behind. Glenn Bianco was horrified by what had happened and was trying hard to understand its implications. She put a trembling hand on his arm.

'Are you all right, Mr Hawker?'

'Just about.'

'You might have been killed.'

'That was the general idea.'

'Who *was* that maniac?' she said.

'I think we've both spoken to him on the phone.'

Her trembling became a full shiver as she took the idea on board. Hawker noted the little restaurant further down the street and hustled her towards it. They both needed a restorative drink and some privacy. Over tea and scones, he managed to break down some of her barriers.

'Mrs Bianco,' he said softly. 'Whether you like it or not, we're in this together.'

'What are you doing in Warwick?'

'Following you.'

'Why?' Indignation soared. 'You had no right! I told you to leave me alone and I meant it. Why did you follow me all the way here?'

'Because of that man in the Volvo.'

'I have no idea who he is.'

'I think he's blackmailing you.'

Hawker could not have hurt her more if he had struck her in the face. She recoiled with fear and coloured at once, pulling out a handkerchief to stem the tears that formed in her eyes. He gave her time to recover before he continued.

'Trust me, Mrs Bianco,' he said. 'I'm on your side.'

'How do I know that?'

'You saw what happened to me out in the street.'

She pondered. 'Go on.'

'I don't want to pry, but there are certain things that I must know if I'm to help you.' Hawker sipped his tea. 'As I see it, there are two big problems for me here. The first one is to stay alive, and the second one is to get you off the hook. Unless we pool our resources, we won't solve either of those problems. Do you agree?'

Glenn Bianco thought it over for a long time and had a few sips out of her own cup. She was anxious not to divulge any secrets but she came to accept the wisdom of what he was saying and realised that she had to give him a degree of cooperation. Her tone remained guarded.

'Ask me what you have to, Mr Hawker.'

'Is that man demanding money from you?'

She lowered her head in defeat and nodded.

'How much?' he said.

'Over a hundred thousand dollars.'

'When do you have to pay it?'

'Tomorrow.'

'Where?'

'He'll ring me with the details.'

Hawker had a clear idea of what lay at the root of the blackmail and he put his theory to the test. Slipping a hand into his pocket, he brought out the golf ball that bore the two initials.

'Do you recognise this?' he said.

'Sure. It looks like one of mine. I play with Wilson Ultra and they're all personalised.' She took it from him to scrutinise it more closely. 'Where did you find it?'

'Beside the body of Larry Newmark.'

Glenn Bianco all but fainted. Dropping the golf ball on the table, she swayed violently and put a hand up to her head. Hawker steadied her for a minute then reclaimed the ball to put away in his pocket. He poured more tea and waited until she had drunk it before he spoke again. His theory had been dramatically confirmed.

'How long had you known him?' he asked quietly.

'Almost a year.'

'Had you arranged to meet him here in England?'

'Yes,' she whispered. 'But Larry never got in touch. I knew something was wrong. He always called when he said he would. He was that kind of guy.'

'Your husband had no inkling of what was going on?'

'None at all,' she said quickly. 'And he must never find out. That would ruin everything. No matter what the cost, Tony must never get wind of any of this.'

'He won't, Mrs Bianco,' promised Hawker.

'It's such a nightmare!'

'What about Mr Stone?'

'Uncle Huby?'

'He knew, didn't he? About the affair, I mean?'

'Oh, yes!' she said bitterly. 'He knew all right. Uncle Huby knew every damn thing!'

'I don't imagine that he approved.'

'He hated it, Mr Hawker. He thought it was just a casual relationship and had no idea how deep it went. Uncle Huby never appreciated what a wonderful man Larry was. All he could think of was breaking us up. Also . . .'

'Well?'

She bit her lip as she debated whether or not to yield up the information and he could see how much embarrassment it was causing her. He tried to help her.

'Your uncle was rather possessive, wasn't he?'

'More than that,' she conceded. 'He was a bit of a weirdo, really. Uncle Huby didn't want any man to get near me – except for Tony, that is. When he cottoned on to what was happening between me and Larry, he went crazy.'

'Was that because he and Newmark were partners?'

'How did you find that out?' she said in surprise.

'Complete chance,' he admitted. 'Was it the reason?'

'Partly. It was Uncle Huby who'd introduced me to Larry in the first place and he couldn't bear the thought that he'd sort of set the whole thing up. But there was another side to it as well.'

'He was jealous.'

Her eyelids flickered in affirmation. He waited quietly while she composed herself, then Glenn Bianco talked her way through it in order to try to make sense of it all. Hawker was touched by her story. At every stage, she was something of a victim and yet quite unable to perceive this. It was Hubert Stone who had imbued her with the love of golf that had given her an outstanding amateur career and which had led – through her uncle's manipulation – to a romance with Tony Bianco. Their marriage had been very happy until her husband started to have an affair with a woman in St Louis. Once again, it was Stone who was the motive force, scuppering the illicit relationship by telling his niece about it, then doing his best to weld the estranged couple together. When Glenn found love in the arms of Larry Newmark, it was the first thing she had done entirely on her own account and thus had a special resonance. But that friendship, too, was doomed as soon as her uncle became aware of it.

For a woman of evident sophistication, Glenn Bianco had a streak of innocence that made her very vulnerable. As she related all the facts, she was quite unable to make some of the darker connections between them. Hawker did not have the heart to tell her that she was scrambling around to get money for the very man who had murdered her lover. Nor did he shock her with the news that Hubert Stone himself had been paying off the hired killer when the latter was cut down in a hotel bedroom. Glenn Bianco was too emotionally involved in it all to be able to take an objective view of events. She had to be protected from the full truth until the crisis was over.

Hawker sought elucidation on a final point.

'There was a deal in the offing,' he said. 'Stone was hoping to sign up your husband, wasn't he?'

'I believe so.'

'Did he make a direct approach?'

'Oh, no,' she said. 'Tony had no idea that Uncle Huby had any link with the company. He would never dream of signing up if he thought that. They never really got on.'

'Why didn't you tell your husband?'

'I was sworn to secrecy.'

Hawker saw at once how it had been done. Enraged by her affair with Larry Newmark, her uncle had made full use of it by blackmailing her into silence. He had stalked Tony Bianco for a long time and was determined to buy his name for the company, but he had to move with stealth. Hubert Stone was a practised manipulator who had put his niece in the place where she would be most valuable to him, and had then applied pressure. The uncle who spent so much time and effort trying to keep the couple together had driven a wedge of dishonesty between them.

'So who negotiated with your husband?' said Hawker.

'Someone else.'

'Larry Newmark?'

'He was told to keep a low profile.'

'Then who?'

'It was Gary Lapidus.'

After making plans for the morrow, they drove back to The Belfry in their own vehicles. Hawker was even more alert on the return journey, but there were no more hazards and he reached his destination without any setback. He went straight across to the car park reserved for the players themselves and saw Glenn Bianco backing her Ford Granada into the place she had vacated earlier. Further down the same line was the blue Volvo Estate that had been hired by Gary Lapidus for his sightseeing. Hawker got close enough to establish a salient fact. The mud-flap on the nearside rear wheel had been cut away. He believed he knew where the souvenir was now kept.

A distant explosion of sound told him that play was over for the day. Evidently there was heady excitement on the eighteenth green and he soon learned what had caused it. The information did nothing to still his unease. In a sustained fightback that was led by Tony Bianco, the visiting team had now drawn level with their opponents. Hawker translated the result into his own predicament. Europe and America were now side by side. The driver of the blue Volvo was well placed to move in for the kill.

Chapter Eleven

The atmosphere in the sunken bar at The Belfry Hotel that evening consisted in equal parts of celebration and commiseration. The American team were more inclined to a freewheeling optimism, though it had its anxiety mongers like Vance Dressler and Gary Lapidus to bemoan the errors that had littered their respective games that afternoon. Being caught from behind had diminished the confidence in the European camp and thrown Angus Cameron back into his most combative mood, but there were those like Tom Pickard and Claudio Mundi who had enjoyed a good day out on the course and who sought to lift the spirits of their colleagues. As the resident pianist provided a melodious background of evergreen favourites, the golfers tried to come to terms with the past two days and extract lessons from them which could be usefully applied on the Sunday.

Honours were even. Everything would be decided on the final head-to-head contests of skill and stamina.

Don Hawker nursed a mineral water on the fringes of the action and looked for chances to contrive interviews. Tony Bianco turned him down flat, and he only got within three metres of Alma Lapidus before her husband whisked her away and left the journalist's ears burning with a torrent of scathing remarks. When he was not making people laugh, the American golfer knew how to wound them with words. Bob Jaglom obliged with a few remarks, but he was far too cagey to be pinned down on matters of detail and would say nothing about the private lives of his team. Hawker saw an aspect of himself in the visiting captain. Like him, Jaglom kept his cards close to his chest and could not be drawn out by anyone.

Still dressed like a protester outside a nuclear power plant, Eric Fretton was getting more restless about his employee's idiosyncratic work methods. He sidled up to Hawker and nudged him in the ribs.

'Where were you this afternoon?' he said.

'Practising the art of survival.'

'Yes, well it may interest you to know that our bloody magazine has to do that. Readers like something to read. How can you write an article about a match that you're not even here to cover?'

'Calm down, Eric. Remember the ulcer.'

'What I remember is the sod who gave it to me.'

'Me?' said Hawker innocently.

'Who else?' barked the other. 'What the hell were you doing driving away from The Belfry? And, more to the point, why did you take leave of your senses and actually clean that death-wagon you call a car?'

'All will be revealed in the fullness of time.'

'Bollocks!'

'Don't be like that,' said Hawker. 'You ought to be pleased with me. Apart from anything else, I'm going to give you a lift back to your hotel.'

'Whatever for?'

'Because I'm spending the night there with you!'

'My God! That's all I need!'

Eric Fretton went off to replenish his glass of wine and to find another editor who understood the miseries of employing wayward journalists. Hawker watched him with wry amusement, then let his eye settle on Tom Pickard. His friend had just entered the bar and Hawker had to check his impulse to go across

213

and offer to buy him a drink. Having promised to give the golfer plenty of leeway, he did not want to go back on his word, and staying where he was turned out to bring its own kind of reward. Karen Maxwell broke away from a group of journalists who were besieging her and slipped over to speak to Pickard. They could not have been together for more than a couple of minutes but there was something about their body language and their manner towards each other that made Hawker think about a brown envelope containing a golf magazine.

He now realised why Karen's handwriting had seemed so familiar. He had seen another example of it in the Visitors Book at Corley Hall. On that occasion, she had signed herself as a Miss Smith and the purpose was clear. Tom Pickard had taken the photograph because she was up in the attic window. Hawker felt a ton weight in the pit of his stomach, and it got even heavier as another possibility intruded. Even for a woman of her proven ability, Karen Maxwell had done remarkably well to land the job at the Ryder Cup and she must have had assistance from someone. Hawker now identified that person. No player in British golf exerted as much influence as Tom Pickard and he had used it to advance the interests of his mistress. Hawker felt let down by both of them.

Karen came bouncing over with her bright smile.

'Did you get that magazine, Don?'

'Yes. Thanks a lot.'

'How's it all going?'

'The pieces are slowly fitting together.'

'Wish I could say the same. I feel as if everything is disintegrating around me.' She laughed shrilly. 'Who was the sadist who talked me into being press officer?'

It was a rhetorical question but he gave an answer.

'I think it was Tom Pickard.'

Hawker knew how to kill a conversation.

Tony Bianco flowed through the American team like a wave of sheer exuberance. Having recaptured his touch that afternoon and been without doubt the most scintillating player on the course, he tried to fire his compatriots with his dynamism. Backed up by Bob Jaglom, he toured the whole contingent to spread the gospel of success and to assure them that the Ryder Cup was now within their grasp. His good humour was infectious, his advice was sensible and his example was inspiring. Jaglom once again applauded his decision to select Bianco. The key player was indeed opening the door for the other eleven. Dinner together was a joyous affair for all of them, with the wives and girlfriends responding positively to the spirit of the occasion. America was now walking on air.

When Bianco got back to his room, his mood altered somewhat. He had not been too absorbed in his role as the team's power source to take his attention completely off his wife. He closed the door behind them and sounded a trifle displeased.

'Who was that journalist you talked to?' he said.

'Oh, I don't know. He's English.'

'Name's Hawker. I froze him off earlier but he stayed around to get a few comments out my wife. It was almost as if he knew you.'

'How could he, Tony?'

'This the first time you met him?'

'Of course.'

'I didn't like the way he looked at you.'

'That's not my fault,' she argued.

'Sure hope not.' He rallied and gave her a kiss. 'I guess I'm as jealous as hell deep down. Can't bear the thought of any man taking an interest in you, let alone actually touching you.' He enfolded her in his arms.

'You're all mine, baby! Aren't you?'

'If you say so.'

'I do say so. Isn't that the way you want it?'

'You're hurting me . . .'

'Tell me, Glenn. I need to hear it.'

She made the effort. 'I'm all yours, Tony.'

'That Hawker guy means nothing to you?'

'I've never set eyes on him before.'

'And there's no one else, is there?'

'No, Tony.'

'I'd go plumb crazy if there was,' he warned. 'You know that. I'd kill the bastard!' He softened at once as tears streamed down her cheeks. 'Am I holding you too tight?' he said, releasing her at once. 'Sorry, hon. I didn't mean to do that. I get carried away. It's all the excitement of the match.'

'I'm okay,' she said, dabbing at her eyes with a tissue. 'Just . . . give me some breathing space, huh?'

'Sure, sure . . .'

He waited until she had used the bathroom before he spoke to her again, tossing the words over his shoulder as he undressed and hung his clothes in the wardrobe.

'What did you do all day?' he said.

'Stayed here. Lay around. Watched the TV.'

'Did you see me this afternoon?'

'Yes, Tony. You were great.'

'I tamed the tenth and eighteenth,' he boasted. 'No course in the world can hold any terrors for me when I'm in that kind of form. I was out on my own.' He turned around. 'Come and watch me tomorrow.'

'I'll try, Tony.'

'It'd make such a difference. All the other women are there, even Alma, and she hates golf. It kinda makes me feel like the odd one out.' He burst out laughing. 'Hell, if I can play like that *without* you, just imagine what I'll be like with you in my corner! Hot as shit!'

'Leave it with me,' she said.

'Try, that's all I ask. Try, honey.'

'I will.'

His affection switched into its aggressive mode again and he crossed the room to pick her up and pull her to him. The words gushed out of him in a waterfall.

'Tomorrow's gonna belong to us, believe me. This trip is not just about winning that damn cup, important as it is. No, Glenn, it's about you and me. It's our chance to bury the mistakes of the past once and for all. This is a second honeymoon. Know what I think? We should grab ourselves a few days' holiday. Instead of flying straight back on Concorde with the rest of the guys, what say we hightail it to Paris or Rome or somewhere? Wouldn't that be just freaky!' He sat her on the edge of the bed and knelt down in front of her. 'Let's make it Paris. We'll have dinner in some fancy restaurant to celebrate our success – and I don't mean winning the Ryder Cup. This will be for us, Glenn. I'll put on my tux and you can wear every damn piece of jewellery I ever gave you. Hit them with the whole lot! Isn't it a swell idea?'

Glenn Bianco was racked by a thousand separate agonies. Mention of the jewellery made her swoon and she thought she would keel over. As her husband kept urging her to agree to the trip, she could see only one way out of her beleaguered position. She grasped at the straw.

'Tony, is there a service here tomorrow?'

'Service?'

'Out on the course,' she said. 'You know, a Christian service led by a parson. Where people can pray . . .'

In the wake of the murder, Sheila Dowling had lost five of her guests prematurely and felt the impact on her advance bookings. When the telephone rang it was more likely to be a cancellation than a booking, and so

217

she was delighted when Hawker called to book a room at the Whitehall Hotel. It was only for one night, but she chose to see it as a hopeful pointer for the future. The tide was turning in her favour. They would live down the gruesome death.

Her daughter's view was nowhere near as sanguine.

'This will finish us off for good, Mum,' she said.

'Of course, it won't, Jenny.'

'Everyone's running out on us.'

'We've only lost five,' said Sheila happily. 'Six, if you count poor Mr Stone. But then he didn't leave of his own accord. He loved it here.'

'Don't go on about him, Mum.'

'I'm bound to mention him from time to time.'

'You talk of nothing else,' complained Jenny. 'It's downright morbid, if you ask me.'

Sheila Dowling heaved a sigh and mythologised away.

'He was one of our best guests ever,' she decided. 'I know he was only here for a short time but he made an indelible mark. Hubert – Mr Stone, that is – was such a sociable man. I think that's where the Americans always have it over the English. They know how to get on.'

Jenny spluttered. 'He was an awkward old sod!'

'Speak as you find, dear. I found him a fascinating character. Larger than life and quite lovable in his own way. He's not the sort of man you forget in a hurry.'

Jenny gritted her teeth and said nothing. She always marvelled at her mother's eagerness to be taken in by revolting men and she was seeing yet another case of it. Though an irascible old man had run her ragged, upset all her other guests and probably ruined her business by his untimely death, she still insisted on thinking well of him. The only way she could come to terms with the appalling mess left behind in one of her rooms was to deify the man who had occupied it.

The two women were in the hall when Hawker came in with Eric Fretton. Sheila gave them a cordial welcome and showed them into the lounge where they ordered coffee. Jenny went off to fetch it and her mother broached a topic that had been at the back of her mind all day.

'Will it ever be safe to use that room again?'

'What room?' said Hawker.

'The room where . . .'

'Oh, that. Yes, of course. Why not, Mrs Dowling?'

'There was a murder in there,' she reminded. 'And they say that a ghost will always linger where there's been a violent death. Will Mr Stone linger?'

'I bloody well hope not!' muttered Eric.

'Quite frankly, I don't think I'd be afraid if he did. Mr Stone would be a benign presence as a ghost. Just as he was in life.' She fell short of a giggle. 'I might even get to like it. So might some of the guests. We could advertise it as the haunted room and charge extra.' She smiled at Hawker. 'Do you believe in ghosts?'

'Not really.'

'What about you, Mr Fretton?'

'Only after ten glasses of whisky.'

The coffee arrived and the women faded away so that the men could continue their argument. Eric was still protesting vociferously about the fact that Hawker had taken such a circuitous route back to the hotel, twice pulling the Cavalier into a lay-by for a few minutes to make sure that they were not being followed. Not wishing to alarm his editor with the truth, Hawker invented an excuse for their strange drive back that only incensed his companion more. After a final vituperative burst, the editor finished his coffee and stalked off to bed.

Hawker took time over his own drink and considered the situation. The blue Volvo Estate was still in the players' car park when they left The Belfry, and he was confident that they had not been trailed back to Sutton Coldfield. He was safe for the night. His appointed executioner obviously knew Corley and the surrounding area very well, which meant that he could pick his spot for an ambush. A change of hotel would shake the man off the scent and enable Hawker to take the initiative. When he next met the bearded American, he wanted it to be a fair fight. To ensure his safety even further, Hawker now took the trouble to walk around the ground floor of the hotel and its garden in order to familiarise himself with its geography. If there were any emergency, he wanted to be able to find his way around in the dark.

Sheila caught him at the bottom of the stairs.

'Good night, Mr Hawker.'

'Good night.'

'Sleep well. Most of my guests usually do.'

'I'm sure.' His memory was jogged. 'Oh, something I meant to ask you. Did Mr Stone ever discuss his business affairs with you, by any chance?'

'Not in so many words,' she said, 'but he hinted.'

'Hinted?'

'Yes, I thought he was a gentleman of leisure but he went out of his way to tell me he was still active, so to speak. We were very close, you see. He kept hinting that there was some big deal on the horizon.'

'Did he say what it was?'

'No. But he gave me the distinct impression that, if it came off, he'd be sitting pretty.' Her eyes widened with the force of revelation. 'Mr Hawker, I just thought of something. That money we found in the hotel safe. Do you think he brought it to England to invest it?'

'I'm certain that he did.'

Hawker did not dare to tell her how he thought that money had been spent. He simply took his leave and went up to his room on the first floor. Before going in,

220

he did another swift tour to take stock of the area, noting the window at the rear which gave access to the fire escape. Once inside his room, he locked the door and moved the little armchair against it. Through the bay window he could look out on Anchorage Road and see a row of cars parked at the kerb. There was no Volvo Estate among them. It was well past eleven now and he was grateful for the brightness of the street lamps. From his vantage point in the hotel he could see as far as the traffic lights on the main road in one direction, and as far as the Town Hall in the other. Nobody could approach on foot or in a car without being seen by him.

Hawker was travelling light, having left the bulk of the contents of his suitcase back at Corley Hall. All that he had brought was a tracksuit, a change of underwear and a toothbrush. Eric Fretton would lend him a battery shaver. He put on his tracksuit and running shoes, switched off the lights and drew the curtains again, keeping his vigil at the window until he heard the town clock booming out the chimes at midnight. It signalled a magic release from the fear that had dogged him. He had actually come through the day on which his death had been decreed, and could afford to relax. The immediate danger was past.

He lay on the bed with his hands behind his head and stared up at the ceiling. Occasional vehicles passed by and intensified the glow around the edges of the curtains for a few seconds. By the time the clock was marking the first hour of the new day, Hawker had fallen into a light sleep. He did not slumber for long. A faint rattling sound brought him instantly awake and made him turn over to face the door. The lock held fast, the armchair did not move and the sound faded. He was about to dismiss it all as a figment of his imagination when a draught blew in under the door. At first, it was quite pleasant but its force was strong enough to lift the carpet slightly and blow down the cards that decorated the mantelpiece.

Getting up from the bed, he reached for the rubber-cased torch which he had brought with him and moved to the door. The armchair was lifted silently out of the way and then he reached for the door knob with a mixture of trepidation and curiosity. He stood well to the side of the door and unlocked it with an outstretched arm, holding the torch ready in his other hand. But there was no cause for alarm. His door swung gently open and he came out on to the landing to see that the draught was coming in through the window at the rear. It had been lifted right up and the stiffening breeze was ventilating the whole house. Putting his head out, he checked the fire escape both above and below, but it was quite deserted. Hawker closed the window as quietly as he could and went back to his room. Light was still spilling in around the fringes of his curtains. It was to be his salvation.

As he closed the door behind him, the attack came from the direction he had least expected. There was a thunderous crash as glass splintered everywhere and a powerful figure came diving through the curtains to launch himself at the bed. The knife had jabbed away three or four times before the interloper realised that his quarry was not in the bed. Hawker did not wait for polite introductions. Enough light now flooded in for him to be able to see the glinting eyes and the dark beard, but he already knew who his visitor was. Stepping in quickly, he swung the torch as hard as he could and caught the man a glancing blow on the side of the head. It dazed him for a moment but he recovered to lunge at Hawker with the stiletto which had just ripped some of the hotel bedding to shreds. The journalist evaded the thrust and countered with a firmer blow to the head, following it up with a kick to the groin which made the man roar in pain.

Hawker's heavy torch swished through the air again to hit the wrist that held the knife. As the weapon was dropped to the floor, the journalist kicked it under the bed, then moved in on his adversary. But the man had had enough. Now at a disadvantage and gulping for breath, he opted for retreat, grabbing a large flower vase to hurl at Hawker and racing out on to the landing while the latter ducked to avoid the missile. By the time that Hawker reached the now-open rear window, footsteps were pounding down the steel steps of the fire escape. The Volvo Estate could soon be heard zooming off into the night.

Terrified faces appeared at other doors or inched downstairs from the top floor. Pulling on her mauve dressing-gown, Sheila Dowling spoke for them all.

'What on earth is going on, Mr Hawker?'

Sunday morning at The Belfry began with a short *alfresco* service taken by the Canon of Coleshill Parish Church. Held on the course itself, it was designed to accommodate all denominations, and there was a respectable turn-out for the occasion. Nearly all the American players appeared with Bob Jaglom and his wife, taking the event seriously and drawing both comfort and inspiration from it. Tony Bianco stood alongside his compatriots, brought along less by his Catholic conscience than by the insistence of his wife, who sang the hymn with feeling and committed herself wholeheartedly to the service. While Glenn Bianco was gaining sustenance, her husband was observing that the last time the two of them had stood before a priest was at their wedding. It revived pleasant memories.

Angus Cameron was in the front row but his team was not as well represented. The Welsh golfers brought their noncomformist zeal along and the two Roman Catholics from Ireland knew their duty, but there were notable absentees. Tom Pickard was nowhere to be seen and Kohlmar was lying in a foam bath back at the hotel. Don Hawker was the most unlikely member of the congregation, standing there in his tracksuit with head bowed and hands fiddling restlessly with the hymm-book. Karen Maxwell could not make up her mind if she was pleased or discomfited to see him, but she made the effort to exchange a few words with Hawker as the service ended.

'I see you put on your Sunday-best tracksuit, Don.'

'Yes,' he said. 'I ran here.'

'All the way from Corley?'

'I stayed the night in Sutton Coldfield.'

'What about your car?'

'Eric will drive it over in a while.' He grinned at the thought. 'It will be a new experience for him.'

'Like this was for you,' she said.

'Mm?'

'Religion. Have you seen the light?'

'Dawn was just breaking when I got up.'

Other people came to speak to Karen, and he took the opportunity to steal away quietly. He was glad that they had been able to chat without any awkwardness and felt something of the old warmth towards her, but he could not linger at the impromptu church any more. He had to seek out another worshipper. Expecting to find him at the service, Hawker now had to look elsewhere. It did not take him long to track down the private chapel.

Gary Lapidus was engaged in his devotions in the bunker near the sixth green. He practised with his sand wedge for half an hour until he was satisfied. The most gregarious member of the American team was a determined loner when it came to the finer points of preparation. Not even a caddie was allowed to distract him. It was only when he was pulling his golf cart towards the clubhouse that Lapidus noticed his audience. He could have wished it to be anyone but Don Hawker. When the journalist fell in beside him, the golfer had to make an effort to control his irritation.

He forced a smile and nodded at the tracksuit.

'When's the big race?' he said. 'You in training for when the bars open?'

Hawker fell in beside him. 'Any chance of a word?'

'You just had one, pal. Several, to be exact.'

'I was after a quote about Larry Newmark.'

'Great guy. Only sorry I never met him. Who was he?'

'I think you know, Mr Lapidus.'

'Not today, mister,' said the other. 'Eighteen holes on the Brabazon course – that's the full extent of my knowledge right now.' He gave Hawker a playful nudge. 'Come back to me tomorrow when I've flown off home.'

'It will be too late then.'

'That's the idea.'

Hawker tried to probe for information but Lapidus fobbed him off with jokey retorts. A frontal assault was the only course left. The journalist marshalled his facts, then launched straight into his accusation.

'I think you're both in this together.'

'What are you on about?'

'The murder of Larry Newmark for starters.'

Lapidus chortled. 'You crazy?'

'Then there was Hubert Stone.'

'Who the hell *are* these guys?'

'Business associates of yours,' said Hawker. 'They signed you up, then used you to winch in other big names. Tom Pickard turned you down but you had more luck with Tony Bianco.' He stopped the golfer with his arm. 'Do you deny that you were working for Newmark's company?'

'My lawyer handles that side of things.'

'What about your hit man?'

'Seems to me I'd have a contract for him right this

225

minute,' said Lapidus, starting to lose his patience. 'Move along, pal. I'm busy.'

Hawker stood in his way as he tried to walk off.

'He used your car,' he challenged.

'Who did?'

'Your accomplice,' said Hawker. 'The man who killed Newmark and Stone then tried to add me to the list.'

'Pity he didn't succeed!'

'You sent him after me.'

'It's not a bad idea at that.'

'He was driving your Volvo Estate.'

'News to me, buddy.'

'Then there was the golf ball,' added Hawker as he thought his way through it. 'I was wrong to believe that it was hers because the initials tallied. She couldn't be certain anyway. My first guess was right.' He pulled the ball from his pocket. Newmark got this from you.'

He expected a more sensational reaction from Lapidus when he handed over the personalised golf ball. Instead of that, he got a blank stare of sheer bewilderment. The American examined the ball then tossed it back to him.

'No, thanks,' he said. 'Prefer to use my own.'

'This *is* one of yours.'

'Not from where I stand.'

'It was found beside Newmark's corpse.'

Lapidus smirked. 'I'd never play such a lousy shot as that. Sand, yes. Water, maybe. But I always keep my ball well clear of dead bodies.' His face hardened and he took a ball from his bag. '*This* is the genuine Gary Lapidus. Compare it with yours and you'll see you've made one hell of a big mistake, mister.'

Hawker took the golf ball. It was a Wilson Ultra 432 and it bore the initials GL but they were more flamboyant than those on the ball he had found. All of a sudden, he began to feel egg on his face. Lapidus was seething.

'Know what?' he said. 'I oughta call a cop and have

you thrown off the fucking course. Who needs all this shit? You got balls, Hawker, I'll give you that.' Lapidus gave a hollow laugh. 'Trouble is, the two of them don't happen to match!'

He grabbed his own golf ball and marched off. The deflated Hawker tried to call after him.

'But you *did* work with Larry Newmark.'

'Not any more.'

'Who borrowed your car?'

The golfer did not even bother to reply. Striding off across the course, he left Hawker to reflect on the stupidity of jumping too hastily to conclusions that were not supported by cast-iron proof. The journalist was livid with himself for bungling the confrontation so comprehensively, and he trudged back to the press tent in a disconsolate mood. More bad news awaited him. Lying on his desk was an object that made his heart constrict. It was a black mud-flap with the VOLVO name in silver. Malcolm was not the only person who could vandalise cars.

Realising that his own vehicle had a giveaway blemish on it, the bearded American had given the Lapidus Volvo the identical treatment. Hawker had been misled over the cars as he had been over the golf balls. In each case, he had unjustly accused Gary Lapidus. The cars looked the same but they were not. The golf balls were remarkably similar and yet they were different.

Hawker now had the nation's egg supply on his face.

Farm life was a never-ending round of chores which filled up a long day and left little room for any leisure. The police presence was not only an irritation in itself, it hampered the plans that Brian Leech had for his land and forced him to make unwelcome changes to his routine. As the number of uniforms gradually diminished, he and his family felt that they were regaining control of their own property again, but it was Malcolm who most appreciated the withdrawal of the duty officers.

Since the slurry lagoon had now told them all that it could, it was allowed to function properly again. The detectives were even talking about letting the cows back into their pasture very soon.

Malcolm thought about this as he came haring down Rock Lane in the tractor with his earphones on and his body gyrating to the pop music. He swung round into the farmyard and screeched to a halt near the high-pressure hose. One of his jobs that morning was to wash the worst of the filth off the tractor, but his break came first and that meant a coffee over at the farmhouse. On his way through the outbuildings, he called into his own room to pick up another packet of cigarettes, flinging open the door and limping straight in. He stopped in his tracks when he saw two men waiting for him.

'Hello, Malcolm,' said Frank Rayment. 'We were hoping you'd drop in some time.'

'Yes,' said Mike Impey. 'We were just admiring your collection of motoring memorabilia. Why don't you come along to the Incident Room with us? Lots to discuss.'

'I done nothing wrong,' said Malcolm truculently. 'None of this stuff was nicked. I just found it.'

Detective Superintendent Frank Rayment held up the blue lamp that had been hewn from a Panda car. He gave a Hitler smile that made the youth take a step backwards.

'What about this?' he said. 'Fall off the roof of a police mobile, did it? Let's go, lad. We think you know more than you're letting on. You're giving us headaches. We believe you might have given Mr Hawker a bit of a headache as well.' Another thin smile. 'Time you started helping us with our enquiries.'

Justice had at last caught up with Malcolm.

Glenn Bianco was on tenterhooks as she waited for the fateful telephone call. Mollifying her husband with the vague promise that she would watch his match – the last of the day – she spent the morning in the hotel room and sweated it out. The Ryder Cup was only feet away on the television screen, but she saw very little of it and cared even less. From her point of view the whole event was an unmitigated calamity. What had brought her to England was not the pleasure of watching quality golf and being able to support her husband and country at the same time, but the chance of a secret meeting with Larry Newmark. Since her uncle found out about their affair, he had hindered it in every way and forbidden his partner even to come to the Ryder Cup. Pretending to obey this dictate, Newmark had travelled incognito and made arrangements to link up with Glenn once she herself arrived. The blissful reunion had never taken place.

All that The Belfry had brought her was heartache. She had lost her lover in the most final way, been thrown back on a husband she despised, and was now a blackmail victim. Unseen hands were working against her on every side and she could see no realistic mode of escape. Having resorted to prayer, she now switched her flimsy hopes to a British journalist who was himself in the line of fire. Hawker injected some spirit into her and she had agreed to be guided by his advice, but she still had many reservations about him, not least the fact that the man against whom they were pitting themselves called all the shots. It was a no-win situation.

When she studied the alternative, however, an even larger chasm opened up at her feet. If Tony Bianco ever found out about his wife's affair, there would be the most unimaginable ructions at a business as well as at an emotional level. It would not only destroy his ego, it would be ruinous for his golf and that weighed heavily with her. Whatever their differences, the game still remained their common denominator. There was a further thought to send shivers through her. Should the truth about her relationship with Larry Newmark be known, she would be embroiled in a murder investigation that would make her grief unendurable. Her survival depended on isolating herself from what had happened.

Before that, the mystery caller had to be appeased. Although she had been sitting over the telephone for two hours, Glenn Bianco was still startled when it rang. She gathered her thoughts before picking up the receiver. It was important to do exactly as Hawker had counselled.

'Hello?' she said.

'Are you on your own?' It was him.

'Of course.'

'Have you got the money?'

'Yes.'

'All of it?'

'All of it,' she lied. 'It wasn't easy but –'

'I'll do the talking,' he interrupted curtly. 'Do you have a pen?'

'Right here.' She picked it up.

'These are your instructions.'

'I'm ready.'

'First off, come alone. Got it? No police, no friends. Or the deal's off.' He became bitter. 'Most of all, no Don Hawker. You bring him along and I'll kill both of you! That clear, baby? This is between you and me. No Hawker!'

She cleared her throat. 'No Hawker,' she said.

'Okay. Here's how to find me . . .'

America was dominating the singles with unnerving

230

skill. It was the area in which Bob Jaglom had predicted success and his team were so far on course to deliver it. In the six matches already under way, the Americans led in three and were level in two. Only one European – the exuberant Claudio Mundi – had the edge over his opponent. Everyone knew that the singles would be the crucial area because all twelve players in each team had to be fielded. The tactical role of the respective captains was limited. All that they could do was to shuffle the order of their players and provide verbal encouragement. The rest was down to the golfers themselves, completely exposed and thoroughly examined, each of them involved in an individual duel to the death that would have a vital bearing on the final result.

Tension and excitement were building all the time. The pressures on the players steadily grew. Don Hawker was hypnotised by what he saw on the screen above his head in the press tent. Unable to plumb the mysteries of golf himself, he was full of admiration for those who had raised their game to the level of an art. He applauded in silence as each new brilliant shot was played. Such was the quality and the exhilaration of it all, he wanted to rush out and watch some of the games live, to join the massive galleries and share in the communal ecstasy. But a deeper duty kept him at his desk and within reach of the telephone. The outcome of his own Ryder Cup match had yet to be decided. In that context, what he was seeing was essentially a bad omen. America ruled the roost.

Hawker was stirred as Ian Roslin chipped the ball in from the fringe of the fifth green to earn his first birdie and to draw level with Vance Dressler. It only cut back the lead slightly, but it was a welcome reassurance. There was still a full afternoon's play to come and that could change the situation entirely. Rolf Kohlmar came up on the screen in earnest discussion with his caddie about a tricky second shot from a bad lie. The German had the misfortune to be up against Hal Mayo when the latter was at his intimidating best. Kohlmar was about to swing his five-iron when Hawker's attention was distracted by the expected ring. Golf was banished from his mind as he snatched up the receiver and heard the breathy voice of Glenn Bianco.

'Mr Hawker?' she said tentatively.

'Has he been in touch?

'Yes. I've got my orders.'

'When do you have to go?'

'Right now.'

'Where's the delivery point?'

'About six or seven miles away. He wants me there in half an hour at the most. It's off the main roads so I should make it easily.'

'Give me the directions,' said Hawker, pencil poised and a map of the area open before him. 'Off you go.'

She paused. 'He was very specific about you.'

'What do you mean?'

'At all costs, he said, you must keep clear.'

'Do you want to face him on your own?' he asked as he sensed her indecision. 'Do you want him to know that you don't actually have the full amount of money?' He could hear her thinking it over. 'I know that I'm not much, Mrs Bianco, but I'm all you've got. Don't throw me away. I promise you he won't see me until it's too late.'

There was another fraught silence as she pondered.

'I'm scared, Mr Hawker.'

'So is he. Now give me those directions . . .'

The rendezvous had been well chosen. It was extremely private, it was on a hill that afforded an excellent view of the surrounding countryside and it was close to a junction from which three lanes diverged as possible exits in the event of speedy withdrawal. Hawker's Ordnance Survey map showed him something else as well. Sweeping down from the hill on the western slope was a small wood that could provide an ideal hiding place for a man awaiting the delivery of some money. Hawker tried to put himself inside the mind of the bearded American and decided that he might well be lurking somewhere along the stipulated route to make sure that Glenn Bianco was not being followed by a Vauxhall Cavalier. There was only one way to obviate that eventuality.

Karen Maxwell was on the telephone as he raced up.

'I need to borrow your car,' he said.

'*Now?*'

'Please, Karen. I'll explain later.'

'What about the golf?'

'This is an emergency.'

She pressed the keys on him and told him where to find the vehicle, torn between anxiety and confusion. Karen knew that he was in trouble but she had no idea how serious it could be. As he sprinted out of the press tent, she wished that she could go with him to help, but she was soon caught up again in the demands of her job. Hawker, meanwhile, found her car and left The Belfry minutes before the Ford Granada. Taking an alternative route to the specified meeting-point, he drove hard to get there well ahead of Glenn Bianco. Almost a mile short of his destination, he tucked his car down a leafy lane, then got out and began to jog across the fields at a steady pace. It took him back to his days as a cross-country runner, and he rose to the challenge of the uneven terrain and the occasional fence that had to be cleared.

He was approaching the hill from the other side of the wood and was certain that he could not be seen. Once among the trees, he slowed to a walk and picked his way along with immense caution. Hawker had no illusions about what lay ahead. This time he would not be involved in a simple trial of strength with a young farm labourer. He was up against a professional killer who had already disposed of two victims in the most callous way. The one weapon that Hawker had was surprise. In order to get close to the man, he was using Glenn Bianco as a decoy and thus putting her life in danger as well. He only hoped that she could cope with the exigencies of the situation. Otherwise a lot of blood might be left on the hillside.

Off to his left, Hawker heard the Ford Granada arrive and come to a halt in a gateway. As he peered through the foliage, he could just pick out the slim figure of Glenn Bianco as she clambered over the five-barred gate and walked across the field in the direction of the hill. There was a bag in her hand and a hesitancy in her stride but she followed her instructions to the letter. She was well short of the summit before a voice called out.

'Stop there!' ordered the man. 'Got the dough?'

She held it up. 'Right here.'

'It better be all there, sweetheart.'

'What do I do?'

'Don't move. Just wait a few minutes.'

The man wanted to be absolutely sure that she had come alone. Glenn Bianco was left shivering in the open while her tormentor watched and waited. It was time for Hawker to go into action. He picked up a stout piece of wood to use as a cudgel, then climbed on through the undergrowth towards the point from which the voice had come, travelling as swiftly as he could without making any undue noise. When he got closer to the summit, he came into a little clearing and stiffened as he saw someone sitting on the ground with his back to a tree. But it was not the bearded American. He relaxed slightly when he saw that it was an old tramp in torn clothes and a battered trilby, swigging at a flagon of cider as he drank himself into a stupor, quite unaware that he was about to be in the middle of some high drama.

As Hawker crept towards him, the tramp emptied his bottle and dropped it beside him, belching loudly before subsiding into a heap. There was no dark beard under the hat, just a rough stubble and a face that had been grimed by outdoor life. Hawker stepped on past him and went in pursuit of his prey, but his advantage had been cast away.

There was a sudden rustle of leaves and the tramp got up with the flagon in his hand. If Hawker had not reacted instinctively, spinning around and raising an arm to protect himself, his head would have been split open by the flying glass. As it was, the flagon burst into pieces against his left forearm, slicing through his tracksuit to the bone, but leaving him conscious to fight back.

The bearded American had shaved. Hawker had been fooled by the disguise and caught off guard. He was quick to respond, lashing out with his cudgel and catching the man a blow on the head which dislodged the hat to reveal a big fleshy face that was lit by two gleaming brown eyes and which terminated in a square jaw. They grappled at once, trying to bang each other against the gnarled trunks around them, kicking, punching, gouging and biting. Blood was gushing from Hawker's forearm and weakening his resistance with every second, but he fought on bravely. The superior strength and guile of his attacker was now beginning to tell. The man was a born street-fighter who would stop at nothing and he winded Hawker with a punch to the solar plexus before hurling him to the ground.

The journalist dropped his cudgel and curled up like a ball, taking several hard kicks before he was able to grab the man's foot and drag him down as well.

They wrestled in the grass, then rolled over into some bushes that lacerated them even more. Hawker was struggling, but the man had lost some of his venom as well and he howled in anguish as an elbow smashed his nose into a bleeding pulp. It put frightening new energy into his muscles and he lifted Hawker bodily from the ground to hurl him at the trunk of an oak tree. Grabbing his hair, he pounded the journalist's head against the timber until the latter was almost unconscious, then he half-carried him across the clearing towards a more hideous fate.

Hawker saw it just in time to rouse himself again. He was being dragged towards the stump of a young tree that had been snapped in two by a recent gale. A thin metre of wood stood upright like a spiked railing and he was about to be impaled upon it. As the man bent to hoist him in the air, however, Hawker brought a knee up under his jaw with such force that the grip on him was released. He tried to scramble away on his hands and knees but the other was soon after him, diving on to his back and winding him even more. Hawker managed to thresh about enough to turn over but he was near to exhaustion now and had only one burst of energy left. Gathering all his strength, he manoeuvred his feet up into the man's stomach then waited his moment, thinking of Larry Newmark and Hubert Stone, recalling two attempts on his life by a blue Volvo, remembering a knife attack in a hotel bedroom in Sutton Coldfield, pushing as hard as he possibly could while thrusting away with his hands at the same time, fighting for his life with every sinew.

The American's weight was used against him for once. As he was propelled back over Hawker's head, he landed on the tip of the razor-sharp tree stump and was skewered beyond recall, writhing in agony until his last cries had echoed through the unforgiving woodland. Hawker got one fuzzy glimpse of the grotesque death before he passed out into a seductive oblivion.

Another bed in another hospital gave him another unsought opportunity of looking up at Superintendent Frank Rayment and his baby-faced assistant. As Don Hawker came out of his coma, they were standing beside his bed with grim expressions, like two undertakers appraising their latest cadaver. When they saw signs of life, relief was mingled with disappointment. Rayment stepped in close. He had the cheated look of a man whose job has been done by someone else when his back was turned. Hawker was in far worse condition than on his previous visit to hospital. Pain was opening up branch offices all over his body and they were frenetically busy. His head had been rented out to the army as a firing range and they were testing some of their latest artillery. When he dared to glance down, he saw that he was all but mummified by bandaging. When he tried to move, his limbs refused to obey.

Rayment took a mournful pleasure in his discomfort.

'You were warned, sir,' he said fussily. 'Leave it to the professionals next time. You were very lucky.'

'What happened?' murmured Hawker.

'The police at Coleshill got an anonymous call from some woman about two men fighting in a wood. They went to investigate, found you and him, brought us in on it at once.' Rayment became self-important. 'We were able to tidy up a number of things in one fell swoop. Forensic are still working on the American's car, but there were clear signs of bloodstains in the rear and other evidence to suggest that he may well have been Larry Newmark's killer.'

'He was,' said Hawker. 'He murdered Stone as well.'

'All will be revealed in the fullness of time, sir.'

'Where is the man now?'

'You saved us the cost of a trial,' muttered Impey.

'Who was he?'

Rayment took over again. 'His name was Wendell Taylor and they have quite a file on him back home in his native Arizona. He kills people for a living. He was not cheap but he offered an efficient service.'

'I can vouch for that,' said Hawker ruefully.

'Does it hurt?'

'All over, Superintendent.'

'Excuse me if I show no sympathy whatsoever.'

'Not even a bunch of grapes and a smile?'

'I see that your brain is functioning again. Though you should train it to work along more law-abiding lines. I guarantee that you'd spend less time in hospital.'

'And miss out on these little visits of yours?' said Hawker with the ghost of a grin. 'Never!'

'Let's get down to brass tacks,' snapped the other. 'Tell us everything. Fill in the few gaps we have left.'

'I'm not sure that I can . . .'

'And don't come the dying soldier with us, Mr Hawker. The doctors say you're as strong as an ox or you'd have perished out in that wood along with Taylor.' He used his Hitler voice. 'Make a clean breast of it, man.'

Hawker took time to collect his thoughts and to edit the facts. Having worked out that Glenn Bianco was the anonymous caller who tipped off the police, he wanted to prevent her being dragged into the investigation at all. She had suffered enough on her doomed trip to England and should be allowed to return home without the trauma of interrogation by the police and the consequences it would mean for her marriage. He gave another version of events.

'It all comes back to business,' he said. 'Larry Newmark and Hubert Stone were partners in an expanding enterprise. Newmark was the public face but it was the old man who controlled things from behind the scenes. They fell out – don't ask me how – and Stone hired a professional killer to eliminate his partner. It was to be done in England in such a way that no traces were found until they had all gone back to America.'

'But Wendell Taylor bungled it,' said Impey.

'Yes, Sergeant. He didn't use a big enough boulder to hold down the body in the lagoon. A hand stuck out.'

'And you saw it,' agreed Rayment. 'We know that much. Take us on to the Whitehall Hotel.'

'Stone refused to pay the full amount,' said Hawker. 'He'd brought a quarter of a million dollars, but he only gave Taylor half of it because the job hadn't been done properly. Taylor killed him and took his wallet to make it look as if robbery had brought him to the hotel.' He gritted his teeth as his wounded arm smarted. 'On the next day, Taylor rang up, pretended to be Stone's cousin and tried to bluff the rest of the money out of Mrs Dowling. Fortunately she'd given it to the police.'

'Nice to hear that someone knows where her duty lies,' said Rayment. 'Okay, supposing we buy your story so far – and it's only *supposing*, believe me – where do you fit in? How come you and Taylor finish up slugging it out in that wood?'

Hawker sighed. 'He took against me.'

'Now why would he do that?' mocked the other. 'Can you think of any reason, Mike?'

'About three dozen, sir.'

'He knew that I was on his tail,' said Hawker.

Rayment bristled. 'Well, that's not going to win you any popularity, is it? Not with Taylor. And not with us.'

'We got him in the end, Superintendent.'

'But not by the book!' protested the detective. 'By

some half-assed heroism that almost got you killed. Do you realise what you were up against in Wendell Taylor? He wasn't just a hit man, he was a psychopath. Do you recall what happened to Larry Newmark?'

'You said the body was mutilated.'

'He was castrated. Taylor cut off his balls and stuffed them down his throat.' He jabbed an index finger. 'That's the sort of man you took on up in those woods. Be grateful you're not talking to us in a high voice.'

Though Hawker shuddered with relief, he knew that the killer had been acting on Stone's orders. It was the old man who had specified the symbolic death. Glenn Bianco had said enough about her uncle's feelings towards her to show that he was a very sick man. She had given her lover a personalised golf ball as a keepsake. Consumed by rage and jealousy, Hubert Stone had insisted on castration, but Wendell Taylor had added the final lurid touch himself. Having first robbed Newmark of his testicles, the killer had then sent him to his grave holding an initialled surrogate. In the long run, that cruel joke had been Taylor's undoing.

Rayment and Impey had a wordless conference before turning back to the patient. They regarded him with an exasperation that was softened by a grudging respect. It was important to let Hawker know that their enquiries were leading them in the right direction.

'We'd have got him,' said Rayment smugly. 'Don't think that you were *that* far ahead of us, sir. We put the pinch on young Malcolm and he told us all about that mud-flap from the Volvo. We were coming up fast behind you.'

'Comforting to know, Superintendent.'

The door opened and a nurse slipped into the room to hold a brief whispered conversation with the detectives. They nodded reluctantly and she went straight out. Impey crossed to the door, but Rayment hovered for a last word with the wounded man.

'We'll be needing a full statement from you, sir.'

'I've just given you one.'

'Too many things missed out, Mr Hawker. I'm a bit of a perfectionist. I like to fill in all the blanks.' He gave an off-duty smile. 'Anything you want to ask me?'

'Such as?'

'The name of this hospital.'

Hawker groaned. 'Don't say it's the George Eliot!'

'No, sir. Things are looking up. The ambulance brought you to Sutton Coldfield.'

'So what's this hospital called?'

'Good Hope.'

The two men vanished through the door. Hawker was still relishing his change of venue when he had another visitor. She let herself in and tripped across the floor with an affectionate concern. He was delighted to see Karen Maxwell, but alarmed that she should see him in such distress. Sitting on the chair beside the bed, she took his right hand in her own and squeezed it gently.

'I suppose you want your car back?' he said.

Her eyes smiled. 'Who cares about that?'

'Thanks for coming.'

'They wouldn't let me in any sooner. How are you?'

'No comment.'

'You're too brave for your own good, Don Hawker.'

'And too stupid.'

'Eric is having kittens.'

'Name them after me.'

She squeezed his hand again and ran a sorrowful eye over his wounds. Karen Maxwell was not just upset by the sight of a friend in great pain. She was activated by guilt as well and it made her lean in close to him.

'I should have mentioned Denver to you,' she said.

'It might have saved me a shock.'

'I lived there for six months.' She shrugged. 'What

241

stopped me telling you was shame, if you'll pardon such an old-fashioned word. I suppose that I didn't want you to think badly of me.'

'Why on earth should I do that?'

'Because I led a double life,' she said. 'I took this job in Denver and told my husband it was a big career move for me but that wasn't the reason. There was somebody else. A husband in Kansas, a lover in Denver. I lost them both.' Her brow furrowed with remorse. 'I did *want* the marriage to work, Don, and I tried hard at first. I hoped that we could be like you and Elaine, so wrapped up in each other that the rest of the world didn't even matter. But I couldn't manage it.'

'Nor could we,' he admitted to himself.

'I behaved very badly,' she said, 'and I wanted to keep that little episode well and truly buried. Denver was not a happy place for me.'

'When did Tom Pickard come into the frame?'

She gulped slightly. 'Soon after I split up with my husband. I was lonely, bored, looking for a way to get back to England. Tom was playing in a tournament in Colorado and I was handling the PR. His wife wasn't around and he was . . . nice to me. We spent a week together, that was all. Apart from one night back here.'

'I've seen the photograph . . .'

The subject closed itself. Nothing more needed to be said and they held hands in silence, drawing closer and finding out about each other all over again. Hawker was about to drift off into a haze of pleasant memories when she spoke again.

'I learned more about Larry Newmark's company.'

'Go on.'

'They were just about to explode,' she said, 'and the Ryder Cup was part of that explosion. Having signed up Gary Lapidus, they had Tony Bianco in their sights. With names like that on their merchandise, they'd buy themselves credibility in the golf world.'

'How does the Ryder Cup come into it?'

'In two ways, Don. It was the event that was going to rehabilitate Bianco – and it certainly did that! But it had a special significance for Newmark. His company was on the verge of landing the contract to provide the outfits for the 1991 Ryder Cup when it's held in the States. That would really mean they'd arrived.'

'I'm with you,' he said. 'Having Bianco and Lapidus in their stable would strengthen their bid for that contract. No wonder Stone was determined that nothing would ripple the waters at The Belfry. He needed an American win with Tony Bianco at the head of it.'

'He almost got it, Don.'

'Did he?' He was flustered. 'Is the match over?'

'Hours ago.'

'Who won?'

'It was a draw.'

'That means Europe retain the Ryder Cup.'

'It also means you've got a terrific new chapter for your book,' she pointed out. 'Bianco was phenomenal but Tom Pickard stole his limelight. They played the final match of the singles and got to the eighteenth hole all square. But the Americans were one up. If Bianco simply halved the hole, he'd pack that cup into his suitcase. Tom had to win.'

'Death or glory. He'd like that.'

'It brought out his Yorkshire grit,' she said. 'He hit a marvellous tee shot over the water and didn't lose his nerve when he saw Bianco's second shot land ten feet from the pin. Tom was as relaxed as if he was playing the game for fun. He just seemed to stroke the ball. The next minute, it hits the green and the fans go delirious. His shot rolled to within six inches of the cup.'

'Bianco missed his putt?'

'By a millimetre. Tom was the hero of the hour. You could write the whole book about that second shot of his. It was inch-perfect.'

'That's the way to hit 'em.'

'Stone dead.'

Don Hawker gave a wry chuckle, then fell gently asleep.

THE JUDGE'S SONG

Bernard Bannerman

It was, as Dave Woolf said, 'the sort of thing that doesn't happen in England'. High-court corruption, gangsters, fire-bombs and a bit of murder on the side – all of it against the backdrop of a family drama raging through London, the West Country and the South of France.

It's not the sort of thing that solicitors ought to be investigating. But Woolf is no ordinary solicitor. Back in the legal fold after a spell as a private eye, he's roped into a spot of detection for the usual reasons – an irresistible fee. Sustained by hefty slugs of Southern Comfort, Camels and his new Aussie sidekick, he's ready to haul a few skeletons out of family cupboards. The trouble is, they're still alive . . .

0 7474 0520 4
CRIME

A MATTER OF DEGREE

Tom Philbin

There's a sex-killer on the loose in Precinct Siberia – and no one is safe . . . Bloodthirsty, cunning and brilliantly elusive, the bizarre criminal will kill until he is caught.

Detective George Benton – known in the 53rd as 'The Bent One' – is an intensive hypochondriac, a dapper dresser, and a truly brilliant detective who has spent his career studying the intricate workings of sex-killers' minds.

As he begins to pursue the threads that might lead him to the killer, George Benton understands the factors in his own life that make him not so very different from his prey . . .

An unusual and exciting new novel in the popular *Precinct Siberia* series: a fascinating psychological journey into the mind of a killer and the mind of the cop who must catch him . . .

0 7474 0284 1
CRIME

TALKING GOD

Tony Hillerman

A toothless corpse dumped in the Arizona desert and a
museum curator's dangerous obsession with his roots
make two seemingly separate cases for detectives Jim
Chee and Joe Leaphorn. But as they follow the different
trails, they are reluctantly drawn together into a lethal
web of international crime and cultural apartheid. For
tribal magic, earthed in New Mexico, connects the two
and begins to shed light on a rich stew of greed, murder,
assassination plots and South American terrorism . . .

0 7474 0629 4
CRIME

Sphere now offers an exciting range of quality fiction and non-fiction by both established and new authors. All of the books in this series are available from good bookshops, or can be ordered from the following address:

Sphere Books
Cash Sales Department
P.O. Box 11
Falmouth
Cornwall TR10 9EN.

Please send cheque or postal order (no currency), and allow 60p for postage and packing for the first book plus 25p for the second book and 15p for each additional book ordered up to a maximum charge of £1.90 in U.K.

B.F.P.O. customers please allow 60p for the first book, 25p for the second book plus 15p per copy for the next 7 books, thereafter 9p per book.

Overseas customers including Eire please allow £1.25 for postage and packing for the first book, 75p for the second book and 28p for each subsequent title ordered.